FLESH

ALSO FROM TITAN BOOKS

CLASSIC NOVELS FROM

PHILIP JOSÉ FARMER

WOLD NEWTON SERIES

The Other Log of Phileas Fogg

Tales of the Wold Newton Universe (coming soon)

PREHISTORY

Time's Last Gift

Hadon of Ancient Opar

SECRETS OF THE NINE: PARALLEL UNIVERSE

A Feast Unknown

Lord of the Trees

The Mad Goblin

GRAND MASTER SERIES

Lord Tyger

The Wind Whales of Ishmael

Venus on the Half-Shell (coming soon)

TITAN BOOKS

FLESH

Print edition ISBN: 9781781163016
E-book edition ISBN: 9781781163030

Published by Titan Books
A division of Titan Publishing Group Ltd
144 Southwark Street, London SE1 0UP

First edition: August 2013
1 3 5 7 9 10 8 6 4 2

A CIP catalogue record for this title is available from the British Library.

Printed and bound in the United States.

For Bette,

Courageous and Loving Wife

FLESH

PRELUDE

The crowd in front of the White House talked, shouted, and laughed. Women shrilled; men boomed. The high-pitched cut of children's voices was missing. They were home and being cared for by their older but prepubescent brothers and sisters or cousins. It was not fitting that children should see what would happen tonight. They would not understand the rites, one of the most holy in honor of the Great White Mother.

It also would not be safe for the children to be present. Centuries before the present date (2860 Old Style), when the rites were first held, children had been allowed to attend. Many had been killed, literally ripped apart, during the frenzies.

Tonight was dangerous enough for the adults. Always, a number of women were badly mauled or killed. Always, a number of men were overpowered by long-nailed, sharp-toothed women who ripped off by the roots that which made men men and who ran screaming down the streets with the trophies held high in the air or clenched between their teeth before placing them on the altar of the Great White Mother in the Temple of Dark Earth.

The following week, on Friday Sabbath, the white-robed Speakers for the Mother, priests and priestesses, would reprimand the survivors for carrying their zeal just a little too far. However, harsh words were the worst that those preached to could expect, and not always these were hurled at them. A man or woman truly possessed by the Goddess, and who was not then, could not be blamed. Besides, what else did the Speakers expect? Did not this happen every night a Sunhero or Stag-king was born? Oh, well, the Speakers felt that it was necessary to quiet the worshipers down so that they could resume a normal life. Listen, pray, and forget. And look forward to the next ceremony.

Besides, the victims had nothing to complain about. They would be buried in a shrine, prayers said over them, and deer sacrificed over them. The ghosts of the slain would drink the blood and be thrice-glorified and sustained.

The bloody sun slid down past the horizon; night rushed in with cool dark whispering wings. The crowd became quieter while the representatives of the great frats lined up on Pennsylvania Avenue. There was a violent argument between the chief of the Moose frat and the chief of the Elks. Each claimed that his frat should lead the parade. Were they not both antlered men? Was not the Sunhero antler-bearing this year?

John Barleycorn, green from head to foot in his ritual costume, scarlet in face, staggering, tried to settle the dispute. As usual, he was too far gone by nightfall to speak clearly or to care much whether or not he spoke at all. His few discernible words only succeeded in making both chiefs angry. They were likely to be easily angered since both were more than a little drunk. They even went so far as to grip their knife handles, though it would have taken far greater provocation for them to unsheathe the knives at this time.

A detachment of the White House Honor Guard left their posts to straighten matters out. The tall girls marched from the porch, their high conical helmets shining in the torchlight, long hair hanging down their backs, their white robes gleaming. They carried their bows in one hand and an arrow in the other. Unlike the rest of the virgins in the city of Washington, they exposed only one breast, the left. The robe concealed the other—or, rather, the lack of the other. Traditionally, a White House archer gladly allowed her breast to be removed so it would not interfere with her handling of the bow. The lack was no disadvantage in getting a husband when she retired. Tonight, after the Sunhero planted the seed of divinity in them, they could have their choice of men to marry. A man whose wife had been a one-breasted Honor Guard was a proud man.

The captain of the Honor Guard sternly asked about the disturbance. After hearing both chiefs out, she said, "This is the first time matters have ever been so badly arranged. Perhaps we need a new John Barleycorn!"

She pointed the arrow in her hand at the chief of the Elk frat.

"You will take the lead in the parade. And you and your brothers will have the honor of bringing out the Sunhero."

The chief of the Moose frat was either a brave man or a foolish man. He protested. "I was out drinking with the Barleycorn last night, and he told me the Moose would have the honor! I demand to know why the Elks have been chosen instead of us!"

The captain stared coldly at him, and then fitted the nock of her arrow to the string of her bow. But she was too well trained in politics to shoot one of the powerful Moose frat.

"The Barleycorn must have been possessed with spirits other than those the Goddess gives him," she said. "It has been planned for some time that the Elks would escort the Sunhero to the Capitol. Is not the Sunhero a stag? Isn't he Stagg? You know that a male Elk is a stag, but a male Moose is a bull!"

"That is true," said the chief Moose, pale from the moment the arrow had been fitted. "I should not have listened to John Barleycorn. But it normally would have been the turn of the Moose. Last year it was the Lions, and the year before it was the Lambs. We should have been next."

"And so you would have been—except for that."

She pointed behind him down Pennsylvania Avenue.

He turned to look. The street ran straight for six blocks from the White House and then ended suddenly in a towering baseball stadium. Rising even over it was the shining needle shape of a craft that had not been seen for seven hundred and sixty years. Not until a month ago, when it had come thundering and flaming out of the late November skies and settled in the center of the ball park.

"You are right," said the chief Moose. "Never before has the Sunhero descended to us from the skies, sent by the Great White Mother Herself. And, certainly, She made it clear what frat he honors by being its brother when She named him Stagg."

He marched away at the head of his men and just in time.

There was a scream from the Capitol, now only six blocks away from the White House. The scream silenced the crowd; it paralyzed them and made the men turn pale. The women in the crowd became wide-eyed, eager, and expectant. Several fell on the ground, writhing and moaning. There came another scream, and now it could be seen that the terrible sound was from the throats of many young girls running down the steps of Congress.

They were priestesses, newly graduated from the divinity college of Vassar. They wore tall conical narrow-brimmed black hats, their hair was unbound and hung to their hips, their breasts were as bare as those of any other virgins; but those would have to serve for five years more before they put on the matronly bras. Not for them tonight the seed of the Sunhero; their participation was confined to initiating the ceremonies. They wore flaring bell-shaped white skirts with many petticoats beneath; some of these were belted with live and hissing rattlesnakes, the rest carried the deadly snakes around their shoulders. In their hands they held ten-foot whips made of snake hide.

Drums began beating; a bugle blared out above the drums; cymbals clanged; syrinxes shrilled.

Screaming, wild-eyed, the young priestesses ran down Pennsylvania Avenue, clearing a way before them with their whips. Suddenly they were at the gate surrounding the yard of the White House. There was a brief mock struggle as the Honor Guard pretended to resist the invasion. Some of it was not so harmless, since the archers and the priestesses had well-deserved reputations as vicious little bitches. There was a hair-pulling and scratching and breast-twisting, but the older priestesses applied their whips to the bare backs of the overenthusiastic. Howling, the girls sprang apart and quickly came to a sense of the business at hand.

These pulled out little golden sickles from their belts and brandished them in the air in a threatening but at the same time obviously ritualistic air. Suddenly, as if he had dramatically staged his entrance—and he had—John Barleycorn appeared in the main doorway of the White House. In one hand he carried a half-empty bottle of whiskey. There was no doubt where its contents had gone. He swayed back and forth and fumbled the cord at his neck before he managed to find the whistle at its end. Then he stuck the whistle in his mouth and blew shrilly.

Immediately, a howl rose from the street where the Elks were assembled.

A number of them burst past the Guard and onto the porch. These men wore little deerskin caps with toy antlers protruding from the sides, deerskin capes, and belts from which hung the tails of deer. Their breechclouts were balloons in phallic shapes. They did not run or walk but pranced on the ends of their toes, like ballet dancers, simulating the gait of a deer. They threatened the priestesses; the priestesses shrieked as if frightened and scattered to one side so the Elks could pass into the White House.

Here, inside the great reception room, John Barleycorn blew his whistle once again and lined them up according to their rank in the frat. Then he began walking unsteadily up the broad curving staircase that led to the second floor.

He disgraced himself by losing his balance and falling backwards into the arms of the chief Elk.

The chief caught the Barleycorn and shoved him to one side. In ordinary circumstances he would not have dared to deal so strongly with the Speaker of the House, but knowing that the fellow was in disgrace made him bold. The Barleycorn staggered to one side of the staircase. He fell backwards over the railing and fell on his head on the marble floor of the reception room. There he lay, his neck at an odd angle. A young priestess rushed forward, felt his pulse, looked at the glazing eyes, then drew out her golden sickle.

At that moment, a whip cracked across her bare shoulders and breasts and left a line from which blood oozed.

"What do you think you are doing?" screamed an older priestess.

The young priestess crouched low, head averted, but she did not dare to hold out her hands to protect herself from the whip.

"I was exercising my right," she whimpered. "Great John Barleycorn is dead. I am an incarnation of the Great White Mother; I was going to reap the crop."

"And I would not stop you," said the older priestess. "It would be your right to castrate him—except for one thing. He died by accident, not during the Planting Rites. You know that."

"Columbia forgive me," whimpered the priestess. "I could not help myself. It is tonight's doing; the coming to manhood of the son, the crowning of the Horned King, the defloration of the mascots."

The stern face of the older priestess splintered into a smile. "I am sure that Columbia will forgive you. There is something in the air that takes us all out of our senses. It is the divine presence of the Great White Mother in Her aspect as Virginia, Bride of the Sunhero and the Great Stag. I feel it too, and—"

At that moment there was a bellow from the second story. Both women looked up. Down the steps poured the mob of Elks, and on their shoulders and hands they bore the Sunhero.

The Sunhero was a naked man magnificently built in every respect. Though he was sitting on the shoulders of two Elks, he obviously was very tall. His face, with its prominent supraorbital ridges, long hooked nose, and massive chin, could have been that of a good-looking heavyweight champion. But at this moment anything that might have evoked such terms as "handsome" or "ugly" was gone from his face. It bore a look that could only be described as "possessed." That was exactly the term anybody in the city of Washington of the nation of Deecee would have used. His long red-gold hair hung to his shoulders. Out of the curly masses, just above the forehead and the hairline, sprouted a pair of antlers.

These were not the artificial antlers that the Elk frat wore. They were living organs.

They stood twelve inches above his head and measured sixteen inches from the outer tip of one to the outer tip of the other. They were covered with a pale shiny skin, shot through with blue blood vessels. At the base of each a great artery pulsed with the throb of the Sunhero's heart. It was obvious that they had been grafted onto the man's head very recently. There was dried blood at the base of the antlers.

The face of the man with the antlers would have been distinguished instantly in a crowd of citizens. The faces of the

Elks and of the priestesses were individual, but all had a look that belonged to their era and could be called cervine. Triangular, with large dark eyes and long eyelashes, high cheekbones, small but full-fleshed mouths and tapering chins, they were cast in the mold of their times. But a sensitive onlooker would have known that this man on the shoulders of the cervines, this man with the face emptied of intellect, belonged to an earlier era. Just as a student of the portraits of humanity can say by looking at this face, "He belongs to the Ancient world," or "This man was born during the Renaissance," or "This man lived when the Industrial Age was just getting its stride," so the student could have said, "This man was born when the Earth swarmed with humanity. He looks vaguely insectal. Yet there is a difference. He also bears the look of the original of those times—the man who managed to be an individual among the insects."

Now the crowd carried him down the broad steps and out onto the great porch of the White House.

At his appearance a tremendous shout rose from the mob in the street. Drums thundered; bugles blared like Gabriel's trumpet; syrinxes shrilled. The priestesses on the porch waved sickles at the men dressed like elks, but they did not cut—except by accident. The Elks on the outside of the mob shoved at the priestesses so they staggered back and fell on their backs. There they lay, their legs up in the air, screaming and writhing.

The antlered man was rushed down the sidewalk, out through the iron gates and onto the middle of Pennsylvania Avenue. Here he was seated on the back of a wild-eyed black stag. The stag tried to buck and rear; but the men held on to his antlers and the long hair of his flanks and prevented him from racing headlong down the street. The man on the beast's back grabbed its antlers to keep from being thrown. His own back arched. The muscles on his arms knotted as he forced the mighty neck back. The stag bellowed, and the whites of his eyes shone in the torchlight. Suddenly, just as it seemed his neck must break under the force of the man's arms, he relaxed and stood trembling. Saliva drooled from his mouth, and his eyes were still wide, but they were frightened. His rider was master.

The Elks formed in ranks of twelve behind the stag and rider. Behind them was a band of musicians, also of the Elk frat. Behind them were the Moose and their musicians. Next was a group of Lions wearing panther skulls as helmets and panther skins as cloaks, the long tails dragging on the cement. They held on to the ropes of a balloon that rose twelve feet over them. This had a long sausage-shape and a swelling round nose. Beneath it hung two round gondolas in each of which sat pregnant women, throwing flowers and rice on the crowd lining the street. Behind them were the representatives of the Rooster frat carrying their totem, a tall pole surmounted by the carved head of an enormous rooster with a tall red comb and a long straight beak knobbed at the end.

Behind them, the leader of the other frats of the nation: the Elephants, the Mules, the Jackrabbits, the Trouts, the Billy Goats, and many others. Behind them, the representatives of the great sisterhoods: the Wild Does, the Queen Bees, the Wood Cats, the Lionesses, the Shrikes.

The Sunhero paid no attention to those behind him. He

was staring down the street. Both sides were lined with crowds, but evidently they had not assembled by accident. They were organized into definite ranks. The group closest to the streets was composed of girls from fourteen to eighteen. They wore the high-necked, long-sleeved blouses which opened at the front to exhibit their breasts. Their legs were concealed by white bell-shaped skirts with many petticoats beneath, and their red-nailed feet wore white sandals. Their long hair was unbound and fell to their waists. Each carried a bouquet of white roses in her right hand. They were wide-eyed and eager; they screamed, over and over, "Sunhero! Horned King! Mighty Stag! Great Son and Lover!"

Behind them stood matrons who seemed, from the advice they shouted at them, to be their mothers. Those wore high-necked, long-sleeved blouses too, but their breasts were covered. Their skirts lacked the petticoats to give them the bell shape; they fell straight to the ground except in the front, where they wore, beneath the skirt, bustles to give them a pregnant appearance. Their hair was coiled up into buns and Psyche knots, and in each were stuck the stems of red roses, one for each child they had borne.

Behind the matrons stood the fathers, each clad in the garment of his particular frat and holding in one hand the totem of his frat. In the other he held a bottle from which he drank frequently and occasionally passed forward to his wife.

All were shouting and screaming, straining forward as if they would crowd onto the street. This was not in the plan, since the way had to be left open for the passage of the parade. The

Honor Guards and the Vassar graduates rushed out in front of the stag and its rider. The Guard jabbed with arrows at those who crossed a white line on the curb, and the priestesses struck out with their whips. The virgins in the front ranks did not whimper or shrink at the blood drawn from them, but instead yelled as if they liked the sight of their own blood.

There was a hush. The drums and bugles and Panpipes ceased for a moment.

Maidens appeared from the White House, carrying on their shoulders and hands a chair in which lolled the body of John Barleycorn. These maidens were dressed in the garb of their sisterhood, long stiff cloths dyed green to look like corn leaves and on their heads tall yellow crowns like ears of corn. They belonged to the Corn sisterhood. They were carrying out the single male member. He was dead. But apparently the crowd did not realize it, since they laughed at the sight of the body. It was not the first time he had passed out in public, and nobody except the Corn Maidens knew the difference. They took their appointed place in the procession just behind the Guard and priestesses and just ahead of the Sunhero.

The drums began again; the bugles blared; the syrinxes shrilled; the men roared; the women screamed.

The stag lurched forward with its rider.

The man on its back had to be restrained from climbing down and joining the teen-aged girls who lined the street. They were shouting suggestions that would have made a sailor blush, and he was shouting back at them in kind. His face, which had been emptied of intellect as he came down the steps, was now demoniac. He struggled to leave the beast. When the Elks pushed him back, he hit at them with his fists. They reeled back, their noses broken and bloody, and fell on the street where the marchers trampled them. Others took their places and gripped the Sunhero with many hands.

"Hold on, Great Stag!" they shouted. "Wait until we get to the domes! There we will release you, and you may do what you want! There the High Priestess Virginia waits in the aspect of the Great White Mother as maiden! And there wait also the most beautiful mascots of Washington, tender maidens filled with the divine presence of Columbia and of America, her daughter! Waiting to be filled with the divine seed of the Son!"

The man with the antlers did not seem to hear them or to understand them—part of which might be explained by the fact that his speech, though American, was a variant of theirs. The other part was explained by the thing that possessed him. It made him deaf to anything but the roar of blood in him.

Though the paraders made an attempt to pace slowly toward their destination, six blocks away, they could not help increasing speed as they came closer. Perhaps the insults and threats of the young girls to tear them apart if they didn't hurry had something to do with it. The whips and arrows drew more blood. The girls nevertheless pressed in, and once a girl made a fantastically high jump into the air and knocked over a priestess. She scrambled up and leaped again onto the shoulders of an Elk, but she lost her footing and fell headlong into the group. There she was treated savagely; the men ripped off her clothes, pinched and gripped her everywhere until they drew blood. One man intended to anticipate the Sunhero, but this blasphemy was prevented by others. They knocked him over the head, and then kicked the girl back into line.

"Wait your turn, honey!" they shouted. They laughed, and one yelled, "If the Great Stag isn't enough, the little stags will accommodate you later, baby!"

By the time this incident had passed, the procession was halted at the foot of the steps to the Capitol Building. Here there was some momentary confusion, as the Guards and priestesses tried to shove the girls back. The Elks pulled the Sunhero off the stag and began to lead him up the steps.

"Hold on just a minute, Great Stag!" they said. "Hold on until you get to the top of the steps. And we will let you go!"

Raving, the Sunhero glared at them, but he allowed them to hang on to him. He looked at the statue of the Great White Mother on the top of the steps by the entrance to the building. Carved marble, it was fifty feet high with enormous breasts. She was suckling her baby Son. One of her feet was crushing the life out of a bearded dragon.

The crowd broke into a mighty roar, "Virginia! Virginia!"

The high priestess of Washington had appeared from the shadows of the columns of the immense porch that ran around the Capitol.

The light from the torches gleamed whitely on her long skirt and bare shoulders and breasts. It turned dark her honey-colored hair, which fell to her calves. It turned dark the mouth which in the daylight was red as a wound. It turned dark the eyes which in the sun were a deep blue.

The Sunhero bellowed like a stag who scents a female during rutting season. He shouted, "Virginia! You'll not put me off any longer! Nothing can stop me now!"

The dark mouth opened, and the teeth flashed white in the torchlight. A long slim white arm beckoned to him. He tore loose from the many hands holding him and ran up the steps. He was only faintly aware that the drums and bugles and pipes behind him had risen to a crescendo and that the screaming was the high-pitched lust of a mob of young girls. He was only dimly aware of these… and not at all aware that his bodyguard was fighting for its life, trying to keep from being trampled underfoot or torn apart by the long sharp nails of the virgins. Nor did he see that mingled with the fallen bodies of the men were the white skirts and blouses of the girls, cast aside.

Only one thing made him pause for even a second. That was the sudden appearance of a girl in an iron cage, set at the base of the statue of the Great Mother. She was a young woman, too, but clad differently than the others. She wore a long-billed cap like a baseball player's, a loose shirt with some indistinguishable marking on it, loose calf-length pants, thick stockings, and thick-soled shoes.

Above the cage was a large sign with thick-limbed letters in Deecee spelling:

MAESST
GAKAETI REA KESILAE

Translated:

MASCOT
CAPTURED IN A RAID ON CASEYLAND

The girl gave him one horrified look, then covered her eyes and turned her back on him.

His puzzled look disappeared, and he ran toward the high priestess. She was facing him with her two arms spread out, as if bestowing a benediction upon him. But the arc of her back bending backwards and the outthrust of her hips made plain that his long waiting was over. She would not resist.

He growled so deeply that it seemed to come from the root of his spine, and he seized her robe and pulled.

Behind him the many throats rose to an insane screeching, and, surrounded by flesh, he disappeared from the view of the fathers and mothers assembled at the foot of the steps.

1

Around and around the Earth the starship sped.

Where air ends and space begins, it skimmed from north pole to south pole and around and around.

Finally, Captain Peter Stagg turned away from the viewplate.

"Earth has changed very much since we were here eight hundred years ago. How do you interpret what you've seen?"

Dr. Calthorp scratched his long white beard and then turned a dial on the panel below the viewplate. The fields and rivers and forests below expanded and shot out of sight. Now the magnifier showed a city on both sides of a river, presumably the Potomac. The city was roughly ten miles square, and could be seen in the same detail as if the men on the ship were five hundred feet above it.

"How do I interpret what I see?" said Calthorp. "Your guess would be as good as mine. As Earth's oldest anthropologist, I should be able to make a fair analysis of the data presented—

perhaps even explain how some of these things came to be. But I can't. I'm not even sure that is Washington. If it is, it's been rebuilt without much planning. I don't know; you don't either. So why don't we go down and see?"

"We've little choice," said Peter Stagg. "We're almost out of fuel."

Suddenly, he smacked his palm with his huge fist.

"Once we land, then what? I didn't see a single building anywhere on Earth that looked as if it might house a reactor. Or anything like the machines we knew. Where's the technology? It's back to the horse and buggy—except that they don't have any horses. The horse seems to be extinct, but they've got a substitute. Some sort of hornless deer."

"To be exact, deer have antlers, not horns," Calthorp said. "I'd say the latter-day Americans have bred deer or elk or both, not only to take the place of the horse but of cattle. If you've noticed, there's a great variety among the cervines. Big ones for draft and pack and meat animals, some bred with the lines of race horses. Millions of them." He hesitated. "But I'm worried. Even the seeming non-existence of radioactive fuel doesn't bother me as much…"

"As what?"

"As what kind of reception we'll get when we land. Much of Earth has become a desert. Erosion, the razor of God, has slashed its face. Look at what used to be the good old U.S.A. A chain of volcanoes belching fire and dust along the Pacific coast! As a matter of fact, the Pacific coast all around—both Americas, upper Asia, Australia, the Pacific islands—is alive with active volcanoes. All that carbon dioxide and dust released into the atmosphere has had a radical effect on the terrestrial climate. The icecaps of the Arctic and Antarctic are melting. The oceans have risen at least six feet and will rise more. Palm trees grow in Pennsylvania. The once-reclaimed deserts of the American Southwest look as if they'd been blasted by the hot breath of the Sun. The Midwest is a dust bowl. And…"

"What has this got to do with the reception we might get?" said Peter Stagg.

"Just this. The central Atlantic seaboard seems to be on the road to recovery. That is why I'm recommending we land there. But the technological and social setup there is apparently that of a peasant state. You've seen how the coast is busy as a hive of bees. Gangs planting trees, digging irrigation ditches, building dams, roads. Almost every activity out of which we've been able to make sense is directed at rebuilding the soil.

"And the ceremonies we've seen through the plate were obviously fertility rites. The absence of an advanced technology might indicate several things. One, science as we knew it has been lost. Two, a revulsion against science and its practitioners exists—because science is blamed, fairly or not, for the holocaust that has scourged Earth."

"So?"

"So these people probably have forgotten that Earth once sent out a starship to explore interstellar space and locate virgin planets. They may look upon us as devils or monsters—especially if we represent the science they may have been taught to loathe as the spirit of evil. I'm not just conjecturing on the basis of pure imagination, you know. The images on their temple walls and the statues, and some of the pageants we've witnessed, clearly show a hatred of the past. If we come to them out of the past, we might be rejected. Rather fatally for us."

Stagg began pacing back and forth.

"Eight hundred years since we left the Earth," he muttered. "Was it worth it? Our generation, our friends, enemies, our wives, sweethearts, children, their children and their children's children… shoveled under and become grass. And that grass turned to dust. The dust that blows around the planet is the dust of the ten billion who lived when we lived. And the dust of God knows how many more tens of billions. There was a girl I didn't marry because I wanted this great adventure more…"

"You're alive," said Calthorp. "And eight hundred and thirty-two years old, Earth-time."

"But only thirty-two years old in physiological time," Stagg said. "How can we explain to those simple people that as our ship crept toward the stars, we slept, frozen like fish in ice? Do they know anything about the techniques of suspended animation? I doubt it. So how will they comprehend that we only stayed out of suspended animation long enough to search for Terrestrial-type planets? That we discovered ten such, one of which is wide open for colonization?"

"We could go around Earth twice while you make a speech," said Calthorp. "Why don't you get down off your soapbox and take us to Earth so we can find out what's facing us? And so you might find a woman to replace the one you left behind?"

"Women!" shouted Stagg, no longer looking dreamy.

"What?" said Calthorp, startled by his captain's sudden violence.

"Women! Eight hundred years without seeing a single, solitary, lone, forlorn woman! I've taken one thousand ninety-five S.P. pills—enough to make a capon out of a bull elephant! But they're losing their effect! I've built up a resistance! Pills or not, I want a woman. I could make love to my own toothless and blind great-grandmother. I feel like Walt Whitman when he boasted he jetted the stuff of future republics. I've a dozen republics in me!"

"Glad to see you've quit acting the nostalgic poet and are now yourself," said Calthorp. "But quit pawing the ground. You'll get your fill of women soon enough. From what I've seen in the plate, women seem to have the upper hand, and you know you can't stand a domineering female."

Gorilla-fashion, Stagg pounded his big hard chest.

"Any woman comes up against me will run into a hard time!"

Then he laughed and said, "Actually, I'm scared. It's been so long since I've talked to a woman, I won't know how to act."

"Just remember that women don't change. Old Stone Age or Atomic Age, the colonel's lady and Judy O'Grady are still the same."

Stagg laughed again and affectionately slapped Calthorp's thin back. Then he gave orders to make planetfall. But during the descent, he said, "Do you think there's a chance we might get a decent reception?"

Calthorp shrugged.

"They might hang us. Or they might make us kings."

As it happened, two weeks after he made a triumphal entry into Washington, Stagg was crowned.

2

"Peter, you look every inch a king," Calthorp said. "Hail to Peter the Sixth!"

Calthorp, despite his ironic tone, meant what he said.

Stagg was six feet six inches tall, weighed two hundred and thirty-five pounds, and had a forty-eight inch chest, thirty-two inch waistline, and thirty-six inch hips. His red-gold hair was long and wavy. His face was handsome as an eagle's was handsome. Just now he looked like an eagle in his cage, for he was pacing back and forth, hands behind his back like folded wings, his head bent forward, his dark blue eyes fierce and intent. Now and then he scowled at Calthorp.

The anthropologist was slumped in a huge, gold-plated chair, a long jeweled cigar-holder dangling from his lips. He, like Stagg, had permanently lost his facial hair. One day after landing, they had been showered, shampooed, and massaged. The servants had shaved them by simply applying a cream to their faces and then wiping the cream off with a towel. Both men thought this was a delightfully easy way to shave until they discovered that the cream had deprived them forever of their right to grow whiskers if they felt like it.

Calthorp cherished his beard, but he had not objected to being shaved because the natives made it clear that they regarded beards as an abomination and a stench in the nostrils of the Great White Mother. Now he lamented its disappearance. He had not only lost his patriarchal appearance, he had exposed his weak chin.

Suddenly, Stagg halted his pacing to stand before the mirror that covered one wall of the tremendous room. He looked hard at his image and at the crown on his head. It was gold, with fourteen points, each tipped by a large diamond. He looked at the inflated green velvet collar around his neck, at his bare chest, on which was painted a flaming sun. He regarded distastefully the broad jaguarskin belt around his waist, the scarlet kilt, the enormous black phallic symbol stitched to the front of the kilt, the shiny, white leather, knee-length boots. He looked at the King of Deecee in all his splendor, and he snarled. He jerked off the crown and savagely threw it across the room. It struck the far wall and rolled back across the room to his feet.

"So I've been crowned ruler of Deecee!" he shouted. "King of the Daughters of Columbia. Or, as they say in their degenerate American, *Ken-a dot uh K'lumpaha.*

"What kind of a monarch am I? I am not allowed to exercise any of the powers and privileges a king should have. I have been ruler of this woman-ridden land for two weeks, and I've had all sorts of parties in my honor. I've had my praises sung, literally, everywhere I go with my one-breasted Guard of Honor. I am initiated into the totem frat of the Elks—and, let me repeat, they were the weirdest rites I've ever heard of. And I was chosen Big Elk Of The Year..."

"Naturally, with a name like Stagg, you'd belong to the Elks," Calthorp said. "It's a good thing they didn't find out your middle name was Leo. They'd have had a hell of a time deciding whether you belonged to the Elks or the Lions. Only..."

He frowned. Stagg kept on raving.

"They tell me I am Father of My Country. If I am, why don't I get a chance to be one? They won't allow a woman to be alone with me! When I complain about it, that lovely bitch, the Chief Priestess, tells me I am not allowed to discriminate in favor of any one woman. I am the father, lover and son, of every woman in Deecee!"

Calthorp was looking gloomier and gloomier. He rose from his chair and walked to the huge French windows on the second story of the White House. The natives thought the royal mansion was named so in honor of the Great White Mother. Calthorp knew better, but he was too intelligent to argue. He motioned to Stagg to come by him and look out.

Stagg did so, but he sniffed loudly and made a face.

Calthorp pointed out the window to the street. Several men were lifting a large barrel onto the back of the wagon.

"Honeydippers was the ancient name for them," said Calthorp. "Every day they come by and collect their stuff for the fields. This is a world where every little grunt is for the glory of the nation and the enrichment of the soil."

"You'd think we'd be used to it by now," Stagg said. "But the odor seems to get stronger every day."

"Well, it's not a new odor around Washington. Though in the old days there was less of the human and more of the bull."

Stagg grinned and said, "Who ever thought America, land of the two-bathroom house, would go back to the little house with the crescent on the door? Except the little houses don't have doors. It's not because they don't know anything about plumbing. We have running water in our apartments."

"Everything that comes out of the earth must go back to the earth. They don't sin against Nature by piping millions of tons of phosphates and other chemicals, which the soil needs, into the ocean. They're not like we were, blind stupid fools killing our earth in the name of sanitation."

"This lecture wasn't why you called me to the window," Stagg said.

"Yes, it was. I wanted to explain the roots of this culture. Or try to. I'm handicapped because I've spent most of my time learning the language."

"It's English. But farther from our brand than ours was from Anglo-Saxon."

"It's degenerated, in the linguistical sense, far faster than was predicted. Probably because of the isolation of small groups after the Desolation. And also because the mass of the people are illiterate. Literacy is almost the exclusive property of the religious ministers and the *diradah.*"

"*Diradah?*"

"The aristocrats. I think the word originally was deer-riders.

Only the privileged are allowed to ride deer. *Diradah.* Analogous to the Spanish *caballero* or French *cavalier.* Both originally meant *horseman.* I've several things to show you, but let's look at that mural again."

They walked to the far end of the long room and stopped before an enormous and brightly colored mural.

"This painting," Calthorp said, "depicts the great basic myth of Deecee. As you can see"—he pointed at the figure of the Great White Mother towering over the tiny plains and mountains and even tinier people—"she is very angry. She is helping her son, the Sun, to blast the creatures of Earth. She is rolling back the blue shield she once flung around Earth to protect it from the fierce arrows of her son.

"Man, in his blindness, greed, and arrogance, has fouled the Goddess-given earth. His ant-heap cities have emptied their filth into the rivers and seas and turned them into vast sewers. He has poisoned the air with deadly fumes. These fumes, I suppose, were not only the products of industry but of radioactivity. But the Deecee, of course, know nothing of atomic bombs.

"Then Columbia, unable any longer to endure man's poisoning of Earth and his turning away from her worship, ripped away her protective shield around Earth—and allowed the Sun to hurl the full force of his darts upon all living creatures."

"I see all those people and animals falling down all over Earth," Stagg said. "On the streets, in the fields, on the seas, in the air. The grasses shrivel, and the trees wither. Only the humans and animals lucky enough to have been sheltered from the Sun's arrows survived."

"Not so lucky," Calthorp said. "They didn't die from sunburn, but they had to eat. The animals came forth at night and ate the carrion and each other. Man, after devouring all the canned goods, ate the animals. And then man ate man.

"Fortunately, the deadly rays lasted only a short time, perhaps less than a week. Then the Goddess relented and replaced her protective shield."

"But what *was* the Desolation?"

"I can only surmise. Do you remember that just before we left Earth the government had commissioned a research company to develop a system for broadcasting power over the entire planet? A shaft was to be sunk into the earth deep enough to tap the heat radiating from the core. The heat was to be converted into electricity and transmitted around the world, using the ionosphere as a medium of conduction.

"Theoretically, every electrical system on the planet could tap this power. That meant, for instance, that the city of Manhattan could draw down from the ionosphere all the power it needed to light and heat all buildings, run all TV sets, and, after electric motors were installed, power all vehicles.

"I believe that the idea was realized about twenty-five years after we left Earth. I also believe that the warnings of some scientists, notably Cardon, were justified. Cardon predicted that the first full-scale broadcast would strip away a part of the ozone layer."

"My God!" Stagg said. "If enough ozone in the atmosphere was destroyed... !"

"The shorter waves of the ultraviolet spectrum, no longer

absorbed by the ozone, would fall upon every living creature exposed to the sunlight. Animals—including man—died of sunburn. Plants, I imagine, were sturdier. Even so, the effect on them must have been devastating enough to account for the great deserts we saw all over Earth.

"And as if that wasn't enough, Nature—or the Goddess, if you prefer—struck man just as he was shakily getting to his feet. The ozone imbalance must have lasted a very short time. Then natural processes restored the normal amount. But about twenty-five years later, just as man was beginning to form small isolated societies here and there—the population must have dropped from ten billion to a million in a year's time—extinct volcano ranges all over Earth began erupting.

"I don't know. Maybe man's probings into the Earth caused this second cataclysm—twenty-five years delayed because Earth works slowly, but surely.

"Most of Japan sank. Krakatoa disappeared. Hawaii blew up. Sicily cracked in two. Manhattan sank under the sea a few meters and then rose again. The Pacific was ringed by belching volcanoes. The Mediterranean was a lesser inferno. Tidal waves roared far inland, stopping only at the feet of the mountains. The mountains shook, and those who had escaped the tidal waves were buried under avalanches.

"Result: man reduced to the Stone Age, the atmosphere filled with the dust and carbon dioxide that make for the magnificent sunsets and subtropical climate in New York, melting icecaps..."

"No wonder there was so little continuity between our

society and that of the survivors of the Desolation," Stagg said. "Even so, you'd think they would have rediscovered gunpowder."

"Why?"

"Why? Because making black gunpowder is so simple and so obvious!"

"Sure," Calthorp said. "So simple and so obvious it only took mankind a mere half a million years to learn that mixing charcoal, sulfur, and potassium nitrate in the proper proportions resulted in an explosive mixture. That's all.

"Now, you take a double cataclysm like the Desolation. Almost all books perished. There was a period of over a hundred years in which the extremely few survivors were so busy scratching out a living they didn't have time to teach their youngsters the three R's. The result? Abysmal ignorance, an almost complete loss of history. To these people, the world was created anew in 2100 A.D. or 1 A.D. their time. A.D. After the Desolation. Their myths say it is so.

"I'll give you an example. Cotton-raising. When we left Earth, cotton was no longer raised, because plastics had replaced fiber clothing. Did you know that the cotton plant was rediscovered only two hundred years ago? Corn and tobacco never vanished. But until three centuries ago, people wore animal skins or nothing. Mostly nothing."

Calthorp led Stagg from the mural back to the open French windows. "I digress, though we've little else to do. Look out there, Pete. You see a Washington, or Wazhtin as it's now called, like none we knew. Washington has been leveled twice since we left, and the present city was built two hundred years ago over the site of the dead cities. An attempt was made to model it after the previous metropolis. But a different *Zeitgeist* possessed the builders. They built it as their beliefs and myths dictated."

He pointed to the Capitol. In some respects, it resembled the one they remembered. But it had two domes instead of one, and on top of each dome was a red tower.

"Modeled after the breasts of the Great White Mother," Calthorp said. He pointed at the Washington Monument, now located about a hundred yards to the left of the Capitol. It was three hundred feet high, a tower of steel and concrete, painted like a barber pole with red, white, and blue stripes and topped with a round red structure.

"No need to tell you what that is supposed to represent. The myth is that it belonged to the Father of His Country. Washington himself is supposed to be buried under it. I heard that story last night, told in all devoutness by John Barleycorn himself."

Stagg stepped through the open French windows onto the porch outside his second-story apartment. The porch ran completely around the second story, but Calthorp walked no farther than around the corner. Stagg, who had delayed following him, found him leaning on the porch railing. This was composed of small marble caryatids which supported broad trays on their heads. Calthorp pointed over the tops of the thick orchard in the White House yard.

"See that white building with the enormous statue of a woman on top? She is Columbia, the Great White Mother, watching over and protecting her people. To us she is just a figure in a heathen religion. But to her people—our descendants—she is a vivid and vital force that directs this nation toward its destiny. And does so through ruthless means. Anybody who stands in her way is crushed—one way or another."

"I saw the Temple when we first came into Washington," Stagg said. "We passed it on the way to the White House. Remember how Sarvant almost died of shame when he saw the sculptured figures on the walls?"

"What did you think of them?"

Stagg turned red, and he growled, "I thought I was hardened, but those statues! Disgusting, obscene, absolutely pornographic! And decorating a place dedicated to worship."

Calthorp shook his head. "Not at all. You have been to two of their services. They were conducted with great dignity and great beauty. The state religion is a fertility cult, and those figures are representations of various myths. They tell stories whose obvious moral is that man has once almost destroyed the earth because of his terrible pride. He and his science and arrogance upset the balance of Nature. But now that it is restored, it is up to man to retain his humility, to work hand in hand with Nature—whom they believe to be a living goddess, whose daughters mate with heroes. If you noticed, the goddesses and heroes depicted on the walls emphasized through their postures the importance of the worship of Nature and fertility."

"Yes? From some of the positions they were in, I'd say they certainly weren't going to fertilize anything."

Calthorp smiled. "Columbia is also the goddess of erotic love."

"I have the feeling," Stagg said, "that you're trying to tell me something. But you're taking a very indirect route. I also have a feeling that I won't like what you're trying to tell me."

At that moment they heard the clanging of a gong in the room they'd just left. They hurried back to see what was going on.

They were greeted by a blast of trumpets and roll of drums. In marched a band of musician-priests from the nearby Georgetown University. These were fat well-fed fellows who had castrated themselves in honor of the Goddess—and, incidentally, to get a lifelong position of prestige and security. Like women, they were dressed in high-necked, long-sleeved blouses and ankle-length skirts.

Behind them walked the man known as John Barleycorn. Stagg didn't know his real name; "John Barleycorn" was evidently a title. Nor did Stagg know Barleycorn's exact position in the government of Deecee. He lived in the White House, on the third floor, and seemed to have much to do with the administration of the country. His function was probably similar to that of the Prime Minister of ancient Great Britain.

The Sunheroes, like the monarch of that country, were more figureheads, binders of loyalty and tradition, than actual rulers. Or so it seemed to Stagg, who had been forced to guess at the meaning of most of the phenomena that flashed and buzzed by him during his imprisonment.

John Barleycorn was a very tall and very thin man of about thirty-five. His long hair was dyed a bright green, and he wore green spectacles. His long ski-slope nose and his face were covered with broken red veins. He wore a tall green plug hat. Around his neck hung a string of ears of corn. His torso was bare. His kilt was green, and the sporran hanging from his belt was made of stiff cloth shaped like the leaves of corn. His sandals were yellow.

In his right hand he carried his emblem of office, a large bottle of white lightning.

"Hail, man and myth!" he said to Stagg. "Greetings to the Sunhero! Greetings to the ramping, snorting stag of the Elk totem! Greetings to the Father of His Country and the Child and Lover of the Great White Mother!"

He took a long swig from the bottle, smacked his lips, and passed it to Stagg.

"I need that," said the captain, and swallowed a mouthful. A minute later, after choking, gasping, and weeping great tears, he returned the bottle.

Barleycorn was elated. "You gave a splendid performance, Noble Elk! You must have been visited by the special potency of Columbia Herself to be so stricken by the white lightning. Indeed, you are divine! Now take me, I am only a poor mortal, and when I first drank white lightning, I was affected. Still, I must confess that when I first assumed office as a lad I was able to feel the holy presence of the Goddess in the bottle and to be affected as much as yourself. But a man may become hardened even to divinity, may She pardon my saying so. Have I ever told you the story of how Columbia first liquified a lightning bolt and then bottled it? And how She gave it to the first man, none other than Washington himself? And how disgracefully he behaved and thereby incurred the wrath of the Goddess?

"I have? Well, to business, then. I am preceding the Chief

Priestess herself to give you a message. To whit and to-whooooo! Tomorrow is the birthday of the Son of the Great White Mother. And you, the child of Columbia, will be born tomorrow. And then what has been will be."

He took another drink, bowed to Stagg, almost fell on his face, recovered, and staggered out of the room.

Stagg called him back. "Just a minute! I want to know what has happened to my crew!"

Barleycorn blinked. "I told you that they were in a building on the campus of Georgetown University."

"I want to know where they are now—at this moment!"

"They are being treated very well. Anything they want they may have, except their freedom. And they will get that day after tomorrow."

"Why then?"

"Because you, too, will be released. Of course, you won't be able to see them then. You'll be on the Great Route."

"What is that?"

"It will be revealed."

Barleycorn turned to leave, but Stagg said, "Tell me, why is that girl being kept in a cage? You know, the one with the sign that says: 'Mascot, Captured in a Raid on Caseyland.'"

"That, too, will be revealed, Sunhero. Meanwhile, I suggest that it is unbecoming in a man of your importance to lower himself by asking questions. The Great White Mother will explain everything in due time."

After Barleycorn had left, Stagg said to Calthorp, "What nonsense is he trying to cover up?"

The little man frowned. "Wish I knew. After all, my chances for an examination into the social mechanisms of this culture have been rather limited. It's just that there is..."

"There's what?" Stagg said anxiously. Calthorp was looking very gloomy.

"Tomorrow is the winter solstice. Midwinter—when the sun is weakest in the northern hemisphere and has reached its most southerly station. On the calendar we knew, it was December twenty-first or twenty-second. As near as I can remember, that was a very important date in prehistoric and even historic times. All sorts of ceremonies connected with it, such as... ahhh!"

It was more a wail than an exclamation of sudden remembrance.

Stagg became even more alarmed. He was about to ask him what was wrong, but he was interrupted by another blast from the band. The musicians and the attendants faced the door and fell on their knees.

They cried in unison, "Chief Priestess, living flesh of Virginia, daughter of Columbia! Holy maiden! Beautiful one! Virginia, soon to lose to the raging stag—heedless, savage, tearing male—your sanctified and tender fold! Blessed and doomed Virginia!"

A tall girl of eighteen walked haughtily into the apartment. She was beautiful, though she had a high-bridged nose and a very white face. Her full lips were red as blood. Her blue eyes were piercing and unflinching as a cat's. Her curling honey-colored hair fell to her hips. She was Virginia, graduate of Vassar College for Oracular Priestesses and incarnate daughter of Columbia.

"Hello, mortals," she said in a high clear voice.

She looked at Stagg.

"Hello, immortal."

"Hello, Virginia," he answered. He felt the blood spurting through his flesh and the ache building up in his chest and loins. Every time he met her, he experienced this almost irrepressible desire for her. He knew that if he were left alone with her, he would take her, no matter what the consequences.

Virginia gave no sign that she was aware of her effect upon him. She regarded him with the cool unfaltering stare of a lioness.

Virginia, like all mascots, was clothed in a high-necked and ankle-length garment, but her garment was covered with large pearls. A large triangular opening in the dress exposed her large but upthrusting breasts. The areola of each was rouged and circled by two rings of blue and white paint.

"Tomorrow, immortal, you will become both Child and Lover of the Mother. Therefore, it is necessary that you prepare yourself."

"Just what do I have to do to prepare myself?" Stagg said. "And why should I?"

He looked at her and ached through his whole body.

She motioned with one hand. Instantly John Barleycorn, who must have been waiting around the corner, appeared. He now carried two bottles, the white lightning and some dark liquor. A priest-eunuch offered him a cup. He filled it with the dark stuff, and handed it to the priestess.

"Only you, Father of Your Country, may drink this," she said, giving the cup to Stagg. "This is the best. Made from the waters of the sticks."

Stagg took the cup. He looked at it dubiously, but he tried to be nonchalant. "Real mountain hooch, hey? Well, here goes. Never let anybody say that Peter Stagg couldn't outdrink the best of them. Aaourrwhoosh!"

The trumpets blew, the drums beat, the attendants clapped their hands and whooped.

It was then that he heard Calthorp protesting. "Captain, you misunderstood! She didn't say sticks. She said *Styx*. Waters of the S-T-Y-X! Get it?"

Stagg had gotten it, but there was nothing he could do about it. The room whirled around and around, and darkness rushed in like a great black bat.

Amid the trumpets and the cheering, he fell headlong toward the floor.

3

“What a hangover!” Stagg groaned.

“I’m afraid they do,” said a voice that Stagg faintly recognized as Calthorp’s.

Stagg sat up and then yelled from the pain and the shock. He rolled out of bed, fell to his knees from weakness, struggled to his feet, and staggered to the three full-length mirrors set at angles to each other. He was naked. His testicles were painted blue; his penis, red; his buttocks, white. He did not think about that. He could think about nothing except the two things he saw sticking at a 45-degree angle from his forehead for a foot and then branching out into many points.

“Horns! What’re they doing there? Who put them there? By God, if I get my hands on the practical joker…” and he tried to pull the things from his head. He yelled with pain and let his hands drop to his side while he stared into the mirror. There was a stain of blood at the base of one of the horns.

“Not horns,” Calthorp said. “Antlers. I like to be specific.

Antlers—and not the hard, dead, horny kind, either. They're fairly soft, warm and velvety, as a matter of fact. If you will put your thumb there, you can feel an artery pulsing, just under the surface. Whether they will later become the hard dead antlers of the mature—pardon the pun—stag, I don't know."

The captain was scared and looking for something at which to get angry.

"All right, Calthorp!" he roared. "Are you in on this monkey business? Because if you are, I'll tear you limb from limb!"

"You not only look like a beast, you're beginning to act like one," Calthorp murmured.

Stagg could have struck the little anthropologist for his ill-timed humor. Then he saw that Calthorp was pale and his hands were shaking. His attitude was a cover-up for his very real fright.

"All right," Stagg said, calming down somewhat. "What happened?"

Voice trembling, Calthorp told him that the priests had carried his unconscious body toward his bedroom. But a mob of priestesses had rushed in and seized him. For a terrible moment Calthorp had feared that Stagg would be torn apart by the two factions. However, the fight was a mock one, a ritual; the priestesses were supposed to win the body.

Stagg had been carried into the bedroom. Calthorp tried to follow, but he was literally thrown out.

"I soon got the point. They didn't want a man in the room—except you. Even the surgeons were women. I tell you, when I saw them enter your room carrying saws and drills and bandages and all sorts of paraphernalia, I about went out of my mind. Especially when I saw that the surgeons were drunk. In fact, all the women were drunk. What a wild bunch! But John Barleycorn made me leave. He told me that at this time the women were likely to tear apart—literally—any man they encountered. He hinted that some of the musicians had not voluntarily qualified for candidacy as priests; they had just not been spry enough to get out of the way of the ladies on the evening of the winter solstice.

"Barleycorn asked me if I were an Elk. Only the totem brothers of the Great Stag were comparatively safe during this time. I replied that I wasn't an Elk, but I was a member of the Lions Club—though my dues hadn't been paid for a long time. He said I would have been safe last year, when the Sunhero was a Lion. But I was in great danger now. And he insisted on my leaving the White House until the Son—by which he meant you—was born. So I did. I came back at dawn and found everyone gone, except you. I stayed by your bedside until you woke up."

He shook his head and clucked with sympathy.

"Do you know," Stagg said, "some things are coming back to me. It's vague and mixed up, but I can remember coming to after taking that drink. I was weak and helpless as a baby. There was a great noise around me. Women screaming as if they were in the pain of childbirth..."

"You were the baby," Calthorp said.

"Yes. How did you know?"

"Things are beginning to shape a not unfamiliar pattern."

"Don't leave me in the dark when you see the light!" Stagg pleaded. "Anyway, I was only half-conscious most of the time. I tried to resist when they put me on a table and then placed a little white lamb on top of me. I didn't have the slightest idea of what they intended—until they cut its throat. I was drenched in the blood from head to foot.

"Then it was taken away, and I was being forced through a narrow triangular opening. The opening must have had a skeleton of metal, but it was surrounded by some pinkish spongy stuff. Two priestesses had me by the shoulders and were pulling me through the opening. The others were caterwauling like banshees. Dopey as I was, my blood was chilled. You never heard such God-awful shrieks in your life!"

"Yes, I did," Calthorp said. "All Washington heard them. The entire adult population was standing right outside the White House gates."

"I was stuck in the opening, and the priestesses were pulling violently at me. My shoulders were jammed. Suddenly, I felt water squirting on my back; somebody must have turned a hose on me. I remember thinking that they must have some sort of pump in the house, for the water had terrific pressure behind it.

"Then, I had slipped through the opening—but I didn't fall to the floor. Two priestesses grabbed my legs. I was lifted into the air and held upside down. And I was spanked, spanked hard. I was so surprised I yelled."

"Which was what they wanted you to do."

"Then I was placed on another table. My nose and mouth and eyes were cleaned out. It's funny, but up to then I hadn't noticed that I had a thick mucus-like stuff in my mouth and up my nostrils. I must have had some trouble breathing, but I wasn't aware of it. Then… then…"

"Then?"

Stagg turned red.

"Then they carried me to this enormously fat priestess, lying propped up on pillows on my bed. I'd never seen her before."

"Maybe she came down from Manhattan," Calthorp said. "Barleycorn told me the Chief Priestess there is enormously fat."

"Enormous is the word for her," Stagg continued. "That woman was the biggest I've ever seen. I'll bet that if she'd stood up, she'd have been as tall as I am. And she must have weighed over three hundred and fifty pounds. She was powdered all over her body—it must have taken a barrel of powder to cover her. She was huge and round and white. A human Queen Bee, born to do nothing but lay millions of eggs and..."

"And what?" Calthorp asked after Stagg had been silent for at least a minute.

"They placed me so my head was on one of her breasts. It's the hugest in the world, I'll swear it. It seemed like the curve of Earth itself. Then she took my head and turned it. I tried to fight, but I was so weak, I could not resist. I could do nothing.

"Suddenly, I did feel like a little baby. I wasn't a full grown man; I was Peter Stagg, just born. It must have been the effect of that drug. It's a hypnotic agent, I'll swear. Anyway, I was... I was..."

"Hungry?" Calthorp said quietly.

Stagg nodded his head.

Then, in an obvious desire to get away from the subject, he put his hand on one of the antlers and said, "Hmmm. The horns are rooted solidly."

"Antlers," Calthorp said. "But you may as well continue

misusing the term. I notice the Deecee use the inexact word too. Well, even if they don't distinguish between antlers and horns in common speech, their scientists are wonderful biologists. Maybe not so hot in physics and electronics, but superb artists in flesh. By the way, those antlers are more than symbolical and ornamental. They function. A thousand to one that they contain glands that are pumping all sorts of hormones into your bloodstream."

Stagg winced. "What makes you think that?"

"For one thing, Barleycorn dropped a few hints that they would. For another, there's your phenomenally rapid recovery from a major operation. After all, it was necessary to cut two holes in your skull, plant the antlers, tie off blood vessels, connect the bloodstream of the antlers with your bloodstream, and who knows what else?"

Stagg growled and said, "Somebody's going to be sorry for this. That Virginia is behind this! I'll rip her apart the next time I see her. I'm tired of being kicked around."

Calthorp had been anxiously watching him. He said, "You feel all right now?"

Stagg flared his nostrils and thumped his chest. "I didn't. But now I feel like I could lick the world. Only thing is, I'm hungry as a bear that's just come out of hibernation. How long have I been out?"

"About thirty hours. As you can see, it's getting dark outside." Calthorp put his hand on Stagg's forehead. "You have a fever. No wonder. Your body is roaring like a furnace, building new cells right and left, pumping hormones like mad into your blood. You need fuel for the furnace."

Stagg crashed his fist on a table top. "I need drink, too! I'm burning up!"

He rammed his fist into the gong repeatedly, until the notes rang throughout the palace. As if they'd been waiting for the signal, servants exploded through the door. They carried trays with many dishes and goblets.

Stagg, all politeness forgotten, tore a tray from the hands of a servant and began stuffing the meat, potatoes, gravy, corn, tomatoes, bread, and butter into his rapidly working jaws, only stopping to wash them down with tremendous drafts of beer. The food and beer slopped on his bare chest and legs but, though he'd always been a fastidious eater, he paid no attention.

Once, after a huge belch that almost knocked over a servant, he roared, "I can outeat, outdrink..." Another giant belch interrupted him, and he fell again to eating like a hog in a trough.

Sickened not only at the sight but at its implications, Calthorp turned away. Evidently the hormones were washing away his captain's inhibitions and exposing the purely animal part of the human being. What would come next?

Finally, his belly sticking out like a bull gorilla's, Stagg rose. He thumped his chest and howled, "I feel great, great! Hey, Calthorp, you ought to get yourself a pair of horns! Oh, that's right, I forgot, you got a pair. That's why you left Earth the first time, wasn't it? Haw, haw!"

The little anthropologist, his face flaming and twisted, screeched and ran at Stagg. Stagg laughed and picked him up by his shirt and held him out at arm's length while Calthorp cursed and swung futilely with his short arms. Suddenly, Calthorp felt the room go by him with a rush. He slammed hard into something behind him. There was a loud clang, and he knew dimly, even as he sat half-unconscious on the floor, that he had been thrown into the gong.

He became aware that a huge hand had gripped him painfully around his wrist, hauling him to his feet. Frightened that Stagg was going to finish him off, he clenched his fist to strike a brave but futile blow. Then he dropped his fist.

Tears were running out of Stagg's eyes.

"Great God, what's the matter with me? I must be completely out of my head ever to do anything like that to you, my best friend! What's *wrong*? How could I do that?"

He sobbed and pulled Calthorp close to his great body and squeezed him affectionately. Calthorp shrieked with pain as his ribs threatened to give way. Stagg, looking hurt, released him.

"Okay, you're forgiven," Calthorp said, retreating cautiously. By now he realized that Stagg was not responsible for what he did. He had become a child in some ways. But a child is not absolutely selfish and may often be tenderhearted. Stagg was genuinely sorry and ashamed.

Calthorp went to the French windows and looked out.

"The street is alive with people and blazing with torches," he said. "They must be having another shindig tonight."

Even to himself, he sounded false. He knew well enough that the Deecee were assembled for a ceremony which would have his captain as its guest of honor.

"Skin-dig, you mean," Stagg said. "These people stop at

nothing when they hold a party. Inhibitions are discarded like last year's snakeskin. And they don't care who gets hurt."

Then he made a statement that surprised Calthorp.

"I hope they get the party started soon. The sooner the better."

"For God's sake, why?" Calthorp said. "Haven't you seen enough to scare the living soul right out of your body?"

"I don't know. But there's something in me that wasn't there before. I can feel an eagerness and a power, a real power I've never known before. I feel… I feel… like a god! A god! I'm bursting with the power of all the world! I want to explode! You can't know how I feel! No mere man could!"

Outside, the priestesses screamed as they raced down the street.

The two men stopped talking to listen. They stood like stone statues while they listened to the mock-fight between the priestesses and the Honor Guards. Then, the battle as the Elks beat off the priestesses.

Then, the rush of feet in the hall outside their apartment, the crash as the Elks hit the doors with their bodies so violently they tore them from their hinges.

Stagg was lifted on their shoulders and carried out.

Just for a second, Stagg seemed to be his normal self. He turned and yelled, "Help me, Doc! Help me!"

Calthorp could do nothing except weep.

4

There were eight of them: Churchill, Sarvant, Lin, Yastzhembski, Al-Masyuni, Steinborg, Gbwe-hun, and Chandra.

These, together with the absent Stagg and Calthorp, were the ten survivors of the original thirty that had left Earth eight hundred years ago. They were congregated in the large recreation room of the building in which they had been kept prisoners for six weeks. They were listening to Tom Tobacco.

Tom Tobacco was not his birth-name. What that was, none of them knew. They had asked, but Tom Tobacco had replied that he was not to mention it or hear it spoken. As of the day he had become Tom Tobacco, he was no longer a man but a *dim.* Apparently *dim* was the word for demigod.

"If affairs had gone normally," he was saying, "it would not be me talking to you but John Barleycorn. But the Great White Mother saw fit to end his life before Planting Rites. An election was held, and I, as chief of the great Tobacco frat, took his place as ruler of Deecee. And so I will be until I am too old and feeble—and then what will be will be."

In the short time that the starship personnel had been in Washington, they had learned the phonology, morphology, syntax, and basic vocabulary of standard Deecee speech. The machines in the laboratory of the *Terra* enabled them to speak Deecee with fluency although they could not utter the phonemes exactly as a native would, and probably never would. The structure of English had changed much; there were some sounds that had never been in English or even in its Germanic parent speech; there were many words that had come into being from unknown sources; a combination of stress and tone played an important part in meaning.

Moreover, the lack of knowledge of Deecee culture impeded understanding. To add to the trouble, Tom Tobacco himself could not speak standard Deecee with much ease. He had been born and raised in Norfolk, Virginia, the southernmost city of the nation of Deecee. Nafek, or Norfolkese, differed as much from Wazhdin, of Washingtonese, as Spanish from French, or Swedish from Icelandic.

Tom Tobacco, like his predecessor John Barleycorn, was a tall, thin man. He wore a brown plug hat, a breastplate made of stiff brown cloth in the shape of tobacco leaves, a brown cloak, a greenish kilt from which hung a two-foot-long cigar, and brown calf-length boots. His long hair was brown, his purely decorative spectacles were brown-tinted, and a big brown cigar was stuck in his tobacco-stained teeth. While he talked, he pulled cigars from a pocket in his kilt and passed them around the group. Everybody except Sarvant accepted them and found them excellent.

Tom Tobacco blew out a thick cloud of green smoke and said, "You will be released as soon as I leave. Which will be soon. I am a busy man. I have many decisions to make, many papers to sign, many functions to attend. My time is not my own; it belongs to the Great White Mother."

Churchill puffed on his cigar to allow himself time to think before speaking. The others were all talking at the same time, but when Churchill spoke they were silent. He was the first mate of the *Terra*, and now that Stagg was gone he was not only the official leader but, by force of his personality, the real one.

He was a short stocky man with a thick neck, thick arms, and thick legs. His face was babyish but at the same time strong. He had thick curly red hair and a reddish complexion with a light sprinkling of freckles. His eyes were round and clear blue as a baby's; his nose was short and round. Yet, if he had at first glance all a baby's helplessness, he also had a baby's ability to command those around him. His voice, completely at variance with his appearance, boomed out richly.

"You may be a busy man, Mr. Tobacco, but you are not so busy you can't at least tell us what is going on. We've been prisoners. We've not been allowed to communicate with our captain or with Dr. Calthorp. We have reason to suspect they may have met with foul play. Yet, when we ask about them, we're told that *what will be will be.* Very fine! Very comforting!

"Now, Mr. Tobacco, I demand that we get answers to our questions. And don't think that just because you've guards stationed outside the door, we couldn't tear you apart right now. We want answers, and we want them now!"

"Have a cigar and cool off," said Tom Tobacco. "Certainly, you're mystified and infuriated. But don't talk of rights. You are not citizens of Deecee, and you are in a very precarious situation.

"However, I will give you some answers; that's why I came here. First, you will be released. Second, you will be given a month to fit into the life of Deecee. Third, if, at the end of the month, you show no promise of becoming a good citizen, you will be killed. Not exiled, but killed. If we escorted you across the borders to another country, we would be increasing the population of our enemy states. And we've no intention of doing that."

"Well, at least we know where we stand," Churchill said. "That is, in a vague way. Do we get access to the *Terra*? The results of ten years of unique study are in that ship."

"No, you do not. However, your personal property will be returned to you."

"Thanks," Churchill said. "Do you realize that except for a few books, we *had* no personal property? What will we do for money while we're looking for jobs? Jobs we may not be able to get in this rather primitive society."

"I really can't say," replied Tom Tobacco. "After all, we've allowed you to keep your lives. There were those who didn't want to give you even that."

He stuck two fingers in his mouth and whistled. A man with a small bag in his hand appeared.

"I must go now, gentlemen. Official business. However, in order that you may not break the laws of this blessed nation through ignorance, and also to remove any temptation to steal, this man will enlighten you about our laws and loan you enough coin to buy food for a week. You will repay it after you have jobs—if you have jobs. Columbia bless you."

An hour later, the eight men stood in front of the building out of which they had just been escorted.

Far from being elated, they felt a trifle dazed and more than a little helpless.

Churchill looked at them, and, though he felt as they did, he said, "For God's sake, buck up! What's the matter with you? We've been through worse than this. Remember when we were on Wolf 69 III, crossing that big Jurassic-type swamp on a raft? And the balloon-creature upset us and we lost our weapons in the water and had to make our way back to the ship unarmed? We were far worse off then, and we didn't look nearly so woebegone. What's happened? Aren't you the men you used to be?"

"I'm afraid not," Steinborg said. "It's not that we've lost our courage. It's just that we expected too much. When we were landing on a newly discovered planet, we expected the unexpected and the disastrous. We even looked forward to it. But here, well, we anticipated too much—plus the fact that we are helpless. We're unarmed, and if we run into a bad situation, we can't just shoot our way out and make our way back to the ship."

"So you're going to stand around and hope everything's turned out all right?" Churchill said. "For God's sake! You men were the cream of the crop of Earth, chosen out of tens of thousands of candidates because of your I.Q., your education, your ingenuity, your physical hardihood. And now you're marooned among a people who haven't the knowledge you have in your little finger! You men should be gods—and you're mice!"

"Knock it off," Lin said. "We're still suffering from shock. We don't know what to do, and that's what is scaring us."

"Well, I'm not going to stand around until some kind soul comes along and takes me in hand," Churchill said. "I am going to act—now!"

"And just what are you going to do?" Yastzhembski asked.

"I'm going to walk around Washington until I see something that calls for action. If you men want to come with me, you can. But if you want to go your own ways, that's all right, too. I'll be your leader, but I won't be your shepherd."

"You don't understand," Yastzhembski said. "Six of us don't even belong on this continent. I would like to return to Holy Siberia. Gbwe-hun wants to go back to Dahomey. Chandra, to India. Al-Masyuni, to Mecca. Lin, to Shanghai. But that seems impossible. Steinborg could conceivably get back to Brazil, yet, if he did, he'd find nothing but desert and jungle and howling savages. So..."

"So you have to stay here and do as Tobacco suggested—fit in. Well, that's what I'm going to do. Anybody coming along?"

Churchill didn't wait for more argument. He began walking down the street and did not look back once. When he had turned a corner, however, he stopped to watch a bunch of naked little girls and boys playing ball in the street.

After perhaps five minutes, he sighed. Apparently no one was following him.

He was wrong. Just as he turned to go on, he heard someone calling to him. "Hold on a minute, Churchill."

It was Sarvant.

"Where are the others?" Churchill said.

"The Asiatics have decided to try to get back to their homelands. When I left they were still arguing about whether they should steal a boat and cross the Atlantic, or steal deer and ride up to the Bering Strait, where they'll cross on boat to Siberia."

"I'll give them credit for the greatest guts in the world—or the most stupid brains. Do they really think they can make it? Or that they'll find any better conditions there than here?"

"They don't know what they'll find, but they're desperate."

"I'd like to go back and wish them good luck," Churchill said. "But I'd just end up trying to argue them out of the idea. They are brave men. I knew it when I called them mice, but I was just trying to arouse them. Maybe I succeeded too well."

"I gave them my blessing, even if most of them are agnostics," Sarvant said. "But I fear their bones will bleach on this continent."

"What about you? Are you going to try for Arizona?"

"From what I saw of Arizona while we were still circling Earth, I'd say there's not only no organized government there, there are almost no people. I would try for Utah, but it doesn't look much better. Even the Salt Lake is dried up. There's nothing to go back to. It doesn't matter. There is a lifetime of work here."

"Work? You don't mean preaching?"

Churchill looked incredulously at Sarvant as if seeing his true character for the first time.

Nephi Sarvant was a short, dark, and bony man of about forty. His chin jutted out so far it gave the impression of curving upwards at its end. His mouth was so thin-lipped it was only a thread. His nose, like his chin, was overdeveloped. It hooked downwards as if trying to meet the chin. His crewmates said that in profile he looked like a human nutcracker.

His large brown eyes were very expressive and just now seemed to glow with inner light. They had glowed often during the star-trip when he had extolled the merits of his church as the only true one left on Earth. He belonged to a sect known as the Last Standers, the strictly orthodox core of a church that had undergone the suburbanization most churches had experienced. Once thought a peculiar people, the members of this sect now could be distinguished from other Christians only by the fact that they still attended their church. But the spiritual fires had died out.

Not so the group to which the Sarvant belonged. The Last Standers had refused to adopt the so-called vices of their neighbors. They had collected in a body at the city of Fourth of July, Arizona, and from there had sent out missionaries to an indifferent or amused world.

Sarvant had been chosen to be a crew member of the *Terra* because he was the foremost authority in his field of geology. He had been accepted only after he had promised not to proselytize. He had never explicitly made an attempt to convert. But he had offered to others the Book of his church, asking only that they read. And he had argued with the others about the authenticity of the Book.

"Of course I mean to preach!" he said. "This country is as wide open to the Gospel as it was when Columbus landed. I'll tell you, Rud, that when I saw the desolation of the Southwest I was filled with despair. It seemed that my church had vanished from the face of the Earth. And if that were true, then my church was false, for it was supposed to be eternal. But I prayed, and at once the truth came to me. That is—I still exist! And through me the church can grow again—grow as it never did, for these pagan minds, once convinced of the Truth, will become as the First Disciples. The Book will spread like a flame. You see, we Last Standers could make little headway among Christians because they thought they already had the true church. But the true church meant little more to them than a social club. It wasn't a way of truth and life, the only way. It..."

"I get your point," Churchill said. "The only thing I have to say is, don't implicate me. Things are going to be tough enough. Well, let's go."

"Go where?"

"Someplace where we can trade these monkey suits in for native clothes."

They were on a street called Conch. It ran north and south, so Churchill felt that if they followed it south it would bring them eventually to the port area. Here, unless things changed very much, there would be more than one shop where they could trade their clothes and perhaps make a little profit in the bargain. In this neighborhood, Conch Street was a mixture of well-to-do residences and large government buildings. The residences were set far back on well-tended yards and were of brick or cement. Single-storied, they presented a broad front, and most of them had two wings at right angles to the front buildings. They were painted in many colors and various designs. Every one had a large totem pole in front of it. These were, for the most part, of carved stone, since wood was reserved for shipbuilding, wagons, weapons, and stove fuel.

The government buildings were set close to the street and were of brick or marble. They had curving walls and were surrounded by roofless porches with tall pillars. On top of each dome roof was a statue.

Churchill and Sarvant walked on the asphalt pavement—there was no sidewalk—for ten blocks. Occasionally, they had to step close to the buildings to avoid being run over by men furiously riding deer or driving carriages. The riders were richly dressed and obviously expected the pedestrians to jump out of the way or get trampled. The carriage drivers seemed to be couriers of one type or another.

Abruptly, the street became shabby.

The buildings presented a solid front except for alleys here and there. They were evidently government buildings that had been sold to private agents and had become little shops or tenements. Naked children played in front of them.

These were not nearly as clean as those they had just passed.

Churchill found the shop he was looking for. With Sarvant at his heels, he entered. The inside of the shop was a small room crowded with clothes of every kind. The store window and the cement floor were dirty; the odor of dog excrement filled the shop. Two dogs of indeterminate breed tried to put their paws on the two men.

The owner was a short big-paunched double-chinned bald man with two enormous earrings of brass. He looked much like any shopkeeper of his breed of any century, except that he had the cervine stamp of the times on his features.

"We want to sell our clothes," Churchill said.

"Are they worth anything?" said the owner.

"As clothes, not much," Churchill replied. "As curios, they may be worth a great deal. We are men from the starship."

The owner's little eyes widened. "Ah, brothers to the Sunhero!"

Churchill didn't know all the implications of the exclamation. He knew only that Tom Tobacco had casually mentioned that Captain Stagg had become a Sunhero.

"I'm sure that you could sell each article of our clothing for quite a sum. These clothes have been to the stars, to places so distant that if you were to walk there without stopping to eat or rest it would take you halfway through eternity. The light of alien suns and the air of exotic worlds are caught in the fibers of these suits. And the shoes still bear the traces of earth where monsters bigger than this building have walked like earthquakes."

The shopkeeper was unimpressed. "But has the Sunhero touched these garments?"

"Many times. Once, he wore this jacket."

"Ahhh!"

The owner must have realized that he was betraying his eagerness. He lowered his eyelids and stiffened his face.

"This is all very well, but I am a poor man. The sailors who come to this shop do not have much money. By the time they get past the taverns, they are ready to sell their own clothes."

"Probably true. But I'm sure you have contacts who can sell these to wealthier patrons."

The owner took some coins from the pocket on his kilt.

"I'll give you four columbias for the lot."

Churchill motioned to Sarvant and started to walk out. Before he reached the door, he found the owner blocking his way.

"Perhaps I could offer you five columbias."

Churchill pointed to a kilt and sandals. "How much are those worth? Or I should say, how much are you charging for them?"

"Three fish."

Churchill considered. A Columbia was roughly equal to a five-dollar bill of his time. A fish was equal to a quarter.

"You know as well as I do that you'll be making a thousand-percent-profit off us. I want twenty columbias for these."

The owner threw his hands up in the air in a gesture of despair.

"Come off it," Churchill said. "I'd go from house to house on Millionaire's Row and peddle these. But I haven't the time. Do you want to give us twenty or not? Last offer."

"You're snatching the bread from the mouths of my poor children… but I'll take your offer."

Ten minutes later, the two starmen stepped out of the shop. They wore sandals and kilts and round hats with floppy brims. Their broad leather belts held sheaths with long steel knives, and their pockets contained eight columbias each. They held bags in their hands, and in these bags were rainproof ponchos.

"Next stop, the docks," Churchill said. "I used to sail yachts for the rich during the summers when I was working my way through college."

"I know you can sail," Sarvant said. "Have you forgotten

that you commanded that sailing-ship we stole when we escaped from prison on the planet Vixa?"

"I forgot," Churchill said. "I want to size up the chances for getting a job. Afterwards, we'll start sniffing around. Maybe we can find out what's happened to Stagg and Calthorp."

"Rud," Sarvant said, "there must be more to this than just getting a job. Why boats particularly? I know you well enough to know you're operating on more than one level."

"Okay. I know you're no blabbermouth. If I can find a suitable ship, we'll get hold of Yastzhembski's boys and take off for Asia, via Europe."

"I'm very glad to hear that," Sarvant said. "I thought you'd just walked out on them, washed your hands of them. But how will you find them?"

"Are you kidding?" Churchill said, laughing. "All I have to do is ask at the nearest temple."

"Temple?"

"Sure. It's evident that the government'll be keeping an eye on us. In fact, it's had a tail on us ever since we left our prison."

"Where is he?"

"Don't look around now. I'll point him out to you later. Just keep walking."

Abruptly, Churchill stopped. His way was barred by a circle of men kneeling on the road. There was nothing to keep Churchill from walking around them. But he stopped to look over the shoulders.

"What are they doing?" Sarvant asked.

"Playing the twenty-ninth-century version of craps."

"It's against my principles even to watch gambling. I sincerely hope you're not planning on joining them."

"Yes, I think that's exactly what I'm planning on doing."

"Don't, Rud," Sarvant said, putting his hand on Churchill's arm. "Nothing good can come of this."

"Chaplain, I'm not a member of your parish. They probably abide by the rules. That's all I want." Churchill took three columbias out of his pocket and spoke loudly. "Can I get into this shoot?"

"Sure," a huge dark man with a patch over one eye said. "You can play as long as your money lasts. You just get off the ship?"

"Not so long ago," Churchill said. He sank to his knees and laid a Columbia on the ground. "My turn for the bones, eh? Come on, babies, Poppa needs a pocketful of rye."

Thirty minutes later a grinning Churchill walked toward Sarvant with a handful of silver coins. "The wages of sin," he said.

He lost his grin when he heard a loud shout behind him. Turning, he saw the dice players walking toward him. The big one-eyed man was yelling at him.

"Wait a minute, buddy, we got a couple of questions!"

"Oh, oh," Churchill said out of the side of his mouth. "Get ready to run. These guys are poor losers."

"You didn't cheat, did you?" Sarvant said nervously.

"Of course not! You ought to know me better than that. Besides, I wouldn't take a chance in that rough bunch."

"Listen, buddy," the one-eyed man said. "You talk kinda funny. Where you come from? Albany?"

"Manitowoc, Wisconsin," Churchill said.

"Never heard of that place. What is it, some small burg up north?"

"North by west. Why do you want to know?"

"We don't like strangers that can't even talk Deecee straight. Strangers got queer tricks, especially when they are shooting craps. Only a week ago we caught a tar from Norfolk who was using magic to control the dice. We knocked his teeth out and threw him off the dock with a weight around his neck. Never saw him again."

"If you thought I was cheating, you should have said something while we were playing."

The one-eyed sailor ignored Churchill's remark and said, "I don't notice no frat mark on you. What frat you belong to?"

"Lambda Chi Alpha," Churchill said. He put his hand on his knife-blade.

"What kind of lingo is that? You mean the Lamb frat?"

Churchill could see that he and Sarvant would be considered lambs for the slaughter unless they could prove they were under the protection of some powerful frat. He didn't mind telling a lie in a situation like this if it got him out of it. But a resentment that had been building up for the past six weeks broke into a sudden fury.

"I belong to the human race!" he shouted. "And that's more than you can say for yourself!"

The one-eyed sailor turned red. He growled, "By the breasts of Columbia, I'll cut your heart out! No stinking foreigner can talk that way to me!"

"Come on, you thieves!" Churchill snarled. He pulled his

knife from its sheath and at the same time shouted at Sarvant, "Run like hell!"

The one-eyed sailor had also pulled his knife and came at Churchill with the blade. Churchill threw the handful of silver coins in the man's eyes and at the same time stepped forward. The palm of his left hand struck outwards against the wrist of the other man's knife-hand. The knife fell, and Churchill sank his blade into the bulging paunch of the sailor.

He withdrew the knife and stepped back, crouching, to face the others. But they knew dirty fighting as well as any sailor. One of them picked up a loose brick from a pile of rubble and threw it at Churchill's head. The world grew dim, and he was vaguely aware that blood was streaming over his eyes from a cut on his forehead. By the time he regained his senses, he found his knife taken away and his arms gripped by two strong sailors.

A third, a short skinny fellow with a broken-toothed snarl, stepped up and shoved his blade straight at Churchill's belly.

5

Peter Stagg awoke. He was flat on his back, lying on something soft, with the branches of a large oak tree above him. Through the branches he could see a bright, cloudless sky. There were birds on the branches, a sparrow, a catbird—and a huge jay which sat on its rear and dangled bare and human legs.

The legs were brown and slim and nicely curved. The rest of the body was disguised in the costume of a giant jaybird. Shortly after Stagg opened his eyes, the jay took off its mask and revealed the pretty face of a dark, big-eyed girl. She reached behind her and pulled a bugle that had been hanging from a cord from over her shoulder. Before Stagg could stop her, she blew a long wavering call.

Immediately, a hubbub arose from somewhere behind him.

Stagg sat up and turned around to face the source of the noise. It came from a mob of people standing on the other side of the road. The road was a broad cement highway running past farm fields. Stagg was sitting a few feet from its edge on a thick pile of blankets which someone had thoughtfully placed beneath him.

He had no idea of when or how he had gotten to this spot. Or where it was. He remembered only too vividly events up to shortly before dawn; after that, all was blank. The height of the sun indicated that the time was about eleven in the morning.

The jay-girl lowered herself from the branch, hung for a moment, then dropped the five feet to the ground. She picked herself up and said, "Good morning, Noble Stag. How do you feel?"

Stagg groaned and said, "I'm stiff and sore in every muscle. And I've an awful headache."

"You'll be all right after you have breakfast. And may I say that you were magnificent last night? I've never seen a Sunhero who could come up to you. Well, I must go now. Your friend, Calthorp, said that when you woke you'd want to be alone with him for a while."

"Calthorp!" Stagg said. He groaned again. "He's the last man I want to see." But the girl had run off across the road and joined the group of people.

Calthorp's white head appeared from behind a tree. He approached with a large covered tray in his hands. He was smiling, but it was obvious he was desperately trying to cover up his concern.

"How do you feel?" he shouted.

Stagg told him. "Where are we?"

"I'd say we're on what used to be U.S. 1 but is now called Mary's Pike. We're about ten miles out of the present limits of Washington. Two miles down the road is a little farming town called Fair Grace. Its normal population is two thousand, but just now it's about fifteen thousand. The farmers and the farmers' daughters from miles around have gathered here. Everyone in Fair Grace is eagerly awaiting you. But you are not at their beck and call. You are the Sunhero, so you may rest and take your ease. That is, until sundown. Then you must perform as you did last night."

Stagg looked down and for the first time became aware that he was still nude.

"You saw me last night?" He looked up pleadingly at the old man.

It was Calthorp's turn to stare at the ground. He said, "Ringside seat—for a while, anyway. I sneaked around the edge of the crowd and went into a building. There I watched the orgy from a balcony."

"Don't you have any decency?" Stagg said angrily. "It's bad enough that I couldn't help myself. It's worse that you'd witness my humiliation."

"Some humiliation! Yes, I saw you. I'm an anthropologist. This was the first time I'd ever had a chance to see a fertility rite at close range. Also, as your friend, I was worried about you. But I needn't have; you took care of yourself. Others, too."

Stagg glared. "Are you making fun of me?"

"God forbid! No. I wasn't expressing humor, just amazement. Perhaps envy. Of course, it's the antlers that gave you the drive and the ability. Wonder if they'd give me just a little shot of the stuff those antlers produce."

Calthorp placed the tray in front of Stagg and removed the

cloth over it. "Here's a breakfast such as you never had."

Stagg turned his head to one side. "Take it away. I'm sick. Sick to my stomach and sick to my soul with what I did last night."

"You seemed to be enjoying yourself." Stagg growled with sheer fury, and Calthorp put out a reassuring hand. "No, I meant no offense. It's just that I saw you, and I can't get over it. Come on, lad, eat. Look what we have for you! Fresh baked bread. Fresh butter. And jam. Honey. Eggs, bacon, ham, trout, venison—and a pitcher of cool ale. And you can have second helpings of anything you want."

"I told you, I'm sick! I couldn't eat a thing." Stagg sat silent for a few minutes, staring across the road at the brightly colored tents and the people clustered around them. Calthorp sat down by him and lit up a large green cigar.

Suddenly, Stagg picked up the pitcher and drank deeply of the ale. He put the pitcher down, wiped the foam off his lips with the back of his hand, belched, and picked up a fork and knife.

He began eating as if this were the first meal in his life—or the last.

"I have to eat," he apologized between bites. "I'm weak as a new-born kitten. Look how my hand's shaking."

"You'll have to eat enough for a hundred men," Calthorp said. "After all, you did the work of a hundred—two hundred!"

Stagg reached up with one hand and felt his antlers. "Still there. Hey! They're not standing up straight and stiff like they did last night. They're limp! Maybe they are going to shrink up and dry away."

Calthorp shook his head. "No. When you get your

strength back, and your blood pressure rises, they'll become erect again. They're not true antlers. Those of deer consist of bony outgrowth with no covering of keratin. Yours seem to have a bony base, but the upper part is mainly cartilage surrounded by skin and blood vessels.

"It's no wonder they're deflated. And it's a wonder that you didn't rupture a blood vessel. Or something."

"Whatever it is the horns pump into me," Stagg said, "it must be gone. Except for being weak and sore, I feel normal. If only I could get rid of these horns! Doc, could you cut them off?"

Sadly, Calthorp shook his head.

Stagg turned pale. "Then I have to go through that *again*?"

"I'm afraid so, my boy."

"Tonight, at Fair Grace? And the next night at another town? And so on until… when?"

"Peter, I'm sorry, I have no way of knowing how long."

Calthorp cried out with pain as a huge hand bent his wrist bones towards each other.

Stagg loosened his grip. "Sorry, Doc. I got excited."

"Well, now," Calthorp said, rubbing his wrist tenderly, "there's one possibility. It seems to me that, if all this business started at the winter solstice, it should end at the summer solstice. That is, about June 21 or 22. You are the symbol of the sun. In fact, these people probably regard you as being literally the sun himself—especially since you came down in a flaming iron steed out of the sky."

Stagg put his head in his hands. Tears welled out from between his fingers, and his naked shoulders shook. Calthorp patted his golden head, while tears ran from his own eyes. He knew how terribly grieved his captain must be, if he could weep through the armors of his inhibitions.

Finally, Stagg rose and began walking across the fields toward a nearby creek. "Have to take a bath," he muttered. "I'm filthy. If I have to be a Sunhero, I'm going to be a clean one."

"Here they come," Calthorp said, pointing to the crowd of people who had been waiting about fifty yards away. "Your devout worshipers and bodyguards."

Stagg grimaced. "Just now I loathe myself. But last night I enjoyed what I was doing. I had no inhibitions. I was living the secret dream of every man—unlimited opportunity and inexhaustible ability. I was a *god*!"

He stopped and seized Calthorp's wrist again.

"Go back to the ship! Get a gun, if you have to sneak it past the guards. Come back and shoot me in the head—so I won't have to go through this again!"

"I'm sorry. In the first place, I wouldn't know where to get the gun. Tom Tobacco told me that all weapons have been taken from the ship and locked in a secret room. In the second place, I can't kill you. While there's life, there's hope. We'll get out of this mess."

"Tell me how," Stagg said.

He didn't have time to continue the conversation. The mob had come across the field and surrounded them. Continuity of talk was difficult to maintain when bugles and drums were roaring in your ears, Panpipes shrilling, men and women chattering away at the tops of their voices, and a group of beautiful girls was insisting on bathing you and afterward toweling you down and perfuming you. In a short time the pressure of the crowd forced the two apart.

Stagg began to feel better.

Under the skillful hands of the girls, his soreness was massaged away, and, as the sun climbed toward the zenith, Stagg's strength rose. By two o'clock he was brimming over with vitality. He wanted to be up and doing.

Unfortunately, this was siesta hour. The crowd dispersed to seek shade under which to lie down.

A few faithful stood around Stagg. From their sleepy expression Stagg decided that they, too, would like to lie down. They couldn't; they were his guards, lean hard men armed with spears and knives. A few yards away stood several bowmen. These carried strange arrows. The shafts were tipped with long needles instead of the broad, sharp steel heads. Undoubtedly, the tips were smeared with a drug that would temporarily paralyze any Sunheroes who might dare to run away.

Stagg thought that it was foolish of them to post a guard. Now that he felt better, he didn't care one bit about escaping. Indeed, he wondered why he could have contemplated such a stupid move.

Why should he want to run and take a chance of being killed—when there was so much living to be done?

He walked back across the field, his guards trailing along at a respectful distance. There were about forty tents pitched on a meadow and three times that many people stretched out sleeping. Stagg was not at the moment interested in them.

He wanted to talk to the girl in the cage.

Ever since he had been moved into the White House, he had wondered who she was and why she was kept prisoner. His questions had invariably been answered with the infuriating *What will be will be.* He remembered seeing her as he approached Virginia, the Chief Priestess. The memory brought back a pang of the shame he had felt a little while ago, but it quickly faded.

The wheeled cage was under the shadow of a plane tree, the deer that drew it browsing nearby. There were no guards within earshot.

The girl was sitting on a built-in cucking stool at one end of the cage. Near her stood a peasant smoking a cigar while he waited for her to finish. When she was through, he would remove the chamber pot from the recess underneath the stool and carry it off to his fields to enrich the soil.

She wore the long-billed jockey cap, gray shirt, and calf-length pants that all mascots wore, though the pants were now down around her ankles. Her head was bowed, but Stagg did not think it was because she was ashamed to be performing this need in public view. He had seen too much of the casual, animal-natural—to him—attitude of these people. They could feel shame and inhibition about many things but public excretion was not one of them.

A hammock was pulled tight against the ceiling. A broom stood in the corner and in the opposite corner a cabinet was bolted to the floor. Probably it contained toilet articles, since a rack on the side of the cabinet contained a washbasin and towels.

He looked again at the sign rising from the top of her cage

like a shark's fin. "Mascot, captured in a raid on Caseyland." What did it mean?

He understood that "mascot" was the word the Deecees used for human virgins. The term "virgin" was reserved for maiden goddesses. But there was much he did not understand.

"Hello," he said.

The girl started as if she had been dozing. She raised her head to look at him. She had large dark eyes and petite features. Her skin was white, and it went even whiter when she saw him, and she turned her head away.

"Hello, I said. Can't you speak? I won't hurt you."

"I don't want to talk to you, you beast," she replied in a shaky voice. "Go away."

He had taken a step toward the cage, but now he stopped.

Of course, she had had to witness last night. Even if she kept her head turned and eyes shut, she couldn't have stopped up her ears. And curiosity would have forced her to open her eyes. At least for brief periods.

"I couldn't help what happened," he said. "It's these that did it, not me." He touched the antlers. "They do something to me. I'm not myself."

"Go away," she said. "I won't talk to you. You're a pagan devil."

"Is it because I'm not clothed?" he said. "I'll put a kilt on."

"Go away!"

One of the guards walked up to him. "Great Stag, do you want this girl? You may have her, eventually, but not now. Not until the end of the journey. Then the Great White Mother will give her to you."

"I just want to talk to her."

The guard smiled. "A little fire applied to her cute little ass might get her to talking. Unfortunately we're not allowed to torture her—yet."

Stagg turned away. "I'll find some way to make her talk. But later. Just now, I want some more cold ale."

"At once, sire."

The guard, not caring that he was waking most of the camp, blew shrilly on his whistle. A girl ran from around the corner of a tent.

"Cold ale!" the guard cried.

The girl ran toward the tent and quickly returned with a tray on which stood a copper pitcher, its sides beaded with sweat.

Stagg took the pitcher without thanking the girl and held it to his mouth. He did not lower it until it was empty.

"That was good," he said loudly. "But ale bloats you. Do you have any lightning on ice?"

"Of course, sire."

She returned from the tent with a silver pitcher full of chunks of ice and another pitcher brimming with clear whiskey. She poured the lightning into the pitcher of ice and then handed it to Stagg.

He drank half of the pitcher before he set it back on the tray.

The guard became alarmed. "Great Stag, if you continue at this rate, we'll have to carry you into Fair Grace!"

"A Sunhero can drink as many as ten men," said the girl, "and he will still tumble a hundred mascots in one night."

Stagg laughed like a trumpet blaring. "Of course, mortal,

don't you know that? Besides, what's the use of being the Great Stag if I can't do exactly what I want to do?"

"Forgive me, sire," the guard said. "It's just that I know how anxious the people of Fair Grace are to greet you. Last year, you know, when the Sunhero was a Lion, he took the other road out of Washington. The people of Fair Grace could not attend the ceremonies. So they would feel very bad if you did not show up."

"Don't be a fool," the girl said. "You shouldn't talk this way to the Sunhero. What if he got mad and decided to kill you? That's happened, you know."

The guard blanched. "With your permission, sire, I'll join my friends."

"Do that!" Stagg said, laughing.

The guard trotted away to a group standing about fifty yards off.

"I'm hungry again," Stagg said. "Get me some food. Lots of meat."

"Yes, sire."

Stagg began to prowl around the camp. When he came across a gray-haired fat man snoring away in a hammock stretched between two tripods, he turned the hammock over and dumped the fat man on the ground. Roaring with laughter, he strode around the camp and began shouting in the ear of every sleeper he came across. They sat up, their eyes wide and their hearts beating with shock. He laughed and moved on and seized the leg of a girl and began tickling her on the sole of her foot. She shrieked with laughter and wept and begged him to let her go. A young man, her fiancé, stood by but made no move to free her. His fists were clenched, but it would have been blasphemy to interfere with the Sunhero.

Stagg looked up and saw him. He frowned, released the girl, and rose to his feet. At that moment the girl whom he'd sent for food came with a tray. There were two pitchers of ale on it. Stagg took one and calmly poured it over the head of the young man. Both girls laughed, and that seemed to be a signal to the whole camp. Everybody howled.

The girl with the tray took the other pitcher of ale and poured it over the fat man who had been dumped out of the hammock. The cold liquid brought him sputtering to his feet. He ran into his tent and came out with a small keg of beer. Holding it upside down, he drenched the girl with its contents.

A beer-throwing party exploded across the camp. There wasn't a person on the meadow who wasn't dripping with ale and beer and whiskey, except for the girl in the cage. Even the Sunhero was showered. He laughed when he felt the cool liquid and ran for more to throw back. But on the way he got a new idea. He began pushing the tents over so they would imprison the occupants. Howls of anguish rose from the interiors of the collapsed tents. The others began imitating Stagg's actions, and shortly there was hardly a tent standing on the meadow.

Stagg seized the girl who had served him and the girl whose foot he'd tickled. "You two must be mascots," he said. "Otherwise you'd not be half-naked. How did I happen to miss you last night?"

"We weren't beautiful enough for the first night."

"The judges must be blind," Stagg roared. "Why, you're two

of the most beautiful and desirable girls I've ever seen!"

"We thank you. It's not just beauty that enables you to be chosen as the bride of the Sunhero, sire, though I hesitate to say it for fear of what might happen if a priestess overheard me. But it's true that if your father happens to have wealth and connections, you stand a much better chance of being picked."

"Then why were you two chosen to be in my entourage?"

"We were second-place winners in the Miss America contests, sire. Being in your entourage isn't as great an honor as having one's debut in Washington. But it is still a great honor. And we are hoping that tonight at Fair Grace..."

Both were looking at him with wide eyes. Their lips and nipples were swelling, they were breathing heavily.

"Why wait until tonight?" he bellowed.

"It's not customary to do anything until the rites begin, sire. Anyway, most Sunheroes don't recover from the previous night until evening..."

Stagg downed another drink. He drew the empty pitcher as high in the air as he could and laughed.

"I'm a Sunhero like you've never had! I'm the genuine Stagg!"

He picked up the two girls by their waists, one in each arm, and carried them into the tent.

6

Churchill reared back and tried to kick more teeth out of the snaggle-toothed sailor's mouth. The blow from the brick had taken more than he realized out of him. He could barely lift his legs.

"Yer would, wouldjer?" Snaggletooth squeaked.

He had jumped back at Churchill's threatening move. Now he stepped forward confidently and shoved the knife toward Churchill's solar plexus.

There was a screech, and a little man jumped forward and thrust his arm in the path of the blade. The point went through the open palm and came out redly on the other side.

It was Sarvant, who had taken this clumsy but effective means of keeping his friend from death.

The knife was stopped for only a moment. Another sailor pushed Sarvant so hard he fell backwards, the knife still protruding from his hand. The sailor drew back to plunge his blade into the original target.

A whistle sounded shrilly almost in his ear. He stopped. The whistler reached out a long shepherd's staff and crooked the end around Snaggletooth's scrawny neck.

The whistler was dressed in light blue, and he had light blue eyes to match. They were as cold as eyes could get.

"These men are protected by Columbia Herself," he said. "You men will disperse at once, unless you want to be strung up by the neck inside ten minutes. And you will not attempt to take revenge on these two later on. Do you understand?"

The sailors had turned pale under their deeply tanned skins. They nodded, gulped, and then ran.

"I owe you my life," Churchill said, shakily.

"You owe the Great White Mother," the man in blue said. "And She will collect as it pleases her. I am merely Her servant. For the next four weeks, you are under Her protection. I hope you will prove yourself worthy of Her consideration."

He looked at Sarvant's dripping hand. "I think you owe this man your life, too. Though he was only the tool of Columbia, he served Her well. Come with me. We will fix up that hand."

They followed him down the street, Sarvant moaning with the pain, Churchill supporting him.

"That's the man who was tailing us," Churchill said. "Lucky for us. And—thanks for what you did."

Sarvant's face lost its look of pain and became ecstatic.

"I was glad to do it for you, Rud. It's something I'd do again, even knowing how it would hurt. It made me feel justified."

Churchill didn't know how to reply to that statement, so he said nothing.

Both men were silent until they walked out of the dock area and came to a temple set far back off the street. Their guide led them into the cool interior. He spoke to a priestess in long white robes, who, in turn, led them to a small room. Churchill was asked to wait while Sarvant was taken away.

He didn't object. He was certain they had no evil intentions against Sarvant—at the present.

He paced back and forth for an hour by a huge sandglass on a table. The chamber was quiet and dark and cool.

He was just in the act of turning the big sandglass over when Sarvant reappeared.

"How's the hand?"

Sarvant held it up for Churchill to see. There was no bandage on it. The hole had been glued together, and a transparent film of some substance covered the wound.

"They tell me I can use it at this very moment for hard work," Sarvant said wonderingly. "Rud, these people may be backwards in many respects, but when it comes to biology, they bow to no one. The priestess told me this thin stuff is a pseudoflesh that will grow and make the wound as if it had never been. They gave me a blood transfusion, and then made me eat some food that seemed to charge me with energy at once. But it wasn't for nothing," he concluded wryly. "They said they'd send me the bill."

"The impression I get is that this culture just doesn't tolerate freeloaders," Churchill said. "We'd better get a job of some kind, and fast."

They left the temple and resumed their interrupted journey

toward the docks. This time they passed without incident to the Potomac River.

The docks extended along the banks for at least two kilometers. There were ships tied up alongside the wharves and many anchored in the river itself. "Looks like a picture of an early nineteenth-century port," Churchill said. "Sailing ships of every size and type. I didn't expect to find any steamships, though it's unreasonable to suppose that these people don't know how to build one."

"The coal and oil supplies were exhausted long before we left Earth," Sarvant said. "They could burn wood, but the impression I have is that, while there's no scarcity of trees, they aren't chopped down except for the utmost necessity. And it's evident they either have forgotten the techniques of making nuclear fuel, or else are suppressing the knowledge."

"Wind power may be slow," Churchill said. "But it's free for the taking, and it'll get you there in time. Man, here comes a beautiful ship!"

He gestured at a single-masted yacht with white keel and scarlet sail. It was tacking to come into a slip just below the wharf on which they were standing.

Churchill, motioning to Sarvant, walked down the long steps running down the bank. He liked to talk to sailors, and the people on this yacht looked as if they were the type he had worked for during his college summers.

The man at the wheel was a gray-haired, heavily built man of about fifty-five. The other two looked like his son and daughter. The son was tall, well-built, handsome, a blond of about twenty; his sister was a short girl with a well-developed bust, slim waist, long legs, extremely beautiful face, and long honey-blond hair. She could have been anywhere from sixteen to eighteen years old. She wore loose bell-bottomed trousers and a short blue jacket. Her feet were bare.

She stood in the prow of the boat, and, seeing the two men waiting on the slip, she flashed white teeth and called, “Catch this rope, sailor!”

Churchill caught it and pulled the yacht alongside the slip. The girl leaped down onto the boards and smiled. “Thanks, sailor!”

The blond youth reached into the pocket of his kilt and tossed Churchill a coin. “For your trouble, my man.”

Churchill turned the coin over. It was a Columbia. If these people could tip so generously for such a small service, they must be worth making acquaintance.

He flipped the coin back at the youth, who, though surprised, deftly caught it with one hand.

“I thank you,” Churchill said, “but I am no man’s servant.”

The eyes of the girl widened, and Churchill saw that they were a dark blue-gray.

“We meant no offense,” she said. She had a rich throaty voice.

“No offense taken,” Churchill said.

“I can tell by your accent you’re not a Deecee,” she said. “Would it offend you if I asked what your native city is?”

“Not at all. I was born in Manitowoc, a city that no longer exists. My name is Rudyard Churchill, and my companion is Nephi Sarvant. He was born in Mesa, Arizona. We are eight hundred years old and remarkably well preserved for our advanced age."

The girl sucked in her breath. "Oh, the brothers of the Sunhero!"

"Shipmates of Captain Stagg, yes." Churchill was pleased that he was making such a strong impression.

The father held out his hand, and by that gesture Churchill knew he and Sarvant were accepted as equals, at least for the time being.

"I am Res Whitrow. This is my son, Bob, and my daughter, Robin."

"You have a beautiful ship," Churchill said, knowing that was the best way to stimulate a flow of talk.

Res Whitrow at once began explaining the virtues of his craft, and his children added their enthusiastic comments. After a while, there was a brief pause in the conversation, and Robin said, breathlessly, "Oh, you must have seen so many things, so many wonderful things, if it's true that you have been out to the stars. I wish I could hear of them!"

"Yes," Whitrow said, "I'm eager to hear of them too. Why don't you two become my guests for the evening? That is, unless you've an engagement for tonight?"

"We would be honored," Churchill said. "But I'm afraid we're not dressed to sit at your table."

"Don't worry about that," Whitrow said, heartily. "I shall see that you are dressed as a brother of the Sunhero should be!"

"Perhaps you can tell me what has happened to Stagg?"

"You mean you don't know? Ah well, I suppose not. We

can talk about that tonight. Evidently there are some things you do not know about the Earth you left behind such a fantastically long time ago. Can it be true? Eight hundred years! Columbia preserve us!"

Robin had taken off her jacket and stood stripped to the waist. She had a magnificent bust but seemed no more self-conscious about it than she would have been about any other attribute of hers. That is, she knew she was worth looking at, but she wasn't going to let the knowledge interfere with her grace of movement or impose any coquettishness upon her.

Sarvant seemed quite affected, since he would not allow his gaze to rest upon her except for very brief intervals. That was strange, thought Churchill. Sarvant, despite his condemnation of the dress of Deecee virgins, had not seemed to be bothered when they were walking through the streets. Perhaps it was because he could look at the other girls impersonally, as savage natives of a foreign country, until acquaintanceship made a personal relationship.

They walked up the steps to the top of the bank, where a carriage waited. It was drawn by a team of two large reddish deer, and had, besides a driver, two armed men who stood on a little platform at its rear.

Whitrow and his son sat down and invited Sarvant to a place beside them. Robin placed herself without hesitation beside Churchill and very close to him. One breast was against his arm. He felt heat radiate from it up his arm to his face and he cursed himself for showing how she affected him.

They drove at a fast clip through the streets, the driver

taking it for granted that the pedestrians would get out of his way or suffer the consequences. In fifteen minutes, they had passed the government buildings and were in a district reserved for the wealthy and the powerful. They turned into a long gravel-strewn driveway and then stopped before a large white house.

Churchill jumped down and held out his hand to help Robin down. She smiled and said, "Thank you," but he was examining the huge totem pole in the yard. It bore stylized heads of several animals, the most numerous of which was the cat.

Whitrow recognized what Churchill was doing. He said, "I am a Lion. My wife and daughters belong to the Wood Cat sorority."

"I was just wondering," Churchill answered. "I know that the totem is a powerful factor in your society. But the idea is strange to me."

"I noticed you were wearing nothing to identify you with a frat," Whitrow said. "I think that perhaps I can do something to get you into mine. It is better to belong to one. In fact, I know of no one, besides you two, who doesn't belong."

They were interrupted by five youngsters who burst out of the front door and threw themselves affectionately upon their father. Whitrow introduced the naked boys and girls and then, as they reached the porch, he introduced his wife, a fat middle-aged woman who had probably once been very beautiful.

They went into a small anteroom, then stepped into a room that ran the length of the house. This was a combination living room, recreation room, and dining hall.

Whitrow charged his son Bob to see that his guests were

washed. The two went into the interior of the house, where they took a shower and then put on the fine clothes that Bob insisted were theirs to keep.

Afterwards, they went back to the main room, where they were handed two glasses of wine by Robin. Churchill intercepted Sarvant's refusal to drink.

"I know it's against your principles," he whispered, "but turning it down might offend them. At least take a little sip."

"If I give in on a little thing, I'll give in later to the big things," said Sarvant.

"All right, be a stubborn fool," Churchill whispered savagely. "But you can't get drunk on one glass, you know."

"I'll touch the glass to my lips," said Sarvant. "That's as far as I'll go."

Churchill was angry but not so angry he couldn't appreciate the exquisite bouquet of the wine. By the time he was down to the bottom of the glass, he was called to the table. Here Whitrow directed them to sit on his right, the place of honor. He seated Churchill next to him.

Robin sat across the table from him. He was happy; it was a joy just to look at her.

Angela sat at the other end of the table. Whitrow said prayers, carved the meat, and passed it to his guests and family. Angela talked a lot, but she did not interrupt her husband. The children, though they giggled and whispered among themselves, were careful not to annoy their father. Even the twenty or so house-cats that prowled around the room were well behaved.

The table was certainly no indication of a land where food

was rationed. Besides all the customary fruits and vegetables, there were venison and goat steaks, chicken and turkey, ham, fried grasshoppers and ants. Servants kept the glasses full of wine or beer.

"I certainly intend to hear of your journey to the stars," Whitrow boomed. "But let us talk of that later. During the meal, we will have small talk. I will tell you of us, so that you may feel you know us and will be at ease."

Whitrow shoved large gobs of food into his mouth, and while he chewed, he talked. He was born on a small farm in southern Virginia, he said, not too far from Norfolk. His father was an honorable man, since he raised pigs, and as everybody except possibly the starmen knew, a pig raiser was a highly respected man in Deecee.

Whitrow did not cotton to pigs, however. He had a liking for boats, so, as soon as his schooling was over, he left the farm and went to Norfolk. The schooling apparently was equivalent to the eighth grade of Churchill's time. Whitrow implied that education was not compulsory and that it had cost his father a respectable sum to send him. Most people were illiterate.

Whitrow shipped out on a fishing vessel as an apprentice seaman. After a few years, he saved enough money to go back to school in Norfolk, where nautical navigation was taught. From the anecdotes told about his stay there, Churchill knew that the compass and the sextant were still used.

Whitrow, though a seaman, had not been initiated into any of the sailor's frats. Even at that early age he was looking far ahead. He knew that the most powerful frat in Washington was the Lions. It was not an easy frat for a relatively poor youth to get into, but he had a stroke of luck.

"Columbia Herself took me under Her wing," he said. He knocked on the table top three times. "I do not boast, Columbia, I merely let men know of Your goodness!

"Yes, I was only a common seaman, despite being a graduate of the Norfolk College of Mathematics. I needed the patronage of a wealthy man to get an appointment as officer-in-training. And I got my patron. It was while I was on the merchant brigantine *Petrel*, bound for Miami in Florida. The Floridians had just lost a big naval battle and had to sue for peace. We were the first Deecee ship with a cargo to Florida in ten years, so we expected to make quite a haul. The Floridians would welcome our goods, even if they might not like our faces. On the way, however, we were attacked by Karelian pirates."

Churchill thought at first that the Karelians were Carolinians, but some of the details Whitrow gave about them changed Churchill's mind. He got the impression that they were from overseas. If that were true, then America was not as isolated as he had thought.

The Karelian ships rammed the brigantine, and the pirates boarded. It was during the fighting that followed that Whitrow saved a wealthy passenger from being cut in two by a Karelian broadsword. The Karelians were beaten off, though with great loss. All the officers were killed, and Whitrow took command. Instead of turning back, he sailed the ship on to Miami and sold the cargo at profit.

From that time on, he rose rapidly.

He was given a ship of his own. As a captain he had many chances to advance his own fortunes. Moreover, the man whose life he had saved knew what was going on in the business world of Washington and Manhattan, and he steered financial opportunities toward Whitrow.

"I was often a guest at his house," said Whitrow, "and there I met Angela. After I married her, I became her father's partner. And so now you see me, owner of fifteen great merchant ships and many farms and proud father of these healthy and handsome children, may Columbia continue to make us prosper."

"A toast to that," Churchill said, and he drank another wine, his tenth. He had made an effort to be temperate to keep his wits ready. But Whitrow had insisted that every time he drank, his guests drank. Sarvant had refused. Whitrow said nothing, but he no longer talked to Sarvant except when Sarvant directly spoke to him.

The table had become very noisy by now. The children drank beer and wine, even the youngest, a boy of six. They no longer giggled but laughed loudly, especially when Whitrow told jokes that would have delighted Rabelais. The servants, standing behind the chairs, laughed until tears ran from their eyes and they had to hold their aching sides.

These people had few visible inhibitions. They chewed noisily and did not mind talking when their mouths were full. When their father belched loudly, the children tried to outdo him.

At first, seeing the lovely Robin eating like a hog had sickened Churchill. It made him aware of the gulf between them, a gulf that meant more than just years. After his fifth wine, he seemed to lose his revulsion. He told himself that their attitude toward food was really healthier than that of his time. Besides, table manners were not intrinsically good or bad. The custom of the land determined what was or was not acceptable.

Sarvant did not seem to think so. As the meal progressed he became more silent and at the end he would not raise his eyes from his plate.

Whitrow became more boisterous. When his wife passed him on her way to direct a servant in the kitchen, he gave her a hard but affectionate slap on her broad rear. He laughed and said that that reminded him of the night Robin was conceived, and then he proceeded to go into the details of that night.

Suddenly, in the middle of the story, Sarvant stood up and walked out of the house. He left a complete silence behind him.

Finally, Whitrow said, “Is your friend sick?”

“In a way,” Churchill said. “He comes from a place where talking of sex is taboo.”

Whitrow was amazed. “But… how could that be? What a curious custom!”

“I imagine you have your own taboos,” Churchill said, “and they would be just as curious to him. If you’ll excuse me, I’ll go ask him what he intends to do; but I’ll be right back.”

“Tell him to come back. I would like to get another look at a man who thinks so crookedly.”

Churchill found Sarvant in a very peculiar situation. He was halfway up the totem pole, clinging tightly to the head of one of the animals to keep from falling.

Churchill looked once at the moonlit scene and leaped back

into the house. "There's a lioness outside! She's treed Sarvant!"

"Oh, that'd be Alice," Whitrow said. "We let her out after dark to discourage burglars. I'll let Robin take care of her. She and her mother can handle big cats much better than I. Robin, will you take Alice back to her den?"

"I'd rather take her with me," Robin said. She looked at her father. "Would you mind if Mr. Churchill took me to the concert now? He can talk to you later. I'm sure he'll accept your invitation to be our guest for an indefinite period."

Something seemed to pass between father and daughter. Whitrow grinned and said, "Of course. Mr. Churchill, would you be my house guest? You are welcome to stay until you care to leave."

"I am honored," Churchill said. "Does that invitation include Sarvant?"

"If he wishes to accept. But I am not so sure he'll be at ease with us."

Churchill opened the door and allowed Robin to precede him. She walked out without hesitation and took the lioness by the collar. Churchill called up, "Come on down, Sarvant. It's not yet time to throw a Christian to the lions."

Reluctantly, Sarvant climbed down. "I should have stood my ground. But it took me by surprise. It was the last thing I would have expected."

"Nobody's blaming you for getting out of reach," Churchill said. "I'd have done the same thing. A mountain lion is nothing to treat with contempt."

"Wait a minute," Robin said. "I have to get a leash for Alice."

She stroked the lioness' head and chucked her under the chin. The big cat purred like distant thunder and then, at her mistress' command, followed her around the side of the house.

"All right, Sarvant," Churchill said. "Why did you take off like the proverbial bird? Didn't you know you could have gravely offended your hosts? Luckily, Whitrow didn't get mad at me. You could have queered the best stroke of luck we've had so far."

Sarvant looked angry. "Surely you didn't expect me to sit there and tolerate such bestial behavior? And his obscene descriptions of his cohabitations with his wife?"

"I gather there's nothing wrong with that in this time and place," Churchill said. "These people are, well, just earthy. They enjoy a good tumble in bed, and they enjoy rehashing it in conversation."

"Good God, you're not defending them?"

"Sarvant, I don't understand you. You encountered hundreds of customs more disgusting, actually repulsive, when we were on Vixa. Yet I never saw you flinch."

"That was different. The Vixans weren't human."

"They were humanoid. You can't judge these people by our standards."

"Do you mean to tell me you enjoyed his anecdotes about his sexual behavior?"

"I did get kind of queasy when he was talking about conceiving Robin. But I think that was because Robin was there. Certainly she wasn't suffering—she was laughing her beautiful head off."

"These people are degenerate! They need scourging!"

"I thought you were the minister of the Prince of Peace."

"What?" Sarvant said. He was silent for a moment, then he spoke in a quieter voice. "You're right. I hated when I should have been loving. But, after all, I'm only human. However, even a pagan like yourself is right to rebuke me when I talk of scourging."

"Whitrow invited you to come back in."

Sarvant shook his head. "No, I just haven't the stomach for it. God only knows what would happen if I spent the night there. I wouldn't be surprised if he offered me his wife."

Churchill laughed and said, "I don't think so. Whitrow's no Eskimo. And don't think that just because they're loose in talk they may not have a far stricter sexual code, in some ways, than we had in our time. What *are* you going to do?"

"I'm going to find some sort of motel and spend the night there. What are *you* going to do?"

"Just now I think Robin intends to take me out on the town. Later, I'm to spend the night here. I don't want to throw away this opportunity. Whitrow could be the wedge to get us into a nice position in Deecee. Washington hasn't changed in some respects; it still pays to know somebody with pull."

Sarvant held out his hand. His nutcracker face was serious.

"God be with you," he said, and walked away into the darkness of the street.

Robin came back around the corner of the house. She was holding the leash in one hand and in the other she held a large leather bag. Evidently she'd spent time in doing more than snapping the leash on the lioness' collar. Even though the moon furnished the only light, Churchill could see that she had changed her clothes and had put on fresh make-up. She had also exchanged her sandals for high-heeled shoes.

"Where did your friend go?" she said.

"Somewhere to spend the night."

"Good! I didn't like him very much. And I was afraid that I would have to be rude and not invite him to come along with us."

"I can't imagine you being rude—and don't waste too much sympathy on him. I think he likes to suffer. Where are we going?"

"I was thinking of going to the concert in the park. But that would mean sitting still too long. We could go to the amusement park. Did you have such things in your time?"

"Yes. It might be interesting to see if they've changed much. But I don't care where I go. Just as long as I'm with you."

"I thought you liked me," she said, smiling.

"What man wouldn't? But I must admit I'm surprised that you seem to like me so much. I'm not much to look at, just a red-haired wrestler with a face like a baby's."

"I like babies," she replied, laughing. "But you needn't act surprised. I'll bet you've laid a hundred girls."

Churchill winced. He wasn't as insensitive to the direct speech of Deecee as Sarvant had thought.

He was wise enough not to boast. He said, "I can truthfully swear you're the first woman I've touched in eight hundred years."

"Great Columbia, it's a wonder you don't explode all over the place!"

She laughed merrily, but Churchill blushed. He was glad that they were not in a bright light.

"I've an idea," she said. "Why don't we go sailing tonight?

There's a full moon, and the Potomac will be beautiful. And we can get away from this heat. There'll be a breeze."

"Fine, but it's a long walk."

"Virginia preserve us! You didn't think we'd walk? Our carriage is in back, waiting."

She reached into the pocket of her bell-shaped skirt and pulled out a small whistle. Immediately following the shrill sound came the beat of hoofs and the crunch of gravel under wheels. Churchill assisted her aboard. The lioness leaped after them and lay down on the floor at their feet. The driver shouted, "Giddyap!" and the carriage sped down the moonlit street. Churchill wondered why she wanted to bring along the lioness, since two armed servants rode the platform on the rear of the carriage. He decided that having Alice along was being doubly fortified. She would be worth ten men in a fight.

The three got down off the carriage. Robin ordered the servants to wait until she came back from the sail. On the way down the long steps to the ship, Churchill said, "Won't they get bored, just waiting for us?"

"I don't think so. They've got a bottle of white lightning and dice."

Alice leaped aboard the yacht first and settled down in the small cabin where she probably hoped the water wouldn't touch her. Churchill untied the craft, gave her a shove, and jumped on. Then he and Robin were busy unfurling the sails and doing everything necessary.

They had a delightful sail. The full moon gave them all the light they needed or wanted, and the breeze was just strong enough to send them at a good clip when they headed downwind. The city was a black monster with a thousand blazing fitful eyes, the torches of the people in the streets. Churchill, seated with the rudder bar in his hand and Robin by his side, told her how Washington looked in his day.

"It was many towers crowded together and connected in the air with many bridges and underground with many tunnels. The towers soared into the air for a mile, and they plunged into the ground a mile deep. There was no night, because the lights were so bright."

"And now it is all gone, melted and covered with dirt," Robin said.

She shivered as if she thought of all that splendor of stone and steel and the millions of people now gone had made her cold. Churchill put his arm around her and, as she did not resist, he kissed her.

He thought that now would be the time to furl the sails and throw out the anchor. He wondered if the lioness would get upset, but decided that Robin must know how she would act under such circumstances. Perhaps he and Robin could go down into the small cabin, though he preferred to stay above decks. It was possible that she would not object if she were locked in the cabin.

But it was not to be. When he told her bluntly why he wanted to haul down the sails, he was informed that this could not be. Not now, anyway.

Robin spoke in a soft voice and smiled at him. She even said she was sorry.

"You have no idea what you do to me, Rud," she said. "I

think I am in love with you. But I am not sure if it is you I love, or if it is the brother of the Sunhero I love. You are more than a man to me, you are a demigod in many ways. You were born eight hundred years ago and you have traveled to places that are so far away my head spins to think of it. To me, there is a light around you that shines even in the daytime. But I am a good girl. I cannot allow myself—though Columbia knows I want to—to do this with you. Not until I'm sure… But I know how you must feel. Why don't you go to the Temple of Gotew tomorrow?"

Churchill did not know what she was talking about. He was only concerned about having offended her so much she wouldn't see him again. It wasn't lust alone that drew him toward her. He was sure of that. He loved this beautiful girl; he would have wanted her if he had just had a dozen women.

"Let's go back," she said. "I'm afraid this has killed your good spirits. It's my fault. I shouldn't have kissed you. But I wanted to kiss you."

"Then you're not mad at me?"

"Why should I be?"

"No reason. But I'm happy again."

After they'd tied the craft to the slip, and were just beginning to walk back up the steps, he stopped her.

"Robin, how long do you think it'll be before you're sure?"

"I am going to the temple tomorrow. I'll be able to tell you when I get back."

"You're going to pray for guidance? Or something like that?"

"I'll pray. But I'm not going primarily for that. I want to have a priestess make a test on me."

"And after this test, you'll know whether or not you want to marry me?"

"Goodness no!" she said. "I'll have to know you much better than I do before I'd think of marrying you. No, I have to have this test made so I'll know whether or not I should go to bed with you."

"What test?"

"If you don't know, then you'll not be worried about it. But I'll be sure tomorrow."

"Sure of what?" he said angrily.

"Then I'll know if it's all right for me to quit acting like a virgin."

Her face became ecstatic.

"I'll know if I'm carrying the Sunhero's child!"

7

It rained the morning that Stagg was to lead the parade into Baltimore. Stagg and Calthorp were in a large open-walled tent and drinking hot white lightning to keep warm. Stagg was motionless as a model while submitting to the usual morning repainting of his genitals and buttocks, necessary because he wore the paint off at nights. He was silent and paying no attention to the giggles and compliments of the three girls whose only work was this daily redecorating of the Sunhero. Calthorp, who generally talked like a maniac to keep Stagg's spirits up, was also glum.

Finally, Stagg said, "Do you know, Doc, it's been ten days since we left Fair Grace. Ten days and ten towns. By now you and I should have worked out a plan for escape. In fact, if we were the men we used to be, we'd have been over the hills and far away. But the only time I get to thinking is in the mornings, and I'm too exhausted and wretched to do anything constructive. And by noon I just don't give a damn. I *like* the way I am!"

"And I've not been much help to you, have I?" Calthorp said. "I get as drunk as you do, and I'm too sick in the morning to do anything but take a hair of the dog that bit me."

"What the hell's happened?" Stagg said. "Do you realize that I don't even know where I'm going, or what's going to happen to me when I get there? I don't even know, really, what a Sunhero is!"

"It's mostly my fault," Calthorp said. He sighed and sipped some more of his drink. "I just can't seem to get organized."

Stagg looked at one of his guards, who was standing in the entrance of a nearby tent. "Do you suppose that if I threatened to wring his neck, he'd tell me everything I want to know?"

"You could try it."

Stagg rose from his chair. "Hand me that cloak, will you? I don't think they'll object if I wear this while it's raining."

He was referring to an incident of the previous day when he had put on a kilt before going over to talk to the girl in the cage. The attendants had looked shocked, then summoned the guards. These surrounded Stagg. Before he could find out what they intended, a man behind him had torn off his kilt and run off with it into the woods.

He did not reappear all day, apparently dreading Stagg's wrath, but the lesson had been taught. The Sunhero was supposed to display his naked glory to the worshiping people.

Now Stagg slipped the cloak on and strode on bare feet across the wet grass. The guards stepped out from their tents and followed him, but they did not come close.

Stagg halted before the cage. The girl sitting inside looked up, then turned her face away.

"You don't need to be ashamed to look at me," he said. "I'm covered."

There was silence. Then he said, "For God's sakes, speak to me! I'm a prisoner too, you know! I'm in as much of a cage as you."

The girl clutched the bars and pressed her face against them. "You said, 'For God's sake!' What does that mean? That you're a Caseylander too? You can't be. You don't talk like my countrymen. But then you don't talk like a Deecee, either—or like anyone I ever heard before. Tell me, are you a believer in Columbia?"

"If you'll stop talking for a minute, I'll explain," Stagg said. "Thank God, you're talking, though."

"There you go again," she said. "You couldn't possibly be a worshiper of the foul Bitch-Goddess. But if you're not, why are you a Horned King?"

"I was hoping you could tell me that. If you can't, you can tell me some other things I'd like to know."

He held out the bottle to her. "Would you like a drink?"

"I'd like one, yes. But I won't accept one from an enemy. And I'm not sure you're not one."

Stagg understood her with difficulty. She used enough words similar to those of Deecee for him to grasp the main idea of her sentences. But her pronunciation of some of the vowels was different, and the tonal pattern was not that of Deecee.

"Can you speak Deecee?" he said. "I can't keep up with you in Caseylander."

"I speak Deecee fairly well," she replied. "What is your native tongue?"

"Twenty-first-century American."

She gasped, and her big eyes became even wider.

"But how could that be?"

"I was born in the twenty-first century. January 30, 2030 A.D.... let's see that would be..."

"You don't need to tell me," she replied in his native speech. "That would be... uh... well, 1 A.D. is 2100 A.D. So, Deecee style, you were born 70 B.D. Before the Desolation. But what does that matter? We Caseylanders use the Old Style."

Stagg finally quit goggling at her and said, "You spoke twenty-first-century American! Something like it, anyway!"

"Yes. Usually only priests can, but my father is a wealthy man. He sent me to Boston University, and I learned Church American there."

"You mean it's a liturgical language?"

"Yes. Latin was lost during the Desolation."

"I think I need a drink," Stagg said. "You first?"

She smiled and said, "I don't understand much of what you've said, but I'll take the drink."

Stagg slipped the bottle through the bars. "At least I know your name. It's Mary I-Am-Bound-for-Paradise Little Casey. But that's all I ever got out of my guards."

Mary handed back the bottle. "That was wonderful. It's been a long dry spell. You said guard? Why do you need a guard? I thought all Sunheroes were volunteers."

Stagg launched into his story. He didn't have time to go into the details, even though he could tell by Mary's expression that she comprehended only half of what he told her. And occasionally he had to shift back into Deecee because it was evident that Mary might have studied Church American at college but she hadn't mastered it.

"So you see," he concluded, "that I am a victim of these horns. I am not responsible for what I do."

Mary turned red. "I don't want to talk about it. It makes me sick to my soul."

"Me too," Stagg said. "In the mornings, that is. Later..."

"Can't you run away?"

"Sure. And I'd run back even faster."

"Oh, these evil Deecee! They must have bewitched you, it could only be a devil in your loins that could possess you so! If only we could escape to Caseyland, a priest could exorcise it."

Stagg looked around him. "They're beginning to break camp. We'll be on the march in a minute. Then, Baltimore. Listen! I've told you about myself. But I still know nothing about you, where you come from, how you happened to be a prisoner. And there are things you could tell me about myself, what this Sunhero stuff is about."

"But I can't understand why Cal..."

She put her hand over her mouth.

"Cal! You mean Calthorp! What's he got to do with this? Don't tell me he's been talking to you? He told me he didn't know a thing!"

"He's been talking to me. I thought that he must have told you so."

"He didn't say a thing to me! In fact, he said he didn't know any more than I did about what's going on! Why, that..."

Speechless, he turned and ran away from the cage.

Halfway across the field, he regained his voice and began bellowing the name of the little anthropologist.

The people in his path scattered; they thought that the Great Stag had gone amok again. Calthorp stepped out of the tent. Seeing Stagg running toward him, he scuttled across the road. He did not allow himself to be stopped by the stone fence in his path but put one hand on it and vaulted over. Once on the other side, he ran as fast as his spindly legs would carry him across a field and around a farmhouse.

Stagg screamed after him, "If I catch you, Calthorp, I'll break every bone in your body! How could you do this to me?"

He stood for a moment, panting with rage. Then he turned away, muttering to himself. "Why? Why?"

At that moment, the rain ceased. A few minutes later, the clouds cleared, and the midnoon sun shone fiercely.

Stagg tore off his cloak and threw it on the ground. "To hell with Calthorp! I don't need him and never did! The traitor! Who cares!"

He called to Sylvia, an attendant, to bring him food and drink. He ate and drank as he always did in the afternoon, and when he had finished, he glared wildly about him. The antlers, which had been flopping limply with every movement of his head, now rose stiff and hard.

"How many kilometers to Baltimore?" he roared.

"Two and a half, sire. Shall I call your carriage?"

"To hell with the carriage! I can't be slowed down by wheels! I am going to run to Baltimore! I am going to take the city by surprise! I'll be on them before they know it! They'll think the Grandfather of all Stags hit them! I'll ravage among them, lay them all low! It'll not just be the mascots who'll get it this time! I'll not just take what's handed to me! No Miss Americas only for me! Tonight, the whole city!"

Sylvia was horrified. "But, sire, things just… just aren't done that way! Since time immemorial…"

"I am the Sunhero, am I not? The Horned King? I will do as I want to do!"

He seized a bottle from the tray she was holding and began to run off down the road.

At first he stayed on the cement. But even though the soles of his feet were by now as hard as iron, he found the pavement too rough, so he ran on the soft grass by the side of the road.

"It's better this way," he said to himself. "The closer I get to Mother Earth, the better for me and the better I like it. It may be superstitious nonsense that a man is refreshed by direct contact with the earth. But I'm inclined to believe the Deecee. I can *feel* the strength surging up from the heart of Mother Earth, surging up like an electric current and recharging my body. And I can feel the strength coming with such power, such overflowing power, that my body isn't big enough to contain it. And the excess spurts from the crown of my head and flames upward toward the sky. I can feel it."

He stopped running for a moment to uncap the bottle and take a drink. He noticed that the guards were running toward him, but they were at least two hundred yards behind. They just did not have his speed and strength. Besides his native muscle, he had the additional power given him by the antlers. He was, he thought, probably the fastest and strongest human being that had ever existed.

He took another drink. The guards were getting closer but they were winded, their pace slowing. They held their bows and arrows nocked, but he didn't think they would shoot as long as he stayed on the road to Baltimore. He had no intention of straying from it. He just wanted to run along on the curving breast of Earth and feel her strength surge through him and feel the ecstasy of his thoughts.

He ran faster, now and then giving great bounds into the air and uttering strange cries. They were sheer delight, exuberance, and nameless longings and their fulfillment. They were spoken in the language of the first men on Earth, the broken chaotic feeling-toward-speech the upright apes must have formed with clumsy tongues when they were trying to name the things around them. Stagg was not trying to name things. He was trying to name feelings. And he was having as little success as his ancestors a hundred thousand years before.

But he was, like them, gaining joy from the effort. And he was gaining a consciousness of something never before experienced, something new to his kind and perhaps to every creature in the world.

He ran toward a man, woman, and child who had been walking on the road. They stopped when they saw him, and then, recognizing him for what he was, fell on their knees.

Stagg did not stop but raced past them. "I may seem to be alone!" he cried at them. "But I am not! Earth comes along with me, your Mother and mine! She is my Bride and goes with me wherever I go. I cannot get away from Her. Even when I traveled through space to places so distant it takes light-years to get there, She was with me. And the proof is that I am back and now have carried out my eight-hundred-years-old promise to marry Her!"

By the time he had finished speaking, he was far past them. He did not care if they heard or not. All he wanted was to talk, talk, talk. Shout, shout, shout. Burst his lungs if he must, but scream out the truth.

Suddenly, he stopped. A large red stag grazing in a meadow beyond a fence had caught his eye. It was the only male of a herd of hind, and, like those deer bred for milk and meat, the stag had a distinctly bovine quality. Its body was thick, its legs short, its neck powerful, its eyes stupid but lustful. It was probably a thoroughbred male, highly prized as a stud.

Stagg leaped over the fence, though it was five feet high and composed of hard stone that would not have yielded if he had tripped. He landed on his feet and then ran toward the stag. The stag bellowed and stood his ground. The hinds ran off toward a corner of the field and there turned to see what was going to happen. They barked like dogs in their alarm, setting up such a clamor that the owner came running from a nearby barn.

Stagg ran up to the big male. The beast waited until the man was about twenty yards away. Then it lowered its antlers, bugled a challenge, and charged.

Stagg laughed with joy and ran very close. Timing his steps exactly, he leaped into the air just as the great branched horns swept the air where he had been. He drew up his knees so the horns would miss him, and then extended his legs so his feet landed beyond the base of the antlers and on the back of the neck. A second later, the stag reared his head, hoping to catch the man with his horns and throw him high in the air. The stag succeeded only in acting as a springboard for the man and propelling him along the line of his back. The man landed on the stag's broad rump.

There, instead of jumping down to the ground, he somersaulted backwards, intending to come down on the stag's neck. However, his feet slipped, and he rolled off the beast and fell on the ground on his side.

The stag wheeled and trumpeted another challenge and lowered his antlers and charged again. But Stagg was on his feet. As the beast lunged, Stagg jumped to one side, caught one of the big ears in his hand, and swung himself onto its back.

During the next five minutes, the amazed farmer watched the naked man ride the bucking, rearing, wheeling, snorting, bugling stag and stay on its back despite all its furious maneuvers. Suddenly, the stag stopped. Its eyes were bulging, saliva dripping from its open mouth, through which wheezed a tired breath, its sides pumping agonizedly for more air.

"Open the gate!" shouted Stagg to the farmer. "I'm going to ride this beast into Baltimore in style, like a Horned King should!"

The farmer silently swung open the gate to the field. He was not going to object if the Sunhero appropriated his prize stag. He would not have objected if the Sunhero had wanted his house, his wife, his daughter, his own life.

Stagg rode the beast onto the road toward Baltimore. Far ahead, he saw a carriage racing toward the city. Even at the distance he could perceive that it was Sylvia, going ahead to warn the people of Baltimore that the Horned King was arriving ahead of schedule—and doubtless to relay the Horned King's boast that he would ravish the entire city.

Stagg would have liked to race after her and arrive on her heels. But the deer was still breathing heavily, so he allowed it to walk until it could regain its breath.

Half a kilometer from Baltimore, Stagg kicked the beast in the ribs with his bare heels and shouted in its ears. It began trotting, then, under its rider's continued urgings, to gallop. It raced between two low hills, and suddenly was on the main street of Baltimore. This led straight for twelve blocks to the central square, where a large crowd was hastily being assembled. Even as Stagg crossed the city limits, a band struck up *Columbia, Gem of the Ocean,* and a group of priestesses began to march toward the Sunhero.

Behind them, the mascots who had been lucky enough to be chosen as the Sunhero's brides ranged themselves in a solid body. They looked very beautiful in their white bellshaped skirts and white lace veils, and their breasts were edged in white frilly lace. Each carried a bouquet of white roses.

Stagg allowed the big deer to slow to a trot so it could reserve its strength for the final spurt. He bowed and waved his hand at the men and women who lined the street and cheered frantically. He called to the teen-aged girls who stood by their parents, the girls who had failed to get first place in the Miss America contest.

"Don't cry! I won't neglect you tonight!"

Then the blare of bugles, thunder of drums, shrilling of syrinxes swelled and filled the street. The priestesses marched toward him. They were clad in gowns of light blue, the color reserved for the goddess Mary, patron deity of Maryland. Mary, according to the myth, was the granddaughter of Columbia and the daughter of Virginia. It was she who had formed a fondness for the natives of this region and had taken them under her protection.

The priestesses, fifty strong, marched toward Stagg. They sang and threw marigolds before them and occasionally gave long shuddering screams.

Stagg waited until he was about fifty meters from them. He kicked the animal in the ribs and beat on its head with his fists. It bugled and reared, and then began galloping straight toward the group of priestesses. These stopped singing to stand in astonished silence. Suddenly, perceiving that the Sunhero did not intend to pull up his mount, that it was not slackening speed but was increasing it, they screamed and tried to scatter to one side. Here they found that the number of the crowd formed an impenetrable body. And when they turned and tried to outrun the galloping stag, they knocked each other down, tripped over each other, got in each other's way.

Only one priestess did not stampede. She was the Chief Priestess, a woman of fifty who had kept her virginity in honor of her patron goddess. Now she remained, as if bolted by her courage to the ground. She held out one hand as she would have held it out to bless him if he had arrived in normal fashion. She tossed her bouquet of marigolds at him, and with the other hand, which held a golden sickle, she described a religious symbol.

The marigolds landed in front of the hoofs of the stag, were trampled, and then the Chief Priestess was knocked down to the ground and her head split open by a flying hoof.

The impact of the priestess' body scarcely checked the onslaught of the stag, which weighed at least a ton. It rammed head-on into the solidly packed mob of struggling, writhing women.

The animal stopped as if it had run into a stone wall, but Stagg continued.

He rose over the lowered neck and antlers and floated through the air. For a moment, he seemed to be suspended. Beneath was the group of blue-clad priestesses, splitting into two from the crash of the great body, flying in all directions, some of them soaring away on their backs, others upside down, several describing cartwheels. There was a severed head spinning by him, a head that had been caught under the chin by the tip of the antler and ripped off.

He was past the blue ruin and descending upon a field of white veils and red mouths behind the veils, of white flaring bell-shaped skirts and bare virginal breasts.

Then he had fallen into the trap of lace and flesh and disappeared from view.

8

Peter Stagg did not awake until the evening of the following day. Yet he was the first of his group to rise, except for one. That was Dr. Calthorp, who sat by his captain's bedside.

"How long have you been here?" Stagg said.

"In Baltimore? I followed right on your heels. I saw you charge that deer into the priestesses—and everything that went on afterwards."

Stagg sat up and moaned. "I feel as if every muscle in my body has been strained."

"Every muscle has been. You didn't go to sleep until about ten in the morning. But you ought to feel more than muscle-ache. Doesn't your back hurt much?"

"A little. Feels like a slight burn in my lower back."

"Is that all?" Calthorp's white brows rose high. "Well, all I can say is that the antlers must be doing more than pouring out philoprogenitive hormones into your bloodstream. They must also be conducive to cell-repair."

"What does all that mean?"

"Why, last night a man stabbed you in the back with a knife. Yet it didn't slow you down much, and the wound seems to be almost healed. Of course, the knife didn't go in more than an inch. You've got some pretty solid muscles."

"I have a vague memory of that," Stagg said. He winced. "And what happened to the man afterwards?"

"The women tore him apart."

"But why did he stab me?"

"It seems he was mentally unbalanced. He resented your intense interest in his wife, and he stuck a knife into you. Of course, he was committing a horrible blasphemy. The women used tooth and nail to punish him."

"Why do you say he was mentally unbalanced?"

"Because he was—at least, from this culture's viewpoint. Nobody in his right mind would object to his wife cohabiting with a Sunhero. In fact, it was a great honor, because Sunheroes usually devote their time to nobody but virgins. However, last night you made an exception... of the whole city. Or tried to, anyway."

Stagg sighed and said, "Last night was the worst ever. Weren't there more than the usual number mangled?"

"You can hardly blame the Baltimoreans for that. You started things off on a grand scale when you trampled those priestesses. By the way, whatever inspired that move?"

"I don't know. It just seemed a good idea at the time. But I think it might have been my unconscious directing me to get revenge on the people responsible for these."

He touched his antlers. Then he fixed a stare on Calthorp.

"You Judas! Why have you been holding out on me?"

"Who told you? That girl?"

"Yes. That doesn't matter. Come on, Doc, spill it. If it hurts, spill it, anyway. I won't harm you. My antlers are an index of whether I'm in my right mind or not. You can see how floppy they are."

"I began to suspect the true pattern of events as soon as I started understanding the language," Calthorp said. "I wasn't sure, however, until they grafted those antlers on you. But I didn't want to tell you until I could figure out some way of escape. I thought you might try to make a break and would get shot down. I soon began seeing that even if you ran away in the morning, you'd be back by evening—if not sooner. That biological mechanism on your forehead gives you more than an almost inexhaustible ability to scatter your seed; it also gives you an irresistible compulsion to do so. Takes you over completely—possesses you. You're the biggest case of satyriasis known to history."

"I know how it affects me," Stagg said, impatiently. "I want to know just what kind of a role I am playing? Toward what goal? And why is all this Sunhero routine necessary?"

"Wouldn't you like a drink first?"

"No! I'm not going to drown my sorrow in liquor. I'm going to accomplish something today. I would like a big cold drink of water. And I'm dying to take a bath, get all this sweat and crud off me. But that can wait. Your story, please. And make it damn quick!"

"I haven't time now to go into the myth and history of Deecee," Calthorp said. "We can do that tomorrow. But I can elucidate fairly well what position of dubious honor you hold.

"Briefly, you combine several religious roles, that of the Sunhero and that of the Stag-King. The Sunhero is a man who is chosen every year to enact the passage of the Sun around the Earth in symbolic form. Yes, I know the Earth goes around the Sun, and so do the priestesses of Deecee, and so does the unlettered mass, But for all practical purposes, the Sun circles the Earth, and that is how even the scientist thinks of it when he is not thinking scientifically.

"So, the Sunhero is chosen, and he is symbolically born during a ceremony which takes place around December 21. Why then? Because that is the date of the winter solstice. When the Sun is weakest and has reached the most southerly station.

"That is why you went through the birth scene.

"And that is why you are taking the northern route now. You are destined to travel as the Sun travels after the winter solstice, northward. And like the Sun, you will get stronger and stronger. You have noticed how the antlers' effect has been getting more powerful; proof of that is the crazy stunt you pulled when you subdued that stag and rode down the priestesses."

"And what happens when I reach the most northerly station?" Stagg said. His voice was quiet and well controlled, but the skin under the deep brown tan had turned pale.

"That will be the city we used to know as Albany, New York. It is now the northernmost limit of the country of Deecee, And it is also where Alba, the Sow-Goddess, lives. Alba is Columbia in her aspect of the Goddess of Death. The pig is sacred to her because, like Death, it is omnivorous. Alba is also the White

Moon Goddess, another symbol of death."

Calthorp stopped. He looked as if he could not bear to continue the conversation; his eyes were moist.

"Go on," Stagg said. "I can take it."

Calthorp took a deep breath and said, "The north, according to Deecee myth, is the place where the Moon Goddess imprisons the Sunhero. A circuitous way of saying that he..."

"Dies," Stagg finished for him.

Calthorp gulped. "Yes. The Sunhero is scheduled to complete the Great Route at the time of the summer solstice—about June 22."

"What about the Great Stag aspect, the Horned King?"

"The Deecee are nothing if not economical. They combine the role of Sunhero with that of the Stag-King. He is a symbol of man. He is born as a weak and helpless infant, he grows to become a lusty, virile male, lover, and father. But he, too, completes the Great Route and must, willy-nilly, face Death. By the time he meets her, he is blind, bald, weak, sexless. And... he fights for his last breath, but... Alba relentlessly chokes it out of him."

"Don't use symbolic language, Doc," Stagg said. "Give me the facts, in plain English."

"There will be one tremendous ceremony at Albany, the final. There you will take, not the tender young virgins, but the white-haired sag-breasted old priestesses of the Sow-Goddess. And your natural distaste for the old women will be overcome by keeping you restrained in a cage until you are at such a point of lust that you will take any woman, even a hundred-year-old great-grandmother. Afterwards..."

"Afterwards?"

"Afterwards, you will be blinded, scalped, castrated, and then hung. There will be a week of national mourning for you. Then you will be buried in the position of a foetus beneath a dolmen, an archway of great slabs of stone. And prayers will be said to you and stags will be sacrificed over your tomb."

"That's quite a consolation," Stagg said. "Tell me, Doc, why was I picked for this role? Isn't it true that the Sunheroes are usually volunteers?"

"Men strive for the honor, just as the virgins strive to become the Bride of the Stag. The man who is chosen is the strongest, most handsome, most virile youth in the nation. It was your misfortune to be not only that, but the captain of men who had actually ascended to the heavens on a fiery steed and then returned. They've a myth about a Sunhero who did that. I think that the government of Deecee decided that if they got rid of you they'd disorganize all of the crew. And so diminish any danger of us bringing back the old and abominated science.

"I see Mary Casey waving at you. I think she wants to speak to you."

Peter Stagg said, "Why do you look to one side when you talk to me?"

"Because," Mary Casey said, "it's hard for me to keep you two separated."

"What two?"

"The Peter I know in the morning, and the Peter I know at night. I'm sorry, but I can't help it. I shut my eyes at night and try to think of something else, but I can't shut my ears. And even though I know you can't help what you do, I loathe you. I'm sorry. I just can't help it."

"Then why did you call me over to talk to me?"

"Because I know that I am not acting charitably. Because I know that you would like to get out of your cage of flesh as much as I want to get out of this cage of iron. Because I hope we can think of some way to escape."

"Calthorp and I have worked out several plans for getting away, but we don't know how to keep me from running back. As soon as the horns began affecting me, I'd come running back to the women."

"Can't you use your will power?"

"A saint wouldn't be able to resist the horns."

"Then it's hopeless," she said dully.

"Not entirely. I don't intend to go all the way to Albany, you know. Somewhere between Manhattan and Albany, I'm taking off for the wilderness. Better to die trying than going like an ox to the slaughterhouse.

"Let's change the subject. Tell me about yourself and your people. One thing that's handicapping me is my ignorance. I just don't know enough to figure a way out."

Mary Casey said, "I'll be glad to. I need somebody to talk to, even if it's… I'm sorry."

During the next hour, while Stagg stood outside her cage and she kept her eyes on the floor, she told him of herself and Caseyland. He broke in now and then with questions, because she had a tendency to take knowledge of fundamental matters for granted.

Caseyland occupied the area once known as New England. It was not as thickly populated as Deecee or as rich. Its people were engaged in rebuilding the soil, but they depended largely on the raising of pigs and deer and on the sea for their food. Even though at war with the Deecee to the southwest, the Karelians to the north, and the Iroquois to the northwest, they traded with their enemies. They had a peculiar institution known as Treaty War. This limited, by mutual agreement, the number of warriors to be sent across the borders on raids in a year's time, and also regulated the rules of warfare. The Deecee and the Iroquois abided by the rules, but every once in a while the Karelians broke them.

"How can either side expect to win?" Stagg said in amazement.

"Neither side does. I think that the Treaty War was adopted by our ancestors for one reason. To allow an outlet for the energies of belligerent men while keeping the majority of the population busy in rebuilding the Earth. I think that when the population of any country gets too large, you will see wholesale warfare without any rules at all. But in the meantime, no nation feels powerful enough to start a treatyless war. The Karelians break the treaties because they are a people who live by a wartime economy."

She continued with a brief résumé of her nation's origins. There were two myths concerning the reason why Caseyland had been so named. One proposed that, after the Desolation, an organization known as the Knights of Columbus had succeeded in founding a city-state near Boston. This, like the original small city of Rome, had expanded to absorb its neighbors. The city-state was called K.C., and over a period of time the initials had somehow been converted into the name of an eponymous and mythical ancestor, Casey.

The other story was that there actually was a Casey family which had founded a town, named after him. And they had originated the present clan system whereby everybody in their country was named Casey.

There was a third version, not widely accepted, that the truth was a combination of the first two myths. A man named

Casey had been the leader of the Knights of Columbus.

"Perhaps none of those myths are true," Stagg said.

Mary did not seem pleased at this suggestion, but she was essentially fair-minded. She said that it was possible.

"What about the claim of the Deecee?" he said. "They say you worship a father-god named Columbus and you got the name from their goddess Columbia. You masculinized both the goddess and her name. Isn't it true that your god has two names, Jehovah and/or Columbus?"

"That is not so!" she said angrily. "The Deecee have confused the name of our god with that of St. Columbus. It is true that we pray quite often to St. Columbus for intercession with Jehovah. But we do not worship him."

"And who was St. Columbus?"

"Why, everybody knows that he came from the east, from over the ocean, and landed in Caseyland. It was he who converted the citizens of the father-city of Casey to the true religion and founded the Knights of Columbus. If it weren't for St. Columbus, we would all be heathens."

Stagg was beginning to get restless, but he managed to ask her one more question before he left.

"I know that *mascot* is the word used for *virgin*. Do you have any idea how mascot came to be used in its present sense?"

"It has always been used so," she replied, looking directly at him for the first time. "A mascot brings good luck with her, you know. Perhaps you've observed how the Deecee touch the hair of a pubescent mascot when they get a chance. That is because the good luck sometimes rubs off on the toucher. And, of course, a raiding party of men always takes along a mascot for good luck. I was with a war expedition against Poughkeepsie when I was captured. That sign lies when it says I was captured on a raid by the Deecee into Caseyland. It was the other way around. But, of course, you can't expect the truth from people who worship the Mother of Lies."

Stagg decided that the Caseylanders were as mixed up and mistaken as the Deecee. It would be useless to argue or try to entangle myth from history.

The great arteries at the base of his antlers were beginning to pulse strongly, and the antlers themselves were stiffening.

"I have to go now," he said. "See you tomorrow."

He turned and walked swiftly away. It was only by an effort of will that he kept from running.

So the days and the nights passed. Mornings filled with weakness and discussion of plans to escape. Afternoons of eating, drinking, and wild and sometimes savage horseplay. Nights… the nights were visions of screaming white flesh, of being one great pulse that throbbed in unison with the buried heart of earth itself, of transformation from an individual man into a force of nature. Mindless ecstasy, body obeying the will of a Principle. He was an agent who had no choice but to obey that which possessed him.

The Great Route led from Washington to Columbia Pike, once U.S. Route 1, through Baltimore, where it switched to what had once been U.S. Route 40 but was now known as Mary's Way. It turned from Mary's Way outside of Wimlin (Wilmington, Delaware) to follow the former New Jersey Turnpike. This road was also named after one of Columbia's daughters, Njuhzhi.

Stagg stayed a week in Kaept (Camden) and noticed the large number of soldiers in the city. He was told that this was because Philadelphia, across the Dway (Delaware) River, was the capital city of the hostile nation of Pants-Elf (eastern Pennsylvania).

The soldiers accompanied Stagg out of Camden on the former U.S. Route 30 until he was deep enough inland to be safe. There they left him, and he and his entourage continued to the town of Berlin.

After the pageant and the orgies that followed, Stagg continued on ex-U.S. 30 to Talant (Atlantic City).

Atlantic City kept Stagg for two weeks. It was a metropolis of thirty thousand, whose population quintupled when the country people poured in to attend the Sunhero rites. From there Stagg followed the former Garden State Parkway until he turned off at what had been State Highway 72. It led to 70 and 70 led to ex-U.S. Route 206. Stagg took this road to Trint (Trenton), where he was again met by a large bodyguard.

When he left Trenton, he was once more on Columbia Pike, the ex-U.S. Route 1. After making the usual progress through the relatively large cities of Elizabeth, Newark, and Jersey City, he took a ferry to Manhattan Island. He made his most extended stay in the Greater New York area, because Manhattan held fifty thousand people and the surrounding cities were almost as large.

Moreover, this was the beginning of the Great Series.

Stagg not only had to throw the first baseball of the season, he had to attend every game. For the first time, he became aware of how much the game had changed. Now it was conducted in such a fashion that it was an unusual match in which both teams did not suffer numerous injuries and several fatalities.

The first part of the Great Series was taken up by games between the champions of the various state leagues. The final game for national championship was between the Manhattan Big Ones and the Washington Sentahs. The Big Ones won, but they lost so many men they were forced to use half of the Sentahs for their reserves in the international games that followed.

The international half of the Great Series was between the national champions of Deecee, Pants-Elf, Caseyland, the Iroquois League, the Karelian pirates, Florida, and Buffalo. The last-mentioned nation occupied a territory stretching out from the city of Buffalo to include a part of the coastal sections of Lake Ontario and Lake Erie.

The final game of the Great Series was a bloody struggle between the Deecee team and the Caseylanders. The Caseylanders wore red leggings as part of their uniform, but by the end of the game the players were red from head to foot. Feelings were very bitter, not only among the players but among the rooters. The Caseylanders had a section of the stadium reserved for them and enclosed from the other sections by a tall fence of barbed wire. Moreover, the Manhattan Police Force had men stationed nearby to protect them if feelings ran too high.

Unfortunately, the umpire—a Karelian who was supposed to be neutral because he hated both sides equally—made a decision disastrous in its effects.

It was the ninth inning, and the score was 7–7. The Big

Ones were batting. One man was on third base and, though he had a gash in his neck, he was strong enough to run for home if he got a chance. Two men were out—literally. One, covered by a sheet, lay where he had been struck down between second and third. The other was sitting in the dugout and groaning, while a doctor glued up the cuts on his scalp.

The man at bat was the greatest hitter of Deecee, and he faced the greatest pitcher of Caseyland. He wore a uniform that had not changed much since the nineteenth century, and his cheek was swelled with a big quid of tobacco. He swung his bat back and forth. The sunlight glittered on its metal sides, for the upper half of the bat was covered with thin vertical strips of brass. He waited for the umpire to call *Play Ball!* and when he heard the cry, he did not step up to the plate at once.

Instead, he turned and waited until the mascot had run from the dugout to him.

She was a beautiful petite brunette who wore a baseball player's uniform. The only departure from ancient tradition was the triangular opening in her shirt which exposed her small but firm breasts.

Big Bill Appletree, the batter, rubbed his knuckles against the black hair of the mascot, kissed her on the forehead, and then gave her fanny a playful slap as she ran back to the dugout. He stepped into the box, a square drawn with chalk on the ground, and assumed the ancient stance of the batter ready for the pitcher.

Lanky John Up-The-Hill-And-Over-The-River-Jordan Mighty Casey spat tobacco, then began to wind up. He held in his right hand a ball of regulation size. Four half-inch steel spikes projected from the ball, one from each pole of the sphere and two from the equator. John Casey had to hold the ball so he wouldn't cut his fingers when he hurled it. This handicapped him somewhat from the view of an ancient pitcher. But he stood six meters closer to the batter, thus more than making up for the awkwardness of hurling the ball.

He waited until the Caseylander mascot had come to him to have her head knuckled. Then he wound up and let fly.

The spike-bearing ball whizzed by an inch from Big Bill Appletree's face. Appletree blinked, but he did not flinch.

A roar went up from the crowd at this show of courage.

"Ball one!" cried the umpire.

The Caseyland rooters booed. From where they sat, it looked as if the ball, though coming close to Appletree's face, had been exactly in line with the chalk mark of the box. Therefore, the throw should have been a strike.

Appletree struck at the next one and missed.

"Strike one!"

At the third pitch, Appletree swung and connected. The ball, however, soared to the left. It was obviously a foul.

"Strike two!"

The next pitch came sizzling in, directed at Appletree's belly. He sucked it in and jumped back, just far enough to keep from being hit but not so far he stepped outside the box, which would constitute a strike.

The next pitch, Appletree swung and missed. The ball did not. Appletree fell to the ground, the spike of the ball sticking in his side.

The crowd screamed, and then became comparatively silent as the ump began counting.

Appletree had ten seconds to get up and bat or else have a strike called on him.

The Deecee mascot, a tall beautiful girl with exceptionally long legs and rich red hair that fell past her buttocks, round and hard as apples, ran out to him. She brought her knees up high in the prancing gait affected by mascots on such occasions. When she got to Appletree, she dropped to her knees and bent her head over him and threw her hair forward so he could stroke it. The strength of a virgin, of a mascot dedicated to the Great White Mother in her aspect as Unfekk, was supposed to flow from her to him. Apparently this was not enough. He said something to her, and she rose, unbuttoned a flap over her pubes, and then bent down to him again. The crowd roared, because this meant that Appletree was so badly hurt he needed a double dose of spiritual-physical power.

At the count of eight, Appletree rose to his feet. The crowd cheered. Even the Caseylander rooters gave him an ovation—all honored a man with guts.

Appletree pulled the spike from his side, took a bandage from the mascot, and placed it over the wound. The bandage clung without being taped, as its pseudoflesh at once put out a number of little claw-tipped tendrils that anchored it.

He nodded to the ump that he was ready.

"Play ball!"

Now it was Appletree's turn to pitch. He was allowed one try to knock the pitcher down. If he did so, he could walk to first.

He wound up and hurled the ball. John Casey stood within the narrow square used for this occasion. If he stepped outside it, he would be in disgrace—the showers for him—and Appletree could walk all the way to second.

He stood his ground, but his knees were bent so he could sway his body either way.

The ball was a technical miss, though the edge of one of the rotating spikes did cut his right hip.

Then he picked up the ball and wound up.

The Deecee rooters prayed silently, their fingers crossed or their hands stroking the hair on the heads of any nearby mascots. The Caseylanders screamed themselves hoarse. The Pants-Elf, Iroquois, Floridians, and Buffaloes yelled insults at whichever team they hated most.

The Deecee man on third base edged out, ready to run for home if he got a chance. Casey eyed him but made no threatening move.

He threw one straight over the plate, preferring to make Appletree hit for a long one rather than dodge and perhaps get another ball called. Four balls, and Appletree could walk to first.

The big Deecee batter hit the ball square. But, as often happened, one of the spikes was also hit. The ball rose high over the path from home plate to first and then dropped toward a point halfway between home and first.

Appletree threw the bat at the pitcher, as was his right, and sprinted for first. Halfway to first, the ball hit him on the head. The first baseman, running to catch it, also rammed into him. Appletree hit the ground hard but bounced up like a rubber ball, ran several steps, and took a belly skid toward first.

However, the first baseman, while still on the ground, had picked up the ball and made a pass with it at Appletree. Immediately after, he jumped up and threw to home. The ball smacked into the huge and thick mitt of the catcher just before the man who had been on third slid into the plate.

The ump called the Deecee player out, and there was no argument there. But the first baseman walked up to the ump and submitted, in a loud voice, that he had touched Appletree as he ran away. Therefore, Appletree was also out.

Appletree denied that he had been touched.

The first baseman said that he could prove it. He had nicked the Deecee on the side of the right ankle with a spike on the ball.

The ump made Appletree take off his stocking.

"You've a fresh wound there, still bleeding," he said. "You're out!"

"I am not!" roared Appletree, spraying tobacco juice into the ump's face. "I'm bleeding from two cuts on my thigh, too, and that was done last inning! That father-god worshiper is a liar!"

"How would he know to tell me to look at your right ankle unless he had nicked you?" roared the ump back at Appletree. "I'm the ump, and I say you're out!"

He spelled it out in Deecee phonetics. "A-U-T! Out!"

The decision did not go over well with the Deecee rooters. They booed and screamed the traditional, "*Kill the ump!*"

The Karelian turned pale, but he stood his ground. Unfortunately, his courage and integrity did him no good, as the mob spilled out of the stadium and hung him by the neck from a girder. The mob also began beating up the Caseylander team. These might have died under the savage blows, but the Manhattan police surrounded them and beat back the frenzied rooters with the flat of their swords. They also managed to cut down the Karelian before the noose had finished its work.

Meanwhile, the Caseylander rooters had attempted to come to the rescue of their team. Although they never reached the players, they did tangle with the Deecee fans.

Stagg watched the melee for a while. At first he thought of leaping into the mass of furiously struggling bodies and striking blows right and left with his great fists. His bloodlust was aroused. He rose to make the leap into the mob below, but at that moment a group of women, also aroused by the fight, but in a different sense, descended on him.

10

Churchill did not sleep well that night. He could not rid himself of the ecstatic expression on Robin's face when she had said she hoped she would bear the Sunhero's child.

First, he cursed himself for not having guessed that she would have been among the one hundred virgins selected to make their debut during the rites. She was too beautiful, and her father was too prominent, for her to have been rejected.

Then he excused himself on the grounds that he really knew little of Deecee's culture. His own attitudes were too much those of his own time. He had treated her as if she were a girl of the early twenty-first century.

He cursed himself for having fallen in love with Robin. He was reacting more like a youth of twenty than a man of thirty-two—no, a man of eight hundred and thirty-two. A man who had traveled thousands of millions of miles and had made interstellar space his domain. Fallen for a girl of eighteen, who knew only a tiny section of Earth and a tiny section of time!

But Churchill was practical. A fact was a fact. And it was a fact that he wanted Robin Whitrow for his wife—or had, up to that moment last night when she had stunned him with her announcement.

For a while he hated Peter Stagg. He had always had a slight resentment against his captain, because Stagg was so tall and handsome and held a position which Churchill knew he was just as capable of holding. He liked and respected Stagg, but, being honest, he had admitted to himself that he was jealous.

It was almost unendurable to think that Stagg, as usual, had beaten him. Stagg was always first.

Almost unendurable.

As the night crept on, and Churchill rose from bed to smoke a cigar and pace back and forth, he forced himself to be frank with himself.

It was neither Stagg's fault nor Robin's that this had happened. And Robin certainly was not in love with Stagg. Stagg, poor devil, was doomed to a short but ecstatic life.

The immediate fact for Churchill to deal with was that he wanted to marry a woman who was going to bear another man's child. That neither she nor the father could be blamed was beside the point. What mattered was whether he wanted to marry Robin and to raise the child as his own.

Eventually, by lying still in bed and relaxing himself through yogoid techniques, he managed to go to sleep.

He woke about an hour after dawn and left his bedroom. A servant informed him that Whitrow had gone to his offices downtown and that Robin and her mother had left for the temple. The women should be back in two hours, if not sooner.

Churchill asked after Sarvant, but he had not as yet appeared.

Churchill ate breakfast with some of the children. They asked him to tell them a story about his trip to the stars. He described the incident on Wolf when the crew, while crossing a swamp on a raft in their escape from the Lupines, had been attacked by a balloon-octopus. This was an enormous creature that floated through the air by means of a gas-filled sac and seized its prey with long dangling tendrils. The tendrils could deliver an electric shock that paralyzed or killed its victims, after which the balloon-octopus tore the corpse apart with sharp claws on the ends of its eight muscular tentacles.

The children were wide-eyed and silent while he told the tale, and at the end they looked at him as if he were a demigod. He was in a bitter mood by the time he'd finished breakfast, especially when he remembered that it was Stagg who had saved his life by chopping off a tentacle that had seized him.

When he rose from the table, the children begged him for other stories. Only by promising to relate others when he returned that day was he able to free himself.

He gave orders to the servants that they should tell Sarvant to wait for him and tell Robin that he was going in search of his crewmates. The servants insisted on his taking a carriage and team. He did not like to be any more in debt to Whitrow than he was but decided that refusing the offer would probably insult him. He drove away at a fast clip down Conch Avenue, heading toward the stadium in which the *Terra* stood.

Churchill had some difficulty in finding the proper

authorities. Washington had not changed in some respects. A little money here and there got him the correct information, and presently he was in the office of the man in charge of the *Terra*.

"I would also like to know where the crew is," he said.

The official excused himself. He was gone for fifteen minutes, during which time he must have been checking on the whereabouts of the *Terra*'s ex-personnel. Returning, he told Churchill that all but one were at the House of Lost Souls. This, he explained, was a rooming and eating house for foreigners and traveling men who could not find a hostelry run for their particular frats.

"If you were the Sunhero and in a city, you could stay at the Elks' Hall," the official said. "But until you are initiated into a frat, you must find whatever public or private lodging you can. It is not always easy."

Churchill thanked him and walked out. Following the official's directions, he drove to the House of Lost Souls.

Here he found all the men he had left. Like him, they were dressed in native costume. Like him, they had sold their clothing.

They exchanged news of what had happened since the day before. Churchill asked where Sarvant was.

"We haven't heard a word about him," Gbwe-hun said. "And we still don't know what we're going to do."

"If you're willing to be patient," Churchill said, "you might be able to sail back to home."

He outlined for them what he knew about the maritime industry of Deecee and the chances they might have for seizing a ship. He concluded, "If I get a ship, I'll see that you have a berth on it. First, you have to be capable of filling a seaman's position. That means you're going to have to be initiated into one of the nautical frats, and then you will have to ship out for training. The whole plan will take time. If you can't stand the idea, you can always try it overland."

They discussed their chances and, after two hours, decided to follow Churchill.

He rose from the table. "All right. You make this your headquarters until further notice. You know where to contact me. So long and good luck."

Churchill allowed the deer pulling the carriage to set their own preferred slow pace. He dreaded what he might find when he returned to the Whitrow home, and he still did not know what he would do.

Eventually, the carriage pulled up before the house. The servants drove the team off. Churchill forced himself to enter the house. He found Robin and her mother sitting at the table, chattering away like a pair of happy magpies.

Robin jumped up from her chair and ran to him. Her eyes were shining, and she was smiling ecstatically.

"Oh, Rud, it has happened! I am carrying the Sunhero's child—and the priestess said it will be a boy!"

Churchill tried to smile, but he could not do it. Even when Robin had thrown her arms around him and kissed him and then had danced merrily around the room, Churchill could not smile.

"Have a cold beer," Robin's mother said. "You look as if you'd had some bad news. I hope not. Today should be a day of rejoicing. I am the daughter of a Sunhero, and my daughter is the child of a Sunhero, and my grandchild will be the son of a Sunhero. This house has been triply blessed by Columbia. We should reward her with the gratitude of laughter."

Churchill sat down and drank deep of the cold dark beer in the huge stone mug. He wiped the foam from his lips and said, "You must forgive me. I have been listening to the troubles of my men. However, that is no concern of yours. What I would like to know is, what will Robin do now?"

Angela Whitrow looked shrewdly at him as if she guessed what was going on inside him.

"Why, she will accept some lucky young man as her husband. She may have trouble making up her mind, since at least ten men are very serious about her."

"Does she favor anyone in particular?" Churchill asked in what he hoped was a nonchalant manner.

"She hasn't told me so," Robin's mother said. "But if I were you, Mr. Churchill, I'd ask her here and now—before the others get here."

Churchill was startled, but he kept a stiff face.

"How did you know I had that in mind?"

"You're a man, aren't you? And I know that Robin favors you. I think you'd make her the best of husbands."

"Thank you," he murmured. He sat for a moment, drumming his fingers on the table top. Then he rose and walked to where Robin was petting one of her cats, and seized her by the shoulders.

"Robin, will you marry me?"

"Oh yes!" she said, and she went into his arms.

That was that.

Once Churchill had made up his mind, he proceeded on the assumption that he had no grounds for resenting Stagg's child or Robin's conceiving it. After all, he told himself, if Robin had been married to Stagg and borne his child, and then Stagg had died, he, Churchill, would have had nothing to resent. And the situation in effect amounted to the same. For one night, Robin had been married to his former captain.

And though Stagg wasn't dead yet, he soon would be.

The upsetting factor had been his reacting with a set of values to a situation in which they did not apply. Churchill would have liked his bride to be a virgin. She wasn't, and that was that.

Nevertheless, he had more than one moment of feeling that, somehow, he had been betrayed.

There wasn't much time to think. Whitrow was called home from his office. He wept and embraced his daughter and son-in-law-to-be and then got drunk. Meanwhile, Churchill was taken away by the female servants and given a hair-trimming and a bath. Afterwards, he was massaged and oiled and perfumed. When he came out of the bathhouse, he found Angela Whitrow busy with some friends arranging a party to be held that night.

Shortly after supper, the guests began pouring in. By this time, both Whitrow and his daughter's fiancé were deep in their cups. The guests did not mind. In fact, they seemed to expect such a condition, and they tried to catch up with the two.

There was much laughter, much talking, much boasting. Only one ugly incident happened. One of the men who had been courting Robin made an allusion to Churchill's foreign pronunciation and then challenged Churchill to a duel. It was to be knives at the foot of the totem pole, the two to be tied by their waists to the pole, and the winner to take Robin.

Churchill punched the young man on the jaw, and his friends, laughing and whooping, carried off the unconscious body to its carriage.

About midnight Robin left her friends and took Churchill by the hand.

"Let's go to bed," she whispered.

"*Where? Now?*"

"To my room, silly. And now, of course."

"But, Robin, we've not been married. Or was I so drunk I didn't notice?"

"No, the marriage will take place in the temple next weekend. But what does that have to do with our going to bed?"

"Nothing," he said, shrugging his shoulders. "Other times, other mores. Lead on, Macduff."

She giggled and said, "What are you muttering about?"

"What would you do if I backed out before we got married?"

"You're joking, of course?"

"Of course. But you must realize, Robin darling, that I don't know much about Deecee customs. I'm just curious."

"Why, I'd do nothing. But it would be a deadly insult to my father and brother. They'd have to kill you."

"I just wanted to know."

The following week was a very busy one. In addition to the normal preparations for the wedding ceremony, Churchill had to decide what frat he was going to join. It was unthinkable that

Robin would marry a man without a totem.

"I would suggest," Whitrow said, "my own totem, the Lion. But it would be better for you to be in a frat directly concerned with your work and one which is blessed by the tutelary spirit of the animal with which you will be dealing."

"You mean one of the fish frats or the porpoise frat?"

"What? No, I do not! I mean the Pig totem. It would not be wise to be breeding hogs and at the same time have as your totem the Lion, a beast which preys on pigs."

"But," Churchill protested, "what do *I* have to do with pigs?"

It was Whitrow's turn to be surprised. "Then you've not discussed it with Robin? No wonder. She's had so little time to talk. Although you two have been alone every night from midnight until morning. But then I suppose you're too busy tumbling each other. Oh, to be young again! Well, my boy, the situation is this. I inherited some farms from my father, who was also no slouch when it came to making money. I need you to run these farms for me for several reasons.

"One, I don't trust the present manager. I think he's cheating me. Prove to me that he is, and I'll have him hung.

"Two, the Karelians have been making raids on my farms, stealing the best of my stock and the good-looking women. They haven't burned the houses and barns down or left the help to starve, since they don't want to kill the golden goose. You will stop the raids.

"Three, I understand that you're a geneticist. Therefore, you should be able to improve my stock.

"Four, when I return to the bosom of the Great White

Mother, you will inherit some of the farms. The merchant fleet goes to my sons."

Churchill rose. "I'll have to talk to Robin about this."

"Do that son. But you'll find she agrees with me."

Whitrow was right. Robin did not want her husband to be a sea-captain. She couldn't stand being separated from him so frequently.

Churchill protested that she could go with him on his voyages.

Robin replied that that wasn't so. The wives of seamen could not accompany them. They got in the way, they were extra expense, and, worst of all, they brought bad luck to the ship. Even when the ships carried paying women passengers, the ship had to be given an especially strong blessing by a priest in order to avert ill-fortune.

Churchill retaliated with the argument that, if she loved him, she'd put up with his long absences.

Robin retorted that if he really loved her, he wouldn't want to leave her for any length of time. Besides, what about the children? It was well known that children raised in a family where the father was weak or was often absent had a tendency to grow up psychically twisted. Children needed a strong father who was always available for love or discipline.

Churchill took ten minutes to reflect.

If he went back on his promise to marry her, he would have to fight Whitrow and his son. Somebody would be killed, and he had a conviction that eventually it would be he. Even if he could stand his ground against her father and brother and killed them, he'd have to fight the next of kin, who were very numerous.

Of course, he could force Robin to reject him. But he did not want to lose her.

Finally, he said, "All right, darling. I'll be a pig-raiser. I only ask one thing. I want to take one last sea voyage before settling down. Can we take a ship to Norfolk and then travel overland to the farms?"

Robin wiped away her tears, smiled, and kissed him, and said she would indeed be a hardhearted bitch if she denied him that.

Churchill left to tell his crewmates that they must buy passage on the ship that he and Robin would be taking. He'd arrange it so they had money enough for the tickets. After the ship was out of sight of land, they must seize it. They would then sail across the Atlantic and points east. It was too bad they hadn't had a chance to learn seamanship. They must learn as they sailed.

"Won't your wife be angry?" Yastzhembski said.

"More than that," Churchill said. "But if she really loves me, she'll go with me. If she doesn't, we'll put her and the crew ashore before we set out."

As it turned out, the crew of the *Terra* never got a chance to seize the vessel. The second day of their voyage, they were attacked by Karelian pirates.

11

When Stagg entered the campus of Vassar, he heard the same song, or variation thereof, he always heard when being presented the keys to the city, or, in this case, an honorary doctorate. Now, however, there was no large crowd to sing the welcome. A choir of freshmen, novitiates, greeted him. The older women, the priestesses and professors, arrayed in scarlet or blue, stood in a half-moon behind the white-clad choir, massed to form a delta. While the novitiates sang, the others nodded in approval at the quality of the performance or pounded the butts of their caducei on the ground in joy at sight of Stagg.

The Pants-Elf war party took the Vassar College for Oracular Priestesses completely by surprise. Somehow, the raiders had gotten the information that the Sunhero was to attend a private ceremony at midnight on the campus of Vassar. They knew that the people of Poughkeepsie had been warned to stay away. The only male on the college grounds was Stagg, and the priestesses numbered perhaps a hundred.

The war party burst out of the darkness and into the torchlight. The women were too busy chanting and observing Stagg and a young novitiate to notice the raiders. Not until the Pants-Elf gave a concerted scream and began cutting off the heads of those on the outside circle did the priestesses know they were attacked.

Stagg had no memory of what happened immediately after that. He raised his head just in time to see a man jump at him and swing the flat of a broadsword at his head.

He woke to find himself hanging like a slain deer from a pole carried on the shoulders of two men. His arms and legs were numb, the circulation cut off by rawhide strips binding them to the pole. His head felt as if it would burst; it ached not only from the blow but from the excess of blood which had drained into it because of its down-hanging position.

The moon was up and full. By its bright light he could see the bare legs and chest of the man behind him. Twisting his head, he could make out the gleam of moon on deeply tanned skins of men and on the white robes of a priestess.

Abruptly, he was lowered heavily on the hard ground.

"Old Horney is awake," a deep male voice said.

"Can't we cut the big bastard loose so he can walk?" another voice said. "I'm worn out carrying his useless hulk. That pole's cut an inch-deep groove in my shoulder."

"Okay," a third voice said, one that obviously belonged to a leader. "Cut him loose. But tie his hands behind his back, and tie a noose around his neck. If he tries to make a getaway, we can choke him. And be careful. He looks strong as a bull moose!"

"Oh, so strong, so superbly built!" a fourth voice said, higher-pitched than the others. "What a lover-boy!"

"You trying to make me jealous?" one of the men said. "Because if you are, dove, you're doing a good job. But don't push me. I'll cut out your liver and feed it to your mother."

"Don't you dare to say anything about my mother, you hairy thing!" the high-pitched voice said. "I'm beginning not to like you very much!"

"In the name of Columbia, our Blessed Mother! Cut out that lovers' quarreling. I'm sick of it. We're on a war party, not lounging around a totem hall. Go ahead, cut him loose. But watch him."

"I couldn't possibly watch him," the high-pitched voice said breathlessly.

"You trying to put his horns on my forehead?" said the man who had threatened to cut his friend's liver out. "Try it, and I'll gouge your face so another man will never look at you again."

"For the last time I said shut up!" the leader said, gratingly. "Next time, I slit the throat of the first man who provides the reason. Understood? Okay! Let's get going. We've a hell of a long way to go before we get out of enemy territory, and it won't be long before they have the bloodhounds on our trail."

Stagg was able to follow the conversation fairly well. The language was akin to Deecee, probably closer than German was to Dutch. He had heard it spoken before, in Camden. A group of Pants-Elf prisoners, taken on a raid, had had their throats cut during a ceremony in his honor. Some of them had been very brave men, jibing obscenely at Stagg until the knife severed their windpipes.

Just now Stagg wished that every man in Pants-Elf had had his throat cut. His legs and arms were beginning to hurt terribly. He wanted to cry out, but he knew that the Pants-Elf would probably knock him out again to keep him quiet. He also did not want to give them the satisfaction of knowing they had hurt him.

The raiders tied his hands behind his back, placed a noose around his neck and promised to put a knife into his back if he made any suspicious moves. Then they shoved him ahead.

At first, Stagg was not capable of trotting. After a while, as the blood reached its normal circulation and the pains went away, he was able to keep up with the others. It was a good thing, he thought. Every time he stumbled, he felt the noose tighten around his neck and his breath choked off.

They were going downhill in sparsely wooded territory. The raiders numbered about forty, strung out in a double file. They carried broadswords, assegais, clubs, bows and arrows. They wore no armor at all, probably to increase their mobility. They did not wear their hair long, like the men of Deecee, but cut it very short and close to the scalp. Their faces presented an odd appearance, since they all had broad dark mustaches. These were the first men with hair on their faces that he had seen since landing on Earth.

They left the wooded area and approached the bank of the Hudson River. He got a closer and brighter view of the Pants-Elf and saw that the mustaches had been painted or tattooed on.

Moreover, each of them had tattooed across his bare chest, in large letters, the word *Mother.*

There were seven prisoners: himself, five priestesses, and—

his heart skipped a beat—Mary Casey. They, too, had their hands tied behind their backs. Stagg tried to edge over to Mary Casey to whisper to her, but the rope around his neck pulled him back.

The party halted. Some of the men began clearing away a pile of brush. In a short time they exposed a number of large canoes piled in a hollow in the ground. These were carried to the river's edge.

The prisoners were forced to step into the canoes, one prisoner to a canoe, and the fleet paddled toward the other shore.

When the other shore was reached, the canoes were pushed out into the river for the current to carry away. The party set out at a trot through the woods. Occasionally, one of the prisoners stumbled and fell on her knees or face. The Pants-Elf kicked them and threatened to slit their throats on the spot if they didn't quit behaving like awkward cows.

Once, Mary Casey fell. A man kicked her in the ribs, and she writhed in agony. Stagg growled with fury and said, "If I ever get loose, Pants-Elf, I'll tear your arms off and wrap them around your neck!"

The man laughed and said, "Do that, dearie. It'd be a *pleasure* to be manhandled by the likes of *you*."

"For mother's sake, clam up!" the leader snarled. "Is this a war party or a courting?"

There was little said the rest of the night. They trotted a while and then walked a while. By dawn they had covered many miles, though not so many as the crow flies. The path wound through many hills.

Just after the eastern horizon began to pale, the leader

called a halt. “We’ll hole up and sleep until noon. Then, if the neighborhood looks deserted enough, we’ll push on. We can make better time in the daylight, even if there is more chance of being seen.”

They found a semicave formed by the overhang of a cliff. Here each man spread his single blanket on the hard earth and stretched out on it. In a few minutes all were asleep, except the four guards posted to keep an eye on the prisoners and any approaching Deecee.

Stagg was the other exception. He called softly to one of the guards. “Hey, I can’t sleep! I’m hungry!”

“You’ll eat when the rest of us do,” said the guard. “That is, if you get anything to eat.”

“You don’t understand,” Stagg said. “I don’t have the normal requirements for food. If I don’t eat every four hours, and twice as much as everybody else, my body starts to eat itself. It’s these horns that do it. They affect my body so I have to eat like a bull moose to keep alive.”

“I’ll get you some hay,” the guard said, and he snickered.

Somebody behind Stagg whispered, “Don’t worry, honey. I’ll get you something to eat. I couldn’t let a monstrously handsome man like you starve to death. That would be a waste!”

There was a stirring behind him as somebody opened a knapsack. The guards looked curiously and then began grinning.

“Looks like you made a hit with Abner,” said one. “But his buddy, Luke, isn’t going to like it one bit when he wakes up.”

Another said, “Good thing it’s not Abner who’s hungry. Then he could eat you. Haw, haw!”

The owner of the whisper walked into Stagg's view. It was the little man who had openly admired Stagg the previous night. He held a half loaf of bread, two huge slices of ham, and a canteen.

"Here, sit up, baby. Mother will feed big Horneycums."

The guards laughed, though not loudly. Stagg turned red, but he was too hungry to refuse food. He could feel the fire raging within him, flesh devouring flesh.

The little man was a youth about twenty, short and very slim-hipped. Unlike the other Pants-Elf, his hair had not been cut close to the scalp. It was wheat-brown and very curly. His face would have been called "cute" by a woman, though the painted mustache gave him a bizarre appearance. His large brown eyes were fringed by very long dark lashes. His teeth were so white they looked false, and his tongue was very red, probably because of some gum-like substance he was chewing.

Stagg hated to owe a debt to a being like Abner, but his mouth seemed to open automatically and gulp the food.

"There," Abner said, fondling Stagg's antlers and then running his long, slim fingers through Stagg's hair. "Does Horneycums feel better now? What about a big kiss to show big Horneycums' thanks?"

"Horneycums will kick hell out of you if you come any closer," Stagg said.

Abner's big eyes became even larger. He stepped back, his lower lip swelling with resentment.

"Is that any way to treat a buddy after he's kept you from starving to death?" he asked in a very hurt tone.

"Admittedly not," Stagg said. "But I just wanted you to know that if you try what I think you have in mind, you'll get killed."

Abner smiled and fluttered his long lashes. "Oh, you'll get over that absurd prejudice, baby. Besides, I've heard that you horned men are oversexed and once you're aroused you stop for nothing. What're you going to do if there are no women available?"

His lip curled in a sneer when he spoke of women. "Women" was a free translation of the word he used, a word that in Stagg's time had been used in a very derogatory, anatomical sense. Later, Stagg found that the Pants-Elf males always used that word among themselves, though in the presence of their females, they referred to them as "angels."

"Let the future take care of itself," Stagg said, and he closed his eyes and went to sleep.

It seemed to him only a minute later when he was awakened, but the sun was at its zenith. He blinked and sat up and looked around for Mary Casey. She had her hands untied, and was eating, while a man with a sword stood guard beside her.

The leader's name was Raf. He was a big man with broad shoulders and slim waistline and a strikingly handsome but cold face and blond hair. His blue eyes were very pale and very cold.

"That Mary Casey tells me you aren't a Deecee," he said. "She says you came down from the skies in a fiery metal ship, and that you left Earth over eight hundred years ago to explore the stars. Is she a liar?"

Stagg outlined his story, watching Raf closely while he told it. He was hoping that Raf would decide not to give him the usual treatment a Pants-Elf gave a Deecee who was in his power.

"Say, you're quite a dish," Raf enthusiastically said, though his pale blue eyes were as icy as before. "And those horns are *crazy.* They give you a real masculine look. I hear that when you Horned Kings are in heat, you've the staying power of fifty bucks."

"That is a well-known fact," Stagg replied smoothly. "What I'd like to know is, what's going to happen to us?"

"We'll decide that after we get out of Deecee territory and get across the Delaware River. We've two days' hard marching ahead of us, though we'll be fairly safe once we get over the Shawangunk Mountains. Beyond the Shawangunk is a no-man's land, where the only people we'll meet are raiding parties, friendly or hostile."

"What about untying me?" Stagg said. "I can't go back to Deecee, and I'd just as soon throw in my lot with you."

"You kidding?" Raf said. "I'd just as soon let loose a mad elk! I'm a damn good man, baby, but I wouldn't want to tangle with you—that is—not in combat. No, you'll stay tied up."

The party set out at a fast pace. Two scouts ran ahead to make sure they didn't fall into ambush. When they came to the Shawangunk Mountains, they approached the pass cautiously, hiding until the scouts gave the go-ahead signal. At midnight the party bedded down behind a high rocky ridge.

Stagg tried to talk to Mary Casey to raise her morale. She was beginning to look very fatigued. Every time she started to lag, she was struck and cursed. Abner was especially hard on her; he seemed to hate her.

The evening of the third day, they forded the Delaware

River at a shallow place. They slept, rose at dawn, and pushed on. By eight o'clock in the morning, the raiders made a triumphal entry into the small frontier town of High Queen.

High Queen had a population of about fifty, huddled in cubical stone buildings surrounded by a twenty-five foot high stone and cement wall. Each building was windowless on the street side, and its entranceways were set deep within the walls. The windows were on the inside walls, facing the court.

The houses had no front yards, since they were set flush with the street. However, they were separated by vacant weed-grown lots on which goats grazed, chickens pecked, and dirty, naked children played.

The crowd that greeted the raiders was composed mainly of men; the few women present soon left at the orders of their husbands. The women were veiled and wore robes that concealed the body from shoulder to ground. Evidently women held an inferior position in Pants-Elf, despite the fact that the only idol in the town was a granite statue of the Great White Mother.

Later, Stagg found out that the Pants-Elf worshiped Columbia, but that the Deecee regarded them as belonging to a heretical sect. In the theology of the Pants-Elf, every woman was a living incarnation of Columbia and therefore a sacred vessel of motherhood. But the men of Pants-Elf knew also that the flesh was weak. They made sure that their women had no chance to dirty their purity.

They were to be good servants and good mothers, but that was all; therefore, they were to be sealed from view as much as possible and also sealed from temptation. The males had sexual intercourse with their wives only to have children, and as little other type of intercourse, social and familial, as possible. They were polygamous—on the theory that polygamy was an excellent institution for repopulating a sparsely settled country.

The women, shut off from men and confined to each other's company, often became Lesbians. They were even encouraged by the males to become so; but they went to bed with the men at least three times a week. This was enjoined on husband and wife as a sacred duty, distasteful as it might be to either or both. The result was almost perpetual pregnancy.

This was a state which the man desired. According to this heretical sect, a pregnant woman was ritually unclean. She was not to be touched, except by other unclean women or priests.

The prisoners were shut within one of the larger stone buildings. Women came to bring them food, but first Stagg was forced to put on kilts so he wouldn't shock the women. The raiders and townsmen then celebrated by getting very drunk.

At about nine at night, they burst into the cell and took Stagg, Mary Casey and the priestesses to the town square. Here stood the statue of Columbia, and around her were a circle of woodpiles. From the center of each pile rose a stake.

A priestess was bound to each stake.

Stagg and Mary were not tied to a stake, but they were forced to stand and watch.

"It is necessary to purify these evil witches through fire," Raf said. "That is why we brought along those young women. We felt sorry for them. You see, those we killed with the sword are forever lost, doomed souls that will wander through eternity.

But these will be purified through fire. They will go to the land of happy souls.

"It is too bad," he added, "that High Queen doesn't have any sacred bears, because then we'd feed the wretches to the bears. Bears are just as much instruments of salvation as fire, you know.

"You needn't worry about anything happening to you here. We wouldn't waste you on this hick town. You're to go to Pheelee, where the government will take the responsibility for you."

"Pheelee? Philadelphia, the City of Brotherly Love?" Stagg said with the last attempt at humor he made that night.

The fires were touched off, and the purifying ritual begun.

Stagg watched for a moment, then closed his eyes. Fortunately, he couldn't hear the women screaming, because they were gagged. The priestesses who were burned had the habit of calling down curses upon the Pants-Elf; the gags were to prevent this.

The stench of burning flesh could not be shut out. Stagg and Mary both became sick—and then had to endure the amused laughter of their captors.

Finally, the fires went out and the two prisoners were marched back to the cell. Mary was held while two men stripped her, locked an iron chastity belt around her and then put a kilt on over it.

Stagg protested; the men looked at him in amazement.

"What?" Raf said. "Leave her open to temptation? Allow the pure vessel of Columbia to be defiled? You must be mad! Inasmuch as she will be left alone with you, and you're a Horned King, the result would be inevitable. And—knowing your endurance—probably fatal for her. You should thank us for this. You know what you would do!"

"Unless you feed me more than you have," Stagg said, "I could not do anything. I'm weak from starvation."

Stagg did not want to eat, in one sense. His meager diet had considerably diminished the action of the antlers. He still suffered from a drive that was embarrassingly evident and had been the object of numerous amused and admiring comments from his captors; but it was almost nothing compared to the satyriasis that had possessed him in Deecee.

Now he was afraid that, if he ate, he would attack Mary Casey—chastity belt or no chastity belt. But he was also afraid that if he didn't eat he'd be dead by morning.

Perhaps, he thought, he could eat enough to feed his body and antlers but not enough so the compulsion would become uncontrollable.

"Why don't you put me in another room if you're so sure I'll attack her?" he said.

Raf looked amazed. But he overdid it, and Stagg knew that Raf had been maneuvering him into making just such a suggestion.

"Of course! I'm so tired, I'm stupid," Raf said. "We'll lock you up in another room."

The other room was located in the same building, across the inner court. From his window Stagg could see the window of Mary's room. Although she had no light of her own, the moon cast beams into the court. They glimmered palely upon her face, pressed against the iron bars.

Stagg waited for twenty minutes; then the expected sound came, a key inserted into the lock of the iron door.

The door swung open with the creak of unoiled hinges. Abner entered with a huge tray. He set it down on the table and told the guard he'd call him when he wanted him. The guard opened his mouth to object, but, seeing Abner's glare, he withdrew. He was a local and therefore awed by this Philadelphia raider.

"See, Horneycums?" said Abner. "Look at all the nice food for you! Don't you think you owe me something for this?"

"I certainly do," Stagg said. He would have gone along with almost anything for the sake of a meal. "You've got more than enough. But in case I want more later, could you get it easily?"

"You bet. The kitchen is just down the hall. The woman has gone back to her quarters, but I'd be delighted to do a woman's work for *you*. How about a kiss to show your gratitude?"

"I couldn't put anything into it until I eat," Stagg replied, forcing himself to smile at Abner. "Then we'll see."

"Don't be coy, Horneycums," Abner said. "And please, pretty please, hurry up and eat. We don't have too much time. I think that big bitch Raf is planning to come here tonight. And I'm nervous, too, about my buddy, Luke. If he knew I was here alone with you… !"

"I can't eat with my hands tied behind my back."

"I don't know," Abner said, hesitatingly. "You're so big and strong. You could tear me apart with your bare hands—such *huge* hands, too."

"I'd be stupid to do that," Stagg said. "Then I'd have nobody to sneak me food. I'd starve."

"That's right. Besides, you wouldn't hurt little old me, would you? I'm so small and helpless. And you do like me, just a little, don't you? You didn't mean what you said on the trail, did you?"

"Of course not," Stagg said, munching on cold ham, bread and butter, and pickles. "I just said that so your buddy Luke wouldn't get any ideas about us."

"You're not only devastatingly handsome, you're clever, too," Abner said. He was panting slightly. "Do you feel strong enough, now?"

Stagg was about to say that he had to eat everything in sight before he would get his strength back, but thought better of the remark. He did not have to say anything, because there was a commotion just outside the door. He put his ear against the iron to hear.

"It's your buddy, Luke. He's telling the guard he knows you're in here with me, and he's demanding that he be let in."

Abner turned pale. "Oh, Mother! He'll kill me and you, too! He's such a jealous bitch!"

"Call him in. I'll take care of him. I won't kill him; just rough him up a bit. Let him know how things are between you and me."

Abner squealed with delight. "That would be *divine*!"

He squeezed Stagg's arm, and rolled his eyes upward with ecstasy. "Mother, what *biceps*! So big and *hard*!"

Stagg beat on the door with his fist and called to the guard. "Abner says it's all right to let him in!"

"Yes," Abner said behind him. "It's perfectly all right. Let Luke in."

He kissed Stagg on the back of the neck. "I can just see the expression on his face when you tell him about us. I've been getting pretty tired of his jealous moods, anyway."

The door squeaked open. Luke rushed in, sword in hand. The guard slammed the door shut behind Luke, and the three were locked in.

Stagg wasted no time. He chopped down with the edge of his palm against Luke's neck. Luke fell, and the sword clanged as it hit the stone floor.

Abner gave a little shriek. Then he opened his mouth for a scream as he saw Stagg bound at him. Before he could give vent to it, he, too, fell on the floor.

His head lay at a grotesque angle. Stagg had hit him so hard with his fist that he'd broken his neck.

Stagg dragged the bodies to one side so they wouldn't be visible from the doorway. He took Luke's sword and with one hard swing cut off Luke's head.

Then he rapped on the door and called in what he hoped was a passable imitation of Abner's voice, "Guard! Come in here and make Luke quit abusing the prisoner!"

The key was turned, and the guard stepped inside. He had his sword in hand, but Stagg struck from behind the door. The head of the guard rolled a foot from his body, the open neck gushing a stream of blood.

Stagg put the guard's knife in his belt and stepped out into the hall, which was narrow and dimly lit by a torch at the far end. He took a chance that the kitchen was at the far end and walked down to it. The door opened onto a large room well stocked with food. He found a cloth sack and filled it with food and several bottles of wine. Then he went back into the hall.

At the same time, Raf opened the door to the hall and stepped inside.

His manner was furtive, and it was probably his nervousness that made him not notice the guard was gone. He was unarmed except for a knife in a scabbard at his belt.

Stagg ran down the hall toward him. Raf looked up and saw the horned man bearing down on him, a lifted bloody sword in one hand, the other holding a large sack slung over his shoulder.

Raf turned and tried to get out of the door. The blade cut all the way through his neck.

Stagg stepped over the corpse, still spouting blood, and went out into the court. There he found two men sleeping on the pavement. Like most of the men in High Queen that night, they had passed out. Stagg did not care to take a chance on their barring his way later, and besides he wanted to kill every Pants-Elf he came across. He gave two quick strokes across their necks and went on.

He crossed the court and entered another hall, exactly like the one he had left. There was a guard posted outside the door of Mary's room, a bottle tilted to his lips.

He did not see Stagg until Stagg was almost on him. For a second, he was too paralyzed with astonishment to make a move. It was all the time Stagg needed. He threw the sword, point foremost.

The point struck the guard exactly in the "O" of the *Mother* tattooed on his bare chest. The guard staggered backward with the impact, his hand clutching the blade. Strangely, his other hand did not drop the bottle.

The point had not gone in deeply, but Stagg dropped his sack, leaped after the sword, seized it and pushed hard on the hilt. The blade went all the way through the breastbone and deep into the organ beneath.

Mary Casey almost fainted when the door opened and the horned and bloody man stepped inside. Then she gasped. "Peter Stagg! How… ?"

"Later!" he said. "No time to talk!"

Together they ran from the shadow of one building to another until they reached the wall and high gate through which they had entered the town. There were two guards posted at the foot of the gate, and two men in small towers above it.

Fortunately, all four were sleeping off their drunk. Stagg had no trouble in plunging his knife into the throats of the two men on the ground. Then he walked softly up the steps leading to the towers and treated the two there the same way. He did not have any trouble in withdrawing the huge bolt of oak that held the two gates together.

They went back by the path on which they had come. They trotted a hundred steps, walked a hundred, trotted a hundred, walked a hundred.

They came to the Delaware and crossed on the same shallow ford. Mary asked for rest, but Stagg said they'd have to push on.

"When the town wakes up and finds all those headless corpses, they'll be hot on our trail. They won't stop till they find us, unless we can reach Deecee territory before they do. And then we'll have to watch out for the Deecee, too. We're going to try to get to Caseyland."

The time came when they had to slow down to a walk; Mary couldn't keep up the pace. By nine in the morning, she sat down.

"I can't go another step unless I get some sleep first."

They found a hollow about a hundred meters from the path. Here Mary fell asleep at once. Stagg ate and drank first and then he lay down to sleep also. He would have liked to stay on guard, but he knew that he had to have rest to continue in a few hours. He needed his strength because he might have to carry Mary.

He woke before Mary did, and he ate again.

When she opened her eyes a few minutes later, she saw Stagg bending over her.

"What are you doing?"

He said, "Shut up. I'm trying to get your chastity belt off."

12

The face of Nephi Sarvant was an index to his character. It looked in profile like a nutcracker or the curved jaws of a pair of pliers. He was faithful to his face; once he fastened down upon something, he would not let go.

Having left Whitrow's house, he swore that he would never set foot in a place where such iniquity thrived. He swore also to dedicate his life, if need be, to bringing the Truth to the idolatrous heathen.

He walked the five kilometers to the House of Lost Souls and spent a night of uneasy sleep there. Shortly after dawn, he left the house. Though it was so early, the street was alive with wagons piled with freight, sailors, merchantmen, children, women marketing. He looked into several restaurants, found them too dirty, and decided to make his breakfast on fruit from a street stand. He talked with the fruit-merchant about his chances for getting a job and was told that there was an opening for a janitor at the temple of the goddess Gotew. The merchant knew this because his brother-in-law had been fired from the job the previous evening.

"It doesn't pay much but you get your board and room. And there are other compensations, provided you are a man who has fathered many children," the merchant said. He winked at Sarvant. "My brother-in-law was fired because he neglected his sweeping and scrubbing for the other advantages."

Sarvant didn't ask what he meant. He got directions for getting to the temple and left.

This job, if he secured it, would be an excellent post for observation of the Deecee religion. And it would afford a first-rate battleground for proselytizing. Oh, it would be dangerous, but what missionary worthy of his faith ever considered that a drawback?

The directions were complicated; Sarvant lost his way. He found himself far into a wealthy residential district, with no one to ask directions from except a few people who rode by in carriages or on deerback. These did not look as if they would stop to talk to a pedestrian, a man of the lower classes.

He decided to go back to the dock area and start over. He had not gone a block before he saw a woman who had just left a large house. She was dressed strangely, covered from head to foot with a hooded robe. At first, he thought she must be a servant; he knew now that an aristocrat never walked when she could ride. On approaching her, he saw that the robe was of too fine a material to belong to one of the lower class.

He followed her for several blocks before he took a chance of offending her by speaking to her. Finally, he called to her,

"Lady, may I humbly ask a question?"

She turned and looked haughtily at him. She was a tall woman of about twenty-two with a face that would have been beautiful if it had been less sharp. Her large eyes were a deep blue, and her hair, where it was not hidden by the hood, was rich yellow.

Sarvant repeated his question, and she nodded her head. He then asked her directions to the Temple of Gotew.

She looked angry and said, "Are you making fun of me?"

"No, no," Sarvant said. "Why would I do that? I don't understand."

"Perhaps you don't," she said. "You sound like a foreigner. Certainly, you've no reason to deliberately insult me. My people would kill you—even if I am not worthy of the insult."

"Believe me, I had no such intention. If I have offended, I apologize."

She smiled slightly and said, "Accepted, stranger. And now, tell me, why do you want to go to the Temple of Gotew? Do you have a wife who is as wretched and cursed as I am?"

"She has been long dead," Sarvant said. "And I do not know what you mean by saying you are wretched and cursed. No, I am looking for a job as janitor in the temple. You see, I am one of those who came down to Earth..." and he launched into his story, though he told it in the briefest outline.

She said, "Then you may talk to me as an equal, I suppose, though it is hard to think of a *diradah* sweeping floors. A true *diradah* would starve to death first. And I see you're not wearing a totem symbol. If you belonged to one of the great totems, you could find a job worthy of you. Or do you lack a sponsor?"

"Totems are superstitious idolatry!" he said. "I would never join one."

Her eyebrows rose. "You *are* a queer one! I don't know how to classify you. As a brother of the Sunhero, you are a *diradah.* But you certainly don't look or act like one. My advice to you is to behave like one so we may know how to behave toward you."

"I thank you," he said. "But I must be what I am. Now, could you please tell me how to get to the temple."

"Just follow me," she said, and she began walking.

Perplexed, he trailed her by a few steps. He would have liked to have clarified some of the statements she made, but there was something about her attitude that discouraged questions.

The Temple of Gotew was on the borderline between the dock area and a wealthy residential district. It was an imposing building of prestressed concrete, shaped like an enormous half-open oyster shell and painted in scarlet and white stripes. Broad steps of granite slabs ran up to the lower lip of the shell, and the interior was cool and dimly lit. The upper part of the shell was supported by a few slim pillars of stone carved in the likeness of the goddess Gotew, a stately figure with a sad and brooding face and an open hollow where her stomach should have been.

In the hollow sat a large stone reproduction of a hen surrounded by eggs.

At the base of each caryatid of the goddess sat women. Every one wore a robe similar to that of the woman he had followed. Some robes were shabby; some, rich. Wealthy and poor sat together.

The woman walked without hesitation to a group that sat

on the cement floor deep within the gloom. There were about twelve around the caryatid, and they must have been expecting the tall thin blonde, since they had a space reserved for her.

Sarvant found a white-faced priest who was standing at the rear by a row of large stone booths. He inquired about the janitor's job. To his surprise, he found he was talking to the chief official of the temple; he had expected a priestess in charge.

Bishop Andi was curious about Sarvant's accent and asked him the same sort of questions others had. Sarvant replied truthfully, but he sighed relief when the bishop failed to ask him if he was a worshiper of Columbia. The bishop turned Sarvant over to a lesser priest, who told him what his duties would be, how much he'd be paid, where he would eat and sleep and when. He concluded by asking, "Are you the father of many children?"

"Seven," replied Sarvant, neglecting to add that they had been dead for eight centuries. It was possible that the priest himself was one of Sarvant's descendants; indeed, it was conceivable that everyone under the roof could claim him as their grandfather thirty-odd generations removed.

"Seven? Excellent!" the priest said. "In that case, you will have the same privileges as any other man of proven fertility. You will have to undergo a medical examination, however, because we take no man's word for such a grave responsibility. I warn you, do not abuse the privilege. Your predecessor was discharged for neglecting his push broom."

Sarvant began sweeping in the rear of the temple. He had just reached the pillar where the blonde was sitting when he noticed a man talking to a woman by the blonde's side. He could not hear what they were saying, but presently the woman arose and opened her robe. She was wearing nothing under the robe.

The man apparently liked what he saw since he nodded his head. The woman took his hand and led him to one of the booths at the rear. They entered, and the woman closed a curtain over the front of the booth.

Sarvant was speechless. It was minutes before he was able to begin pushing the broom again. By then he saw that the same actions were being repeated everywhere in the temple.

His first impulse was to drop the broom, run out of the temple, and never come back. But he told himself that wherever he went in Deecee he would find evil. He might as well stay here and see if he could do anything in the service of the Truth.

Then he was forced to witness something that almost made him vomit. A big sailor approached the thin blonde and began talking to her. She rose and opened her robe, and in a moment the two had gone into a booth.

Sarvant shook with rage. He had been shocked enough that the others would do this, but that she, *she*... !

He made himself stand still and think.

Why should her actions offend him more than the actions of the others? Because—admit it—he had felt attracted to her. Very much attracted. He had felt about her as he had not felt about a woman since the day he had met his wife.

He picked up his brush, walked to the office of the underling priest, and demanded to be told what was going on.

The priest was astonished. "Are you so new to our religion that you did not know Gotew is the patroness of sterile women?"

"No, I did not," Sarvant replied, his voice shaking. "What does that have to do with this..." He stopped, because Deecee had no words, as far as he knew, for prostitution or whoring. Then he said, "Why do these women offer themselves to strangers, what does the worship of Gotew have to do with this?"

"Why, everything of course! These are unlucky women, cursed with a sterile womb. They came to us after a year's endeavor to conceive by their husbands, and we gave them a thorough physical examination. Some women have troubles we can diagnose and rectify, but not these. There is nothing we could do for them.

"So, when science fails, faith must be called upon. These unfortunate women come here every day—except on holy days, when there is a ceremony to attend elsewhere—and they pray that Gotew will send them a man whose seed will quicken their dead wombs. If, after a year's time, they are not blessed with a child, they usually enter an order where they may dedicate their life to serving their goddess and their people."

"What about Arva Linkon?" Sarvant said, naming the blonde. "It's unthinkable that a woman with her beauty and aristocratic family should lie with any man who comes along."

"Tut, tut, my dear fellow! Not *any* man. Perhaps you didn't observe that those males who come here went into a side room first. My good brothers examine them there to make sure they are brimming with healthy sperm. Also, any man who is diseased or in any way unfit to be a father is rejected. As for ugliness or handsomeness of the male, we pay no attention to that; here the desideratum is the seed and the womb. Personalities and personal taste do not enter. By the way, why don't you take the examination too? No reason to selfishly restrict your offspring to one woman. You owe as much a debt to Gotew as to any other aspect of the Great White Mother."

"I have to get back to my sweeping," muttered Sarvant, and he left hastily.

He did manage to finish the main floor, but it was only by an extreme effort of will. He could not keep from looking at Arva Linkon from time to time. She left at noon and did not return the rest of the day.

He did not sleep well that night. He dreamed of Arva entering the booth with those men—ten in all; he had counted them. And though he knew he should love the sinners and loathe the sin, he loathed every one of the ten sinners.

When morning came, he swore that he would not hate the men who came to her today. But even as he swore he knew he could not keep his vow.

That day he counted seven men. By the time the seventh strolled out, he had to retreat to his quarters to keep from running after the man and closing his hands around his throat.

The third night, he prayed for guidance.

Should he leave the temple, look elsewhere for work? If he stayed, he would be indirectly approving of and directly maintaining this abomination. Moreover, he might have the terrible sin of murder on his conscience, the blood of a man on his hands. He did not want that. Yes, he wanted it! But he must not want it, he must not!

And if he left, he would not have done a thing to wipe out

the evil; he would have fled like a coward. Moreover, he would not have made Arva realize that she was slapping God in the face by carrying on this loathsome travesty of a religious rite. He wanted to get her out of the temple more than he had wanted anything in his life—even more than he had wanted to be on the *Terra* so he could carry the Word to the ignorant heathen of the other planets.

He had not made a single convert during those eight hundred years. But he had tried. He had done his best; he could not help it if their ears were deaf to the Word, their eyes blind to the light of the Truth.

The next day, he waited until Arva began to walk out of the temple at noon. Then he leaned his brush against the wall and followed her out into the sunshine and the buzz and crash of Deecee street life.

"Lady Arva!" he called. "I must speak with you!"

She stopped. Her face was shadowed by the overhanging hood, but it seemed to him that she looked as if she were deeply ashamed and were suffering. Or did she look that way because he wanted her to?

"May I walk home with you?" he asked.

She was startled. "Why?"

"Because I will go crazy if I do not."

"I do not know," she said. "It is true that you are a brother of the Sunhero, so that there should be no loss of dignity in having you walk by my side. On the other hand, you have no totem, and you do the work of the lowest of menials."

"And who are you, of all people, to talk to me about being

lowly!" he snarled. "You, who take on all comers?"

Her eyes widened. "What have I done wrong? How dare you talk to a Linkon in that manner?"

"You are a… a whore!" he shouted, using the English word even though he knew she would not understand.

"What's that?" she said.

"Prostitute! A woman who sells herself for money!"

"I never heard of anything like that," she said. "What kind of country do you come from, that a vessel of the Holy Mother would so dishonor herself?"

He tried to calm down. He spoke in a low but quivering voice.

"Arva Linkon, I just want to talk to you. I have something to say that will be the most important thing you have ever heard in your life. Indeed, the only important thing."

"I don't know. I think you are a little crazed."

"I swear that I would not dream of doing you harm!"

"Swear on the sacred name of Columbia?"

"No, I cannot do that. But I will swear by my God that I will not lay a hand on you."

"God! You worship the god of the Caseylanders?"

"No, not theirs! Mine! The true God!"

"Now I know you are crazy! Otherwise, you would not be talking of this god in this country, and especially not to me. I won't listen to the foul blasphemy that would pour from your wicked mouth."

She walked away.

Sarvant took a step after her. Then, realizing that now

was not the time to talk to her, and that he was not conducting himself as he would have wished, he turned away. His fists were clenched, and he was grinding his teeth together. He walked like a blind man, several times bumping into people. They swore at him, but he paid no attention.

He went back to the temple and picked up his broom.

Again, he did not sleep well at night. He planned a hundred times how he would talk softly and wisely to Arva. He would show her the errors of her belief in a manner she could not refute. Eventually, she would be his first convert.

Side by side, they would begin the work that would sweep the country clean, as the Primitive Christians had swept ancient Rome.

The following day, however, Arva did not come into the temple. He despaired. Perhaps she would never come back.

Then he realized that that was one of the things he had wanted her to do. Perhaps he was making more progress than he had thought.

But how would he get to see her again?

The morning of the next day, Arva, still clad in the hooded robe of the sterile woman, walked into the temple. She averted her eyes and was silent when he greeted her. After praying at the foot of the caryatid at which she customarily sat, she went to the rear of the temple and began talking earnestly to the bishop.

Sarvant was seized with a fear that she was denouncing him. Was it reasonable to expect that she would keep silent? After all, in her eyes, he was committing blasphemy by even being in this—to her—holy place.

Arva resumed her place at the foot of the caryatid. The bishop beckoned to Sarvant.

He put his broom down and walked to him, his legs weak with anxiety. Was this mission to stop here and now, before he had planted one seed of faith that would grow after he was gone? And if he failed now, then the Word was lost forever, since he was the last of his sect.

"My son," said the bishop, "up to now the knowledge that you are not as yet a believer has been confined to the hierarchy. You must remember that you were granted a great privilege because you are a brother to the Sunhero. If you had been anybody else, you would have been hanged long ago. But you were given a month to see the error of your ways and to testify to the truth. Your month is not up yet; but I must warn you that you will have to keep your mouth shut about your false belief. Otherwise, the time will be shortened. I am disturbed, since I had hoped that your application to work here meant that you were about to announce your desire to sacrifice to the Mother of Us All."

"Then Arva told you?"

"Bless her for a truly devout woman, she certainly did! Now, do I have your promise that you will not repeat the incident of the day before?"

"You have it," Sarvant said. The bishop had not asked him to quit proselytizing. He had just asked him not to repeat the incident. From now on he would be cunning as the dove, wise as the serpent.

Five minutes later, he had forgotten his resolution.

He saw a tall and handsome man, an aristocrat by his

bearing and his expensive clothes, approach Arva. She smiled at him, rose, and led him to the booth.

It was the smile that did it.

Never before had she smiled at the men who came to her. Her face had been as expressionless as if cut from marble. Now, seeing the smile, Sarvant felt something well up in him. It spread from his loins, roared through his chest, raced through his throat, cutting off his wind. It filled his skull until it exploded; he could see only blackness before him and could hear nothing.

He did not know how long he had been in that condition, but when he partially regained his senses, he was standing in the office of the priest-physician.

"Bend over, and I'll massage your prostate and get a specimen," the priest was saying.

Automatically, Sarvant obeyed. While the priest was examining the slide through a microscope, Sarvant stood like a block of ice. Inside, he was fire. He was filled with a fierce joy he had never known; he knew what he was going to do, but he did not care. At that moment he would have defied any being or Being who tried to stop him.

A few minutes afterward, he strode from the office, Unhesitatingly, he walked up to Arva, who had just returned from the booth and was about to sit down.

"I want you to come with me!" he said in a loud clear voice.

"Where?" she said, and then, seeing the expression on his face, she understood.

"What did you say about me the other day?" she asked scornfully.

"That was not today."

He seized her hand and began to pull her toward the booth. She did not resist, but when they were in the booth and he had closed the curtain, she said, "Now I know! You have decided to sacrifice to the Goddess!"

She threw off her robe and smiled ecstatically. But she was looking upwards, not at him.

"Great Goddess, I thank You for having allowed me to become the instrument to convert this man to the true faith!"

"No!" said Sarvant hoarsely. "Don't say that! I do not believe in your idol. It is just—God help me!—I want you! I cannot stand seeing you go into this booth with every man that asks you. Arva, I love you!"

For a moment, she stared at him with horror. Then she stopped and picked up her robe and held it in front of her. "Do you think that I would allow you to defile me by touching me? A pagan! And under this holy roof!"

She turned to walk out. He leaped at her, spun her around. She opened her mouth to scream, and he stuffed the hem of the robe into her mouth. He wrapped the rest of the robe around her head and shoved her backwards so she fell upon the bed and he on top of her.

She writhed and twisted to get from his grip, but he held her with fingers that cut deep into her flesh. Then she tried to hold her knees together. He gave a great flop like a giant fish, coming down hard with his hips; it broke the lock of her legs.

She tried to go backwards, like a snake attempting to crawl on its back, but her head was stopped by the wall behind her.

Suddenly, she stopped struggling.

Sarvant moaned and gripped her back with his hands, pressing his face against the robe over her face. He wanted to feel his lips upon hers, but the cloth was doubled where he had shoved it into her mouth; he could feel nothing through the thickness.

There was a spark of sanity, the thought that he had always hated violence and especially rape, and yet he was forcing himself upon this woman he loved. And worse, far worse, she had willingly given herself to at least a hundred men in the last ten days, men who did not care at all about her but merely wanted to spew out their lust upon her. Yet she was resisting him like a virgin martyr of ancient Rome at the mercy of a pagan emperor! It did not make sense; nothing did.

He screamed with the sudden release of eight hundred years.

He did not know that he was screaming. He was absolutely unaware of his surroundings. When the bishop and priest rushed in, and Arva, weeping and sobbing, told her story, he did not comprehend what was happening. Not until the temple was crowded with furious men from the street, and someone appeared with a rope, did he understand what was happening.

Then it was too late.

Too late to try to tell them what had impelled him. Too late even if they could have known what he was talking about. Too late even if they had not knocked him down and beaten him until his teeth were knocked out and his lips too puffed to do anything but mumble.

The bishop tried to intervene, but the mob pushed him to one side and carried Sarvant out into the street. There they dragged him by the legs, his head bumping on the cement, until they came to a square where a gallows stood. This was in the shape of a hideous old goddess, Alba, the Throttler of Men's Breath. Her iron hands, painted a dead-white, reached out as if clutching for every man that passed.

The rope was thrown over one of her hands and its end tied around the wrist. Men brought a table out from a house and set it beneath the dangling rope. They lifted Sarvant upon it and tied his hands behind his back. Two men held him while a third put a noose around his neck.

There was a moment of silence when the cries of outraged men ceased, and they quit trying to get their hands upon him and tear his blasphemer's flesh.

Sarvant looked about him. He could not see clearly, since his eyes were puffed up, and blood was running over them from gashes in his scalp. He mumbled something.

"What did you say?" one of the men holding him asked.

Sarvant could not repeat it. He was thinking that he had always wanted to be a martyr. It was a terrible sin, that desire; the sin of pride. But he had desired martyrdom. And he had always pictured himself coming to the end with dignity and with the courage given him by the knowledge that his disciples would carry on and would eventually triumph.

This was not to be. He was to hang like a criminal of the worst sort. Not for preaching the Word, but for rape.

He had not a single convert. He would die unmourned, die practically nameless. His body would be thrown to the hogs. Not that his body mattered; it was the thought that his name and his deed would die, too, that made him want to scream out to the heavens. Somebody, even if just one soul, should carry on.

He thought, No new religion succeeds unless the old religion first becomes weak. And these people believe without a shadow of a doubt to relieve the blinding intensity of conviction. They believe with a strength that the people of my time certainly did not have.

He mumbled again. By now he was standing alone on the table, swaying back and forth but determined that he would not show any fear.

"Too soon," he said in a language his hearers could not have understood even if he had spoken clearly. "I came back to Earth too soon. I should have waited another eight hundred years, when men might have begun to lose faith and to scoff in secret. Too soon!"

Then the table was dragged out from under him.

13

Two tall-masted schooners, sailing out of the dawn mists, were on the Deecee brigantine before the lookout had time to cry a warning. The sailors aboard *The Divine Dolphin*, however, had no doubt about the identity of the attackers. The simultaneous shout, "The Karelians!" arose; then all was confusion.

One of the pirate vessels ran up alongside *The Divine Dolphin.* Grappling hooks from the Karelian ship secured the two ships tightly. In an incredibly swift time, the pirates were aboard.

They were tall men who wore nothing but brightly colored shorts and broad leather belts bristling with weapons. They were tattooed from head to foot, and they brandished cutlasses and big clubs with spiked knobs. They shouted ferociously in their native Finnish, and they swung cutlass and club as if berserk, sometimes felling their own men in their fury.

The Deecee were caught by surprise but they fought bravely. They did not think of surrender; that meant being sold into slavery and worked to death.

The crew of the *Terra* were among the defenders. Though they knew nothing of swordplay, they slashed away as best they could. Even Robin seized a sword and fought by Churchill's side.

The second schooner closed in on the other side. The Karelians from her swarmed aboard and attacked the Deecee before they could turn around to face them. Gbwe-hun, the Dahomeyan, was the first casualty among the starmen. He had killed a pirate with a lucky stroke and wounded another before a cutlass wielder from behind cut off the Dahomey's sword arm and then lopped off his head. Yastzhembski went down next, bleeding from a gash across his forehead.

Suddenly, Robin and Churchill were struggling in the folds of a net thrown over them from a yardarm. They were beaten unconscious with fists.

Churchill awoke to find his hands tied behind him. Robin was on the deck beside him, also tied. The clang of blade on blade had ceased, and even the shrieks of the wounded were still. The badly wounded Deecee had been thrown overboard, and the badly wounded Karelians refused to cry out.

The pirate captain, a Kirsti Ainundila, stood in front of the captives. He was a tall dark man with a patch over one eye and a scar running across his left cheek. He spoke in a heavily accented Deecee.

"I have been through the ship's log," he said, "and I know who you are. So there is no use lying to me. Now! You two"—he pointed to Churchill and Robin—"are worth a huge ransom. I think that this Whitrow will pay much to get his daughter and son-in-law back unharmed. As for the rest, they will fetch a fair price on the block when we get back to Aino."

Aino, Churchill knew, was a Karelian-held city on the coast of what had once been North Carolina.

Kirsti ordered all the prisoners taken below and chained to the bulkhead. Yastzhembski was among them, since he had been judged fit to recover from his wound.

After they had been chained and the pirates had left, Lin spoke up.

"I see now that it was foolish to think we could go back to our homelands. Not because we've been captured, but because we no longer have homelands. We'd be no better off there than here. We'd find our descendants as alien and hostile as Churchill has found his.

"Now, I've been thinking for some time of a thing that we forgot because of our desire to get back to Earth. That is, what happened to the Earthmen who colonized Mars?"

"I don't know," Churchill said, "but it does seem to me that if the Martians weren't wiped out for some reason or other, they would have sent spaceships to Earth long before this. After all, they were self-supporting. They had their own ships."

"Apparently something prevented them," Chandra said. "But I think I know what Lin is getting at. There are radioactive minerals on Mars. The means for making ore should still be there even if the people no longer are."

"Let me get this straight," Churchill said. "You are proposing that we take the *Terra* there? We *do* have enough fuel to get us to Mars, but there's not enough to get us back. Are you suggesting we use the equipment in the Martian domes to make more fuel? And then leave for the stars once more?"

"We found one planet where the aborigines are not advanced enough, technologically, to fight us," Lin said. "I mean the second planet of Vega. It had four large continents, each about the size of Australia, each separated by a large body of water. One of the land-masses is inhabited by humanoids who are, technologically speaking, at the level of the ancient Greeks. Two are inhabited by Neolithics. The fourth is uninhabited. If we can get to Vega, we can colonize the fourth continent."

They were all silent for a while.

Churchill could see that Lin's proposal had its points; the biggest objection was that they had no means of carrying it out. First, they must get free. Then they must seize the *Terra*—and it was so heavily guarded that the starmen, who had discussed it after being released from their Washington prison, had discarded the idea.

"Even if we can seize the ship," he said, "and that's a big *if*, we must get to Mars. That's the biggest gamble of all. What if conditions there are such that we can't get fuel?"

"Then we hole in and start making equipment," Al-Masyuni said.

"Yes, but assuming that Mars gives us what we want, and we do reach Vega, we have to have women. Otherwise the race dies out. That means I have to take Robin, willy-nilly. And it also means that we have to abduct Deecee women."

"Once they come out of deep-freeze on Vega, there's not much they can do about it," Steinborg said.

"Violence, abduction, rape," Churchill said. "What a way to start a brave new world!"

"Is there any other way?" Wang said.

"Don't forget the Sabine women," Steinborg said.

Churchill did not reply to that but brought up another objection. "We are so few that in a short time our descendants would be highly inbred. We don't want to found a race of idiots."

"We kidnap children as well as women and take them along in deep-freeze."

Churchill frowned. There seemed to be no way to get away from violence. But then it had always been so throughout man's history.

"Even if we take infants who are too small to talk and therefore will not remember Earth, we still have to take along enough women to raise them. And that brings up another problem. Polygamy. I don't know about the other women, but I do know that Robin will strongly object."

Yastzhembski said, "Explain to her it's only temporary. Anyway, you could be the exception, the monogamous one, if you wish. Let us have all the fun. I suggest we raid a Pants-Elf village. I've been told that the Pants-Elf women are accustomed to polygamy, and from what I heard, they'd welcome having husbands who'd pay attention to them. They sure as hell can't like the so-called men they got now."

"All right," Churchill said. "Agreed. But there's one thing that really bothers me."

"What's that?"

"How do we get out of this immediate mess?"

There was a gloomy silence.

Yastzhembski said, "Do you think Whitrow would put up the money to ransom all of us?"

"No. It's going to strain his purse to get Robin and me out of this tight-fisted pirate's hands."

"Well," Steinborg said, "at least you've a way out. What of us?"

Churchill stood up and began banging his manacles against each other and shouting loudly for the captain.

"Why are you doing that?" Robin said. She had not understood more than a few words of the conversation so far because it had been conducted in twenty-first-century American.

"I'm going to try to talk the captain into some sort of a deal," he replied in Deecee. "I think I've a way out. But it depends on how glibly I can talk and how receptive he is."

A sailor stuck his head through the hatch and asked what the hell was going on.

"Tell your captain I've a way for him to make a thousand times more money than he expects," Churchill said. "And enough glory to make him a hero."

The head disappeared. Within five minutes, two sailors came down into the hold and unlocked Churchill.

"See you," he said to the others as he left. "But don't wait up for me."

He did not know how true his joking words would be.

The day passed, and he did not return. Robin was close to hysteria. She speculated that the captain had gotten angry at her husband and had killed him. The others tried to calm her down with the reasonable argument that a good businessman like the Karelian would not destroy such a heavy investment. Nevertheless, despite their reassurances, they were worried. Churchill might have inadvertently insulted the captain and therefore forced him to murder Churchill to save his face. Or he might have been slain trying to escape.

Some of them dozed off. Robin stayed awake to murmur prayers to Columbia.

Finally, close to dawn, the hatch opened. Churchill came down the ladder, accompanied by two sailors. He staggered and almost fell down, and once he hiccupped loudly. After he had been chained, the others could understand his behavior. His breath stank of beer, and he slurred his words.

"Been drinking like a camel about to go on a caravan," he said. "All day, all night. I outtalked Kirsti, but I think he outdrank me. Found out a lot about these Finns. They were spared more than other people during the Desolation, and afterwards they exploded all over Europe, just like the ancient Vikings. They mingled with what was left of the Scandinavians, Germans, and the Baltic peoples. They now hold northwest Russia, the eastern part of England, most of northern France, the coastal regions of Spain and North Africa, Sicily, South Africa, Iceland, Greenland, Nova Scotia, Labrador, and North Carolina. God knows what else, because they have sent expeditions to India and China..."

"Very interesting, but some other time," Steinborg said. "How did you come out with the captain? Make a deal?"

"He's a pretty shrewd fellow and awfully suspicious. I had a hell of a time convincing him."

"What happened?" Robin said.

Churchill told her, in Deecee, not to worry, that they'd all be out soon. Then he switched back to the language of his birth.

"Have you ever tried to explain antigravity generators and antimatter propulsion to a man who doesn't even know there are such things as molecules or electrons? Among other things, many other things, I had to give a lecture in basic atomic theory, and..."

His voice trailed off, and his head dropped. He was asleep.

Exasperated, Robin shook him until he struggled up from his befuddlement.

"Oh, it's you, Robin," he mumbled. "Robin, you won't like this little scheme I've cooked up. You'll hate me..."

He went back to sleep. This time all her efforts to arouse him were in vain.

14

"I wish I *could* get the belt off," Mary Casey said. "It's very cumbersome and irritating. It chafes my skin so I can hardly walk. And it's not very sanitary, either. It has two small outlets, but I have to pour water down it to clean myself."

"I know that," Stagg said impatiently. "That's not what's bothering me."

Mary looked at him and said, "Oh, no!"

His antlers had lost their floppiness and were standing stiff and erect.

"Peter," she said, trying to keep her voice calm, "please don't. You mustn't. You'll kill me."

"No, I won't," he answered, almost sobbing—but whether from his desire or from agony at not being able to control himself, she could not tell.

"I'll be as gentle as possible. I promise it won't be too much for you."

"Once is too much!" she said. "We've not been married

by a priest. It would be a sin."

"No sin if you don't do it willingly," he said hoarsely. "And you've no choice. Believe me, you've no choice!"

"I won't do it," she said. "I won't! I won't!"

She continued protesting, but he paid no attention. He was too busy concentrating on getting the belt open. It presented a problem that only a key or a file could solve; since neither was available, it looked as if he would have to be frustrated.

But he was under the stress of a thing that did not acknowledge rationality.

The belt was composed of three parts. The two parts that went around the waist were made of steel. It was hinged at the back so it could be put on open and then snapped shut with a lock in front. The third part was made of many small links and was fastened to the belt by a second lock. Its chain mail effect allowed a certain amount of flexibility. Like the band around the waist, it was padded with thick cloth on the inside to prevent chafing and cutting. However, the whole contrivance was necessarily tight. Otherwise, the wearer could have slipped out of it or have been pulled out, with force and a little lost skin. This belt was a very snug fit, so tight that Mary complained about breathing.

Stagg managed to work his hands inside the front of the belt, though Mary protested that he was hurting her very much. He did not answer but began trying to work the two ends of the belt back and forth with the intention of twisting them loose from the lock.

"Oh, God!" Mary cried. "Don't, don't! You're crushing my insides! You'll kill me! Don't, don't!"

Suddenly, he released her. For a moment he seemed to have regained control. He was breathing hard.

"I'm sorry, Mary," he said. "I don't know what to do. Maybe I should run away as fast as I can until this thing in me turns me around and sets me to looking for you again."

"We might never find each other again," she said. She looked sad and then spoke softly. "I would miss you, Peter. I like you very much when you're not under the influence of the antlers. But there's no use pretending. Even if you got over this today, you might do the same tomorrow."

"I'd better go now while I still have a grip on myself. What a dilemma! Leaving you here to die because, if I stay, you might die!"

"You can't do anything else," she said.

"There's just one thing," he said slowly and hesitatingly. "That belt doesn't absolutely mean that I can't get what I want. There's more than one way..."

She turned white and screamed, "No, no!"

He turned away and ran as fast as he could down the path.

Then it occurred to him that she would be coming along the same trail. He left the path and went into the forest. It was not much of a forest, since this country was still a wasteland in the slow process of recovering from the Desolation. Its earth had not been seeded and water diverted through it, as much as the Deecee land had been. The trees were relatively scarce; most of the growth was weeds and underbrush and not too much of those. Nevertheless, where there was water at any time of the year, the forest was thicker. He had not run far before he came across a small creek. He lay down in it, hoping that the shock of the water would cool off the fire in his loins, but the water was warm.

He rose and crossed the creek and began running again. He rounded a tree and ran headlong into a bear.

Since he and Mary had left High Queen he had been watching for just such an animal.

He knew they were comparatively numerous in this area, because of the Pants-Elf custom of tying up their prisoners and rebellious women and leaving them for the sacred bears to eat.

The bear was a huge black male. He may or may not have been hungry. Perhaps he might have been as frightened by Stagg's sudden appearance as Stagg was by his. If he'd had a chance, he might have retreated. Stagg was on him so swiftly he must have thought he was being attacked—and being attacked meant attacking back.

He reared back on his hind legs, as was his habit in seizing his helpless human prey. He swung his immense right paw at Stagg's head. If it had connected it would have scattered the man's skull like a jigsaw puzzle dumped on a floor.

It did not land, though it came close enough for the claws to tear across Stagg's scalp. He was knocked to the ground, partly by the force of the blow and partly because his own forward impetus unbalanced him.

The bear dropped to all fours and went after Stagg. Stagg rolled to his feet. He drew his sword and screamed at the bear. The beast, unshaken by the noise, reared up again. Stagg swung his sword, and its edge sliced into the outstretched paw.

Though the bear roared with pain, it advanced. Stagg

swung again. This time the paw flicked out with such stunning force against the blade that it knocked it from Stagg's grip and sent it flying into the weeds.

Stagg leaped after it, bent down to pick it up—and was buried under the enormous weight of the bear. His head was shoved flat into the earth, and his body felt as if it were being pressed flat by a giant iron.

There was a moment when even the bear was confused, for it had overextended its lunge and the man was covered only by its hindquarters. It quickly rolled over and away and then reversed itself. Stagg jumped up and tried to run away. Before he could take two steps, the bear had reared up and folded its front legs around him.

Stagg knew that it was not true that the bear hugs its victim to death, but in that moment he thought that he had met a bear who did not know his natural history. However, the bear was trying to hold Stagg while it raked Stagg's chest open.

He did not succeed because Stagg broke loose from the embrace. He did not have time to be amazed at his Herculean feat of pushing the extremely powerful legs of the bear apart. If he had, he would have known that the superhuman strength given him by the antlers was responsible.

He jumped away and whirled around to face the animal. Fast as he was, he was too close for flight. Inside fifty meters, a bear could outrun even an Olympic champion.

The bear was on him. Stagg did the only thing he could think of. He hit the animal as hard as he could with his fist on its black snout.

The impact would have broken a man's jaw. The bear said, "Oof!" and stopped in its tracks. Blood ran from its nostrils, and its eyes crossed.

Stagg did not stay to admire his fistwork. He ran past the stunned beast and tried to pick up his sword. His right hand would not close round the hilt. It hung numbly, paralyzed by the blow he had given the bear.

He reached down with his left hand, picked up the sword, and turned. He was just in time. The bear had recovered enough to make another lunge, though this time it had lost some of its original speed.

Carefully, Stagg raised the sword and then, just as the bear closed in, he swung the edge downward across the thick short neck.

The last thing he saw was the blade sinking deep into the black fur and the spray of crimson that followed.

He woke some time later to find himself in deep pain, the bear lying dead by his side and Mary weeping over him.

Then the pain became overbearing, and he fainted.

When he regained consciousness, his head was on Mary's lap and water from a canteen was running into his open mouth. His head still hurt abominably. Reaching upward to find out why, he discovered bandages around his head.

The right-hand branch of his antlers was missing.

Mary said, "The bear must have torn it off. I heard the fight from a distance. I could hear the bear roaring and you screaming. I came as fast as I could, though I was scared."

"If you hadn't," he said, "I'd have died."

"I think so," she said matter-of-factly. "You were bleeding terribly from the hole left in the bony base of the torn-off antler. I ripped up part of my kilt and managed to stop the flow with it."

Suddenly, great hot tears fell on his face.

"Now it's over," he said, "you can cry all you want. But I'm glad you're so brave. I couldn't have blamed you if you'd run away from here."

"I couldn't have done that," she sobbed. "I—I think I love you. Of course, I wouldn't have left anyone to die like this. Besides I was scared to be alone."

"I heard what you said the first time," he replied. "I can't see how you could love a monster like me. But if it'll make you feel better, and not worse, I love you, too—even if it didn't look like it a while ago."

He touched the broken-off part of the base of the antlers and winced. "Do you think this will cut my… my compulsion in half?"

"I don't know. I wish it would. Only… I thought that if the antlers were removed, you'd die from the shock."

"I did too. Maybe the priestesses lied. Or maybe the whole set has to be removed before a fatal shock occurs. After all, the bony base is still intact, and one of the antlers is still operating. I don't know."

"You quit thinking about it," she said. "Do you think you could eat? I've cooked some bear steak."

"Is that what I smell?" he said, sniffing. He looked at the carcass. "How long was I out?"

"You were unconscious all day and night and part of the

morning," she said. "And don't worry about the smoke from the fire. I know how to make a small smokeless fire."

"I think I'll be all right then," he said. "The horns have great regenerative powers. I wouldn't be surprised if it grew back."

"I will pray that it won't," she said. She went to the fire and removed two slices of bear steak from a wooden spit. In a moment, he was eating a loaf of bread and the steaks.

"I must be getting better," he said. "All of a sudden I'm hungry enough to eat a bear."

Two days later he could look back on what he had said and laugh, because he *had* eaten the bear. There was nothing left except skin, bones, and entrails; even the brains had been cooked and devoured.

By then he felt ready to move again. The bandage had been removed from the wound just above the bony base of the antlers, and a cleanly healing scar was disclosed.

"At least, it's not going to grow out again," he said. He looked at Mary. "Well, here we are again. Just where we started when I ran away from you. I'm beginning to feel the urge again."

"Does that mean we have to separate again?" From her tone, it was impossible to tell if she wanted him to leave or not.

"I've been doing a lot of thinking while I was convalescing," he said. "One thing that I thought of was that when the Pants-Elf were taking us to High Queen, I felt a definite diminution of the drive. I think it happened because I was underfed. I'm going to propose that we stay together, but I go on a starvation diet. I'll eat just enough to keep me going, but not enough to stimulate this… this desire. It'll be hard, but I can do it."

"That's wonderful," she said. She hesitated, then blushed and said, "We're going to have to do one thing, though. I must get rid of this belt. No, not for the reason you might be thinking. It's driving me out of my mind. It cuts and chafes, and it presses me so tightly around the middle I can scarcely breathe."

"As soon as we get into Deecee territory and find a farmhouse," he said, "I'll steal a file. We'll get rid of that devil's device."

"All right. Just so you don't misunderstand my motives," she said. He picked up the sack, and they started off.

They proceeded as swiftly as they could, considering the handicap the belt gave Mary. They were very cautious, sensitive to any strange noise. There was not only a chance of running into the inevitable party from High Queen searching for them but a chance of encountering hostile Deecee.

They crossed the Shawangunk Mountains. Then, as they came into a glade through which the path ran, they saw the men who had come out of High Queen to avenge the deaths of their friends.

They must have been so intent on running down the two escapees that they had been utterly surprised by the ambushing Deecee. Now they hung from the trunks of trees where they had been tied before their throats were cut, or their bones lay at the foot of the trees. What the bears had not eaten, the foxes had; and what the foxes had overlooked, the crows were now picking.

"We'll have to be more cautious than ever," Stagg said. "I doubt if the Deecee have given up looking for us yet."

He did not speak with his accustomed vigor. He was

pounds lighter, and his eyes were ringed with black. His horn flopped with every motion of his head. When he sat down to eat, he finished his short rations and then looked longingly at Mary's portion. Sometimes, he left the campsite and lay down where he could not see her until she was through eating.

The worst of it was, he could not forget food even when he slept. He dreamed of tables bending beneath the weight of a hundred savory dishes and huge stone mugs filled with cold dark beer. And when he was not distressed by these visions, he dreamed again of the maidens he had met during the Great Route. Though his drive was considerably lessened by lack of food, it was still stronger than most men's. There were times when, after Mary had fallen asleep, he had to go into the woods to relieve the terrible tension. He felt deeply ashamed afterwards, but it was preferable to taking Mary by force.

He did not dare kiss Mary. She seemed to understand this, since she made no attempt to kiss him. Nor did she again refer to having told him she loved him. Perhaps, he thought, she did not love him. She had been overcome with emotion because he had not been killed; the words might just have been an expression of relief.

After coming across the bones of the Pants-Elf, they left the trail and cut straight across the woodlands. Their speed was reduced, but they felt safer.

They reached the banks of the Hudson. That night, Stagg broke into a barn and found a file. He had to kill the watchdog, which he did by strangling it before it managed to bark more than twice. They returned to the woods where Stagg took four hours to cut through the belt with the file. The steel was hard, and he had to be careful not to hurt Mary. Then he gave her some ointment he had found in the barn, and she went into the brush to rub it on the chafed and infected places. Stagg shrugged his shoulders at this incongruous modesty. They had seen each other unclothed many times. But, of course, she had not been able to control the situation then.

When she came back, they walked along the bank until they found a boat tied to a wooden dock. They untied it and rowed across. Stagg shoved the boat out into the current, and they began walking eastward. For two nights they walked, hiding and sleeping during the days. Stagg stole some more food from a farmhouse just outside the town of Poughkeepsie. When he returned to Mary in the woods, he sat down and devoured three times what he was supposed to eat. Mary was alarmed, but he told her that he had to because he could feel his cells turning cannibal.

After he had eaten half of the food and also drank a whole bottle of wine, he sat quietly for a while. Then he said to Mary, "I'm sorry, but I just can't stand it any more. I have to go back to the farmhouse."

"Why?" she said alarmedly.

"Because the men there are gone, probably into town. And there are three women there, two of them good-looking girls. Mary, can you understand?"

15

“No!” she said, “I can’t. Even if I could, do you think you should endanger us by returning there? Those women will tell their men when they return, and the priestesses at Vassar will be notified. And we’ll have them on our track. We’d be sure to get caught if they knew we were in this neighborhood.”

“I know you’re right,” he said. “But I can’t stand it. I ate too much. It’s either those two women or you.”

Mary rose to her feet. She looked as if she were going to attempt something she disliked but must do.

“If you’ll turn around a moment,” she said, her voice quivering, “I think I can solve your problem.”

Ecstatically, he said, “Mary, would you really? You don’t know what this means to me!”

He turned away, and, despite his almost unbearably keen anticipation, he had to smile. How like her to be so modest about unclothing just before she bedded with him.

He heard her stir behind him. “Can I turn around now?”

"Not yet," she said. "I'm not ready."

He heard her approach him and he said, impatiently, "Is it all right to turn around now?"

"Not yet," she said, standing behind him.

"I can't stand waiting much longer…"

Something hit him hard on the back of the head. He blacked out.

When he awoke, he was on his side, his arms bound behind him and his legs tied together at the ankles. She had cut into two the thin rope he had put into the bag before escaping from the Pants-Elf. Near him was a large rock which he supposed she had used to knock him out.

Seeing his eyes open, she said, "I'm terribly sorry, Peter. I had to do that. If you'd put the Deecee on our trail, we might not have escaped."

"There are two bottles of whiskey in the sack," he said. "Prop me up against a tree trunk and put a bottle to my lips. I want to drink the whole quart. One, because I need something to kill this pain in my head. Two, because unless I drink myself unconscious, I'll go crazy from frustration. Three, I want to forget what a black-hearted bitch you are!"

She did not reply but did obey him, holding the bottle to his mouth and withdrawing it from time to time when he quit gulping.

"I'm sorry, Peter."

"To hell with you! Why did I have to get stuck with somebody like you? Why couldn't I have run off with a real woman? Keep feeding me the whiskey."

In two hours, he had drunk two-thirds of the fifth. He sat quietly for a few seconds, his eyes staring straight ahead. Then he groaned and fell asleep.

The next morning, he woke to find himself untied. He did not complain of his hangover or say anything to her. He merely watched her while she placed his rations before him. After breakfast, during which he drank much water, they began walking east in silence.

Toward midmorning, Mary spoke. "No farms in the last two hours. And the forest is thinning out and the land getting rockier. We're in the wastelands between Deecee and Caseyland. We must be more careful than ever, because we're likely to run into war parties of either nation."

"What's wrong with meeting your people?" Stagg said. "They're the boys we want, aren't they?"

"They might shoot first and identify us later," Mary said, nervously.

"Okay," he answered harshly. "So we'll holler out at them from a distance. Tell me, Mary, are you certain I'll not be treated as a Deecee captive? After all, this horn might prejudice them."

"Not after I tell them how you saved my life. And that you can't help being a Sunhero. Of course..."

"Of course what?"

"You'll have to submit to an operation. I don't know if my people have medical skill enough to remove your horn without killing you, but you'll have to take that chance. Otherwise, you'll be locked up. And you know that would drive you crazy. You can't be allowed to run loose in this condition. And, naturally,

I wouldn't think of marrying you while you still have that horn. Oh yes, you must first be baptized in our belief. I wouldn't marry a heathen. I couldn't if I wanted to; we kill heathens."

Stagg didn't know whether to roar with anger, bellow with laughter, or weep with sadness. As a result, he expressed no emotion. Instead, he spoke levelly, "I don't remember asking you to marry me."

"Oh, but you don't have to," she replied. "It is enough that we spent one night together without chaperones. In my country, that means that a man and a woman must get married. In fact, that is often one way to announce your engagement."

"But you've done nothing to justify a forced marriage," he said. "You're still a virgin. At least, as far as I know."

"I most certainly am! But it makes no difference. It is taken for granted that a man and a woman who spend the night together must succumb to the flesh, however strong the will. That is, unless they are saints. And if they're saints, they don't allow such situations to happen."

"Then why in blue skies and rocketing nonsense have you been so determined to be a good girl?" he said loudly. "If you're going to have the name, you might as well have the game."

"Because I wasn't brought up that way. Because," she added somewhat smugly, "it doesn't matter what people think. It is what the Mother sees that counts."

"Sometimes you're so sanctimonious I could wring your pretty little neck! Here I've been suffering agonies of frustration such as you'll never know, and all the time you could have eased my pain without any moral blemish on your part—and had a time such as few women ever get!"

"There's no need to get angry," she said. "After all, it wasn't as if it had occurred at home, where we could be killed before we could be married. And then I would have sinned. Besides, you're not in the normal category. You have that horn. That puts you in a special case. I'm sure it'll take a learned priest to straighten out all the complexities."

Stagg shook with rage. He said, "We haven't reached Caseyland yet!"

Noon came. Stagg ate much more than his normal allowance. Mary said nothing about it, but she kept eyeing him. Every time he came near, she flinched. They repacked the bag and resumed walking. Stagg obviously was beginning to feel the benefit of food. The fleshy upper part of the antler began to swell and to stand stiff. His eyes sparkled, and he gave little leaps into the air, grunting with suppressed joy.

Mary began to lag behind. He was so affected by the approaching rush of desire that he did not notice. When she was about twenty yards behind him, she ran off into the bushes. He walked another twenty yards before he turned around and saw that she was gone. Then he roared and darted after her into the woods, losing all sense of caution and shouting her name.

He found her trail in a bed of crushed weeds, followed it to a small, almost dry creek bed, crossed the creek, and entered a grove of oaks. There he lost the trail. Emerging on the other side, he faced a broad meadow.

He also faced a dozen or more swords, behind every uplifted point of which was the grim face of a Caseylander.

Beyond them he saw a girl of about twenty.

This girl wore a costume such as Mary had worn when he first saw her in the cage. She was a mascot. The men were dressed in the red-soxed uniform of a Caseylander champion baseball team. There was one incongruous item among their clothes. Instead of long-billed caps, they wore feather-plumed hats, like an admiral's headgear.

Beyond them stood deer, nineteen for the first team and substitutes, one for the mascot, four to carry food and equipment.

The leader of the Caseys, titled "Mighty" as all the Casey captains were, was a tall rangy man with a long lean face, one cheek of which was swelled with a quid of tobacco. He grinned savagely at Stagg. "So, Old Horney! You expected to find soft curved young flesh? And instead you find the hard biting edge of a sword. Disappointed, monster? Don't be. We'll give you the embrace of a woman—only her arms are thin and bony and her breasts are flabby and wrinkled, and her breath stinks of the open grave."

"Don't be so damned melodramatic, Mighty," growled one of the men. "Let's hang him and get it over with. We've a game to play in Poughkeepsie."

Stagg understood then what they were doing there. It was no war party but a ball club that had been invited to compete in Deecee. As such, they would have a safe-conduct pass guaranteeing them against being ambushed.

Furthermore, the guarantee involved the promise not to hurt any Deecee they might encounter in the wasteland.

"Let's not talk of hanging," he said to Mighty. "According to the rules, you're not to harm a Deecee unless he attacks you."

"That's true," Mighty said. "But it just so happens that we've heard of you through our spies. You're not a native of Deecee; therefore our promise doesn't hold for you."

"Then why hang me?" Stagg said. "If I'm not a Deecee, I'm also not your enemy. Tell me, didn't you see a woman running ahead of me? Her name's Mary Casey. She'll tell you I should be treated as a friend!"

"A likely story," said the man who had urged hanging Stagg. "You're one of those devil-possessed horned men! That's enough for us."

"Shut up, Lonzo!" Mighty said. "I'm captain here."

He spoke to Stagg. "I wish now I'd had you cut down before you could open your mouth. Then you'd be no problem. But I would like to hear about this Mary Casey." Suddenly he said, "What's her middle name?"

"I-Am-Bound-For-Paradise."

"Yes, that's my cousin's name. But I guess your knowing it doesn't prove anything. She was hauled along with you on the Great Route. We have a good spy system, and we know you and she disappeared after the fairy-boys made a raid on Vassar. But the witches substituted another Horned King and then sent secret war parties out looking for you."

"Mary is somewhere nearby in these woods," Stagg said. "Find her, and she'll verify that I was helping her escape to your country."

"And what were you doing separated?" Mighty said, suspiciously. "Why were you running?"

Stagg was silent. Mighty said, "I thought so. One look at

you would tell anybody why you were chasing her. I'll tell you what, Horned King. I'm going to give you a break. Ordinarily, I'd roast you over a low fire first, then rip out your eyes and stuff them down your throat. But we've the game to make and no time to waste, so I'm going to give you a quick death. Tie his hands, boys, and string him up!"

A rope was thrown over the branch of an oak and a noose put around his neck. Two men seized his arms, while a third prepared to tie them. He did not resist, though he could easily have tossed the two aside.

He said, "Wait! I challenge you to a game according to the rules of One against Five, and I call God to witness that I have challenged you!"

"What?" Mighty said, incredulously. "Columbus' sake, man, we're late now! Besides, why should we accept the challenge? We don't know if you're our equal. We're all *diradah*, you know, and a challenge from a *shet hed* is not acceptable. In fact, come to think of it, it's unthinkable."

"I am not a *shet hed*," Stagg said, also using the term for a peasant. "Have you ever heard of a Sunhero being chosen from any but the ranks of the aristocrats?"

"That's right," Mighty said. He scratched his head. "Well, it can't be helped. Let him loose, boys. Maybe the game won't take long."

There was not even a flicker of thought in his mind to ignore Stagg's challenge and hang him. He had a code of honor, and he would not think of breaking it. Especially since Stagg had called on the name of his deity.

The Caseys who were to play on the first five removed their plumed admiral's hats and put on long-billed caps. They took their equipment from the bags on the sides of their deer and began laying out a diamond on the nearby meadow. From a leather bag they poured out a heavy white powder to mark the lanes from plate to plate and from each plate to the pitcher's box. They drew a narrow square around each plate, since in the rules of One against Five, Stagg might have to bat from any one of the bases during the course of the game. They drew a somewhat larger box for the pitcher.

"Is it okay if our mascot is the ump?" Mighty asked. "She will swear before the Father, Mother, and the Son that she will not favor us over you. If she isn't fair, lightning will strike her down. Worse, she'll become sterile."

"There's not much choice," Stagg said, hefting the brass-bound bat they'd given him. "I'm ready when you are."

His desire for women was gone now, sublimated in an eagerness to spill the blood of these men.

The mascot, wearing a barred iron mask and a heavily padded uniform, waddled up to her place behind the catcher.

"Batter up!"

Stagg waited for the Mighty's pitch. The Mighty stood only thirty-nine meters away from him, holding the hard leather ball with the four sharp steel spikes. He eyed Stagg, then wound up and let fly.

The ball sped like a cannon shot straight toward Stagg's head. It came so fast and so true that it was doubtful if a man of normal reflexes could have avoided it. Stagg, however, bent his knees. The ball skimmed an inch over his head.

"Ball one!" the mascot cried in a high, clear voice.

The catcher made no effort to catch the ball. In this game his duty was to chase after the ball and return it to the pitcher. Of course, he also guarded home plate and would try to catch the ball in his immense padded glove if Stagg ever tried to slide into home.

Mighty Casey wound up again and aimed this time for Stagg's midriff.

Stagg swung. The bat connected with a dull sound that contrasted strangely with the sharp crack he had automatically expected.

The ball bounced off to Stagg's left and rolled out of the diamond, crossing the foul line.

"Strike one!"

The catcher returned the ball. Mighty Casey feinted winding up, then threw it suddenly in one smooth motion.

Stagg was almost caught. He had no time to swing, just barely enough time to stick the bat out. The ball struck the side and clung for a second, one of its spikes embedded in the brass.

Stagg ran for first, clinging to his bat as the rules said he could do if the ball stuck to it. Mighty Casey ran after him, hoping the ball would fall off on the way. Otherwise, if Stagg reached first and had possession of the ball, he became the pitcher and Mighty Casey became the batter.

Halfway toward first, the ball fell off.

Stagg ran like the deer he resembled, launched himself head foremost and slid on the grass into the plate. The bat, which he held out before him in his extended arm, hit the first baseman in the shinbone, knocking him off his feet.

Something struck Stagg in the shoulder. He groaned with pain as he felt the spike sticking in the flesh. But he leaped up, reached behind him, and pulled the spike out, heedless of the warm gush down his shoulder.

Now, according to the rules, if he survived the impact of the ball and had strength enough, he could throw it at either the pitcher or the first baseman.

The first baseman had tried to run away, but he had been so badly hurt by Stagg's bat that he could not even walk. He had removed his own bat from the sheath hanging over his back and stood ready to knock down the ball if Stagg would throw it at him.

Stagg threw, and the first, his face contorted with the pain of his leg, swatted at the ball.

There was a thump. The first swayed back and forth, then slumped, the spike buried in his throat.

Stagg had the choice of staying safe on first or trying to steal second. He chose to run, and again had to slide in face first. The second baseman, unlike the first, stood to one side. So great was Stagg's momentum that he slid past the plate. At once he twisted around and rolled back to touch second base.

There was a smack as the ball caught in the second's enormous thickly padded glove.

Stagg was—theoretically—safe on second. But he did not relax because of the look of fury on the second's face. He jumped up, his bat ready to hit the fellow over the head if he forgot the rules long enough to try to hit Stagg with the ball.

The second, seeing the bat poised, let the ball drop to the ground. Blood dripped from his fingers where he had cut himself on the spikes in his eagerness to get the ball loose from the glove.

Time out was called, while the first baseman had some brief rites said over him as he was being covered with a blanket.

Stagg asked for more food and water because he was beginning to feel faint from hunger. He had a right to demand such if the other side called time out.

He ate. Just as he finished, the mascot called, "Play ball!"

Now Stagg, standing within the narrow box marked around second base, was at bat again. Mighty wound up and let loose. Stagg knocked the ball to his left just inside the foul line. He began running, but this time the fellow who had replaced the dead first baseman was on the ball as soon as it landed and stuck in the ground. Stagg broke his run for a split second, not knowing whether to run on for third or return to second.

The first tossed the ball in an underhand motion to Mighty, who, by now, was crouched close to the lane between second and third, almost in Stagg's path. Stagg's back would be unprotected if he continued. He spun around; his bare feet slipped on the grass, and he fell on his back.

For one terrible second, he thought he was done for. Mighty was very close and had drawn back to throw at his prostrate target.

But Stagg had clung to his bat. Desperately, he raised it before him. The ball hit it glancingly, knocking the bat out of his hand and itself rebounding to a spot a few feet away.

Stagg roared with triumph, leaped to his feet, picked up

the bat, and stood there, swinging the bat warningly. Unless he was actually hit by the ball while between bases, he could not pick it up and hurl it back at his opponents. Nor could he leave the white-marked lane to threaten anyone who tried to pick it up. However, if the ball was lying on the ground close enough for him to bat anybody who tried to pick it up, he could do so.

The ump's feminine voice shrilled over the field as she began counting to ten. Stagg's opposition had ten seconds in which to decide whether to try for the ball or allow him to stroll safe to third.

"Ten!" called the mascot, and Mighty turned away from the swinging bat.

Mighty threw again. Stagg swung and missed. Mighty smiled and threw at Stagg's head. Stagg swung and missed the ball, but the ball also missed him.

Mighty grinned wolfishly because, if Stagg struck out, Stagg would have to throw aside his bat and stand unmoving while Mighty tried to hit him between the eyes with the ball.

However, if Stagg managed to get to home plate, then he became the pitcher. He would still be at a disadvantage because he had no teammates to help; on the other hand, his greater speed and strength made him a one-man team.

There was a hush with only the murmurs of the prayers from the Caseys to be heard. Then Mighty hurled.

Straight for Stagg's belly the ball flew, giving him the choice of trying to bunt it down or else lean to one side and still keep his feet in the narrow box. If he stepped or fell outside, he had a strike against him.

Stagg chose to lean.

The ball shot by his shrinking flesh. So close was it that a whirling spike point ripped out a tiny gobbet. Blood trickled down his stomach.

"Ball one!"

Mighty hurled for the belly again. To Stagg the ball seemed to swell enormously, pregnant with doom, a planet toward which he was falling.

He swung hard, the bat coming around in a swift arc, parallel to the ground. Its tip connected with the ball, and a shock ran down the bat. It broke in two, and the ball soared back to Mighty.

The pitcher was caught off guard. He could not believe that the heavy ball could fly so far. Then, as Stagg raced for home, Mighty ran forward and caught the ball in his glove. At the same time, the other players, breaking out of their paralytic astonishment, closed in for the kill.

Two men stood between Stagg and home, one on each side of the white lines of the path. Both begged for Mighty to throw them the ball. But he chose the honor of tackling Stagg himself.

Desperately, Stagg struck the ball down with the stub end of his bat, the wooden part which had separated from the brassbound half. The ball did not rebound but stuck in the ground at his feet.

A Casey dived for it.

Stagg caved in the hat and the skull beneath it.

The others stopped running.

The mascot had thrown her hands over her mask, shielding

the sight of the dead man from her eyes. But in a moment she put her hands down and looked beseechingly at Mighty. Mighty hesitated for a moment, as if he were going to give the signal to rush at Stagg and dispose of him, to hell with the rules.

Then he took a deep breath and called out, "Okay, Katie, start the count. We are *diradah*. We do not cheat."

"One!" quavered the mascot.

The other players looked at Mighty. He grinned and said, "Okay. Everybody line up behind me. I'll try first. I wouldn't ask you boys to do anything that's my duty."

One of the men said, "We could let him walk home."

"What?" cried Mighty. "And have every henpecked, skirt-wearing, idol-worshiping man in Deecee laughing at us? No! If we must die—and we have to die some time—we'll die like men!"

"Five!" the mascot called, sounding as if her heart were breaking.

"We haven't a chance!" a Casey groaned. "He's twice as fast as any of us. It'll be a lamb to the slaughter."

"I'm no lamb!" Mighty roared. "I'm a Casey! I'm not afraid to die! I'll go to heaven, while this fellow'll roast in hell!"

"Seven!"

"Come on!" Stagg bellowed, swinging the broken half of the bat. "Step up, gentlemen, and try your luck!"

"Eight!"

Mighty crouched for the leap, his lips working in a silent prayer.

"Nine!"

"STOP IT!"

16

Mary Casey ran from the woods, her hands held out in protest. She threw her arms around Mighty and began kissing him, weeping all the while.

"Oh, cousin, cousin, I thought I'd never see you again!"

"Thank the Mother you're safe," he said. "So what this horned man said was true, heh?" He held her away from him and looked carefully at her. "Or did he harm you?"

"No, no! He didn't touch me. He was a true *diradah* all the time," she said. "And he's not a worshiper of Columbia. He swears by God and the Son. I've heard him many times! And you know no Deecee would do that."

"I wish I'd known that," Mighty said. "We'd not have two good men dead for nothing."

He turned to Stagg. "If what she says is true, friend, there's no reason to continue the game. Of course, if you insist, we will."

Stagg threw the stump of the bat to the ground and said, "My original purpose was to go to Caseyland and live there the rest of my life."

"We've no time to talk!" Mary said. "We have to get out of here! Fast! I climbed a tree to get a better look around, and I saw a pack of hellhounds and a group of men and women on deer following them. And the death-hogs!"

The Caseys turned pale.

"Death-hogs!" Mighty said. "Alba is riding! But what's she doing here?"

Mary pointed at Stagg. "They must know he's in this area, and they must have picked up his scent. They were coming too fast just to be casting around."

"We're in a hell of a dilemma," Mighty said. "She won't bother us, I think, because we've a safe-conduct pass. But you never know about Alba. She's above such things as treaties."

"Yes," Mary said, "but even if they don't harm you, what about Peter—and me? I'm not included in the safe-conduct."

"I could give you two a couple of extra deer. You could run for the Housatonic River; once across it, you'd be safe. There's a fort there. But Alba still might catch you."

He twisted his face into a mask of intense concentration. Then he said, "Only one honorable thing to do. We can't allow two God-believers to fall into the foul hands of Alba. Especially when one of them is my cousin!

"All right, men!" he shouted. "What do you say? Shall we give up the safe-conduct and fight for these two? Or be chickens before the hawk and hide in the forest?"

"We live like Caseys and we die like Caseys!" the team roared.

"Okay, we fight," Mighty said. "But first we make a run for it. We'll make them work for their blood."

At that moment, they heard the baying of the hounds.

"On your mounts! Let's go!"

Mary and Stagg untied the packs from the deer given them, climbed on the bare backs of the beasts, and gripped the reins.

"You women ride first," Stagg said. "We'll drop behind a little."

Mary looked despairingly at Stagg. "If he stays behind, I stay behind with him."

"No time to argue," Mighty said. "We'll ride together."

They began galloping down the rough and winding trail. Behind them, the baying increased as the hounds caught the scent of many men and deer. The fugitives had scarcely left the meadow before the first of the hounds burst out of the woods. Stagg, looking back, saw a large dog built like a cross between a greyhound and a wolf. Its body was snow-white, and its wolflike ears were auburn. Behind it came a pack of twenty more like it.

Then he was too busy guiding his deer over the rough trail to risk many more backward glances. He did not have to urge the frightened beast to run at top speed.

Half a kilometer sped beneath the flying hoofs, and then Stagg took another quick look behind him. Now he saw about twenty deer and riders. At their head, riding a white stag with scarlet-painted antlers, was an old woman who wore only a tall black conical hat and a live snake around her neck. Her long white hair trailed out behind her, and her flat hanging breasts bounced with every motion of the beast under her.

She was enough to frighten any man. Alongside of the riders, running swiftly as the deer, was a herd of pigs. These were tall, long-legged, rangy swine, built for speed. They were black, their tusks long and painted with scarlet, and they squealed hideously as they ran.

Stagg had just turned his head when he heard a crash and then a deer screaming with pain in front of him.

He looked ahead. There were two deer on the ground, and beside them their riders. The worst had happened. The deer of the mascot had stepped into a hole and gone down.

Mary, just behind her, had not been able to pull to one side quickly enough.

Stagg reined in his deer and leaped down.

"Are you all right?" he cried.

"A little shaken up," Mary said. "But I think Katie's deer has broken its leg. And mine has bolted into the woods."

"Get on the back of my deer," he said. "One of the others can carry Katie."

Mighty rose from Katie's side and came to Stagg. He said, "She can't move her legs. I think her back is broken."

Katie must have known what he was saying. She called, "Somebody kill me! I won't commit the sin of doing it myself! But if you kill me, I'm sure it would be forgiven. Even the Mother wouldn't want me to fall into Alba's hands!"

"Nobody's going to kill you, Katie," Mighty said. "Not while one of us is alive to defend you."

He barked orders, and the rest of the Caseys dismounted.

"Form into two lines. The dogs will hit us first; use your

swords on them. Then grab your spears because either the hogs or the cavalry will charge next."

His men had just enough time to form in front of the two women when the hellhounds reached them. These dogs were no hangers-back but vicious beasts trained to kill. Snarling, they leaped into the air at the throats of the defenders.

There was confusion for a moment as the dogs bowled over many of the men. But in two minutes, despite all the snarling, shouting, yelping, screaming, it was over. Four dogs, badly wounded, limped to the woods to die. The rest were dead, their heads half severed or their legs cut off.

One Casey was on his back, eyes staring, throat ripped out. Five had been bitten deeply in several places but could still wield their swords.

"Here come the others!" Mighty shouted. "Reform ranks and stand ready to cast spears!"

The Deecee had reined in. The white-haired hag rode out a little in front of them, shouting in a high thin voice.

"Men of Caseyland! We do not want *you*! Give us our Horned King, and all of you, even that girl who was our prisoner, may go back to your country in safety. If you don't, I will release my death-hogs on you—and all will die!"

"Go screw yourself!" Mighty roared. "I'm sure you're the only one you could find to do it, you withered stinking old she-goat!"

Alba shrieked with rage. She turned to her priests and priestesses and signaled with her hand.

They unsnapped the leashes on the big tuskers.

"Use your spears as if you were on a pig-sticking!" Mighty

shouted. "You've hunted wild hogs since you were old enough to hold a spear! Don't let them panic you!"

To Stagg he said, "Use your sword. I saw you fight the dogs. You're quicker and stronger than we—quick enough to wield a sword even on a tusker… okay, men, steady! Here they come!"

Mighty rammed his spear into the neck of a huge boar. The boar slumped to the ground; an enormous sow just behind it charged for Mighty. Stagg leaped over the carcass of the dead boar and brought his broadsword down with such force it cut through the sow's spinal cord just back of the neck.

Then he repeated the feat on another sow that had knocked a man down and was ripping his legs open with her teeth.

He heard a scream from Mary and saw that she was holding onto the end of her spear, the head of which was stuck in the side of a boar. The boar was not hurt badly, he was just angry and was trying to get at Mary. She clung to the end of the spear while she went around and around in a circle with the wheeling boar in its center.

Stagg shouted and leaped through the air. He landed with his feet on the back of the hog, and its legs crumpled under the impact. Stagg rolled off onto the ground. The boar regained its hoofs with lightning speed and swiveled toward Stagg. He thrust the point of his sword out; it drove into the open mouth of the tusker and down its throat.

He rose to his feet, assuring himself with a glance that Mary, though frightened, was not hurt. Then he saw that a hog had reached Katie. The Casey who had been protecting her was also on the ground, screaming because his legs had been ripped open and his ribs were sticking out of his flesh.

Stagg was too late to help Katie. By the time he had chopped off one of the hog's hind legs and slashed its jugular vein, Katie was dead.

He took a quick survey of the situation.

It was bad. The sixteen Caseys left alive after the onslaught of the dogs had been reduced to ten by the swine. Of the ten, only five were still on their feet.

Stagg helped the Caseys dispatch three more hogs. The remainder of the original twenty beasts, four wounded ones, ran squealing for the woods.

Mighty panted, "Alba will charge now, and we'll be done for. But I want to say, Stagg, that this is a fight they'll sing of for a long time to come in the halls of Caseyland!"

"They're not going to get Mary!" Stagg screamed. His eyes were wild, his face emptied of human expression. He was possessed—but it was blood he wanted, not women.

He turned toward Alba's group. They were being marshaled into files of five, their long spears glittering in the sunlight.

"Alba!" he roared, and he ran toward her.

She did not see him at first, but when her retainers warned her, she wheeled the white stag to face him.

"I'll kill you, you bloody old bitch!" he shouted. He swung his sword in great circles above his head. "I'll kill you all!"

And then a strange thing happened.

The priests and priestesses had been conditioned from childhood to regard the Sunhero as a demigod. Now they were in an abnormal and upsetting situation. They were being led by the Death-Goddess, who was invincible. But they were also being asked to battle a man whom their religion told them was also invincible. Every myth about the Sunhero stressed his inevitable triumph over his enemies. One of the myths even told of his victory over Death.

Moreover, they had witnessed his killings of the hellhounds and the death-hogs, animals sacred to Alba, and seen his superhuman swiftness and terrible swordplay. So, when the incarnation of the Death-Goddess ordered them to level spears and charge the Horned King, they hesitated.

Their pause lasted only a few seconds, but that time was long enough for Stagg to be upon Alba.

He slashed at her spear and cut through the wood of the shaft so that the steel head fell on the ground. At the same time, the deer on which Alba sat reared up.

She fell off backwards.

Alba landed on her feet like a cat. For a moment she had a chance to run among her retainers, since her deer was between her and Stagg.

He slashed at it, and the beast fled.

For a second, he stared into her pale blue eyes. He saw a tall, bent-backed old woman, old, old. She looked as if she were two hundred, so lined and seamed and wrinkled was her face. Long thin white hairs sprouted from her chin, and hairs formed a white film like milk on her upper lip. Her eyes seemed to have seen generations of men come and pass, and their stoniness said that she would see more. She was Death Herself!

Stagg felt cold, as if he were facing the inevitable Destroyer.

The rattlesnake, writhing and hissing around her neck, added the extra note of fatality.

Then he shook himself, reminding himself that she was, after all, only human. He charged.

He never reached her.

Her face contorted with pain, she clutched at her chest, and she fell, stricken dead with a heart attack.

There was panic among her followers, a panic of which Stagg took advantage. Running into their midst, he struck left and right. He was berserk, unmindful of the gashes from their spear heads or sabers.

He slashed riders and mounts alike. The deer reared up and threw men and women onto the ground, and Stagg cut them down before they could get to their feet.

For a while, it looked as if he would defeat the whole band. He had killed and wounded at least six on deerback and upset four more and struck them down. Then a rider who had kept cool urged her beast forward. She rode directly toward Stagg. He looked up just in time to see her bearing down on him.

He saw the lovely face of Virginia, the one-time chief virgin of Washington, the woman with the long honey-colored hair and nose like a delicate hawk's and lips as red as blood and breasts that tilted upwards. Her bosom was covered now, for she was full in the belly with his child. She had only four months to go before delivering the baby—and yet she was riding deerback.

Stagg had raised his sword to cut at her.

Then, recognizing her—and realizing that she carried his child, he froze.

That was enough time for her. Her beautiful face cold and expressionless, she slashed out with her weapon, a keen-edged light saber. The edge whistled through the air, thwacked into his antler. And that was the end for Peter Stagg.

17

The plan called for months of careful preparation.

First, spies, disguised as Deecee of various classes, drifted into Washington. They investigated any sources that might be able to inform them about the equipment left on the *Terra.* They also used their many means to find out what had happened to the Sunhero. During their inquiries, they discovered that Doctor Calthorp was back in Washington.

It was not long before he was contacted, and, a few days later, he slipped out by boat down the Potomac to Chesapeake Bay and on out into the ocean. Here a Karelian ketch picked him up and took him to the port of Aino.

He had a happy reunion with Churchill and the others, marred only by news of the deaths of Sarvant and Gbwe-hun and the doubts about Stagg's whereabouts.

Churchill explained the deal he had made with the Karelians. Calthorp chuckled and said that it might work. If it didn't, they would at least have tried. He himself was the most profitable source of information on the conditions of the *Terra.* He knew exactly what they would find in it and what they needed to get elsewhere.

Finally, they were ready.

They left Aino with Captain Kirsti Ainundila and three Karelians to each one of the crew of the *Terra.* The Karelians carried knives which they would use at the first suspicious action of the starmen.

They sailed in a swift brigantine that preceded the vast fleets to follow. This fleet was composed of vessels manned by Karelians from the colonies south of Deecee and the colonies of what had once been called Nova Scotia and Labrador.

The brigantine sailed boldly into Chesapeake Bay and let the small party of invaders out on a sailboat at the mouth of the Potomac. Disguised as a fishing vessel of Deecee, the sailboat tied up at night on a dock near Washington.

At midnight, the party rushed the building where the arms from the *Terra* were stored.

The few guards went down silently, their throats cut. The armory was broken into, and the starmen took the rapid-fire rifles and passed out the rest to the Karelians. These had never handled such weapons before, but they had worked in Aino with mock-ups made by Churchill.

Churchill also armed the starmen with self-propelled grenades.

They walked without hindrance to the great baseball stadium, now a shrine sacred to the Sunhero. Inside it, the *Terra* still reared her needle nose toward the stars she had left.

The group was challenged by the sentries; a fight took place—slaughter, rather. Thirty archers were killed by the automatic rifles, and forty more badly wounded. The invaders, unscratched, blasted open the gate to the stadium.

The starship was designed so that one man could operate it. Churchill sat in the pilot's seat, Kirsti and two Karelians standing beside him, knives in their hands.

"You will see what this ship can do," Churchill said. "It can destroy Washington simply by letting its bulk down on the buildings. Your fleet will have no trouble sacking the city. And we can fly to Camden and Baltimore and New York and do the same there. If we had not been taken in by the Deecee at first, we'd never have been captured. But we let them sweet-talk us into coming out of the ship after they made Stagg their king."

He tested the controls, checked the indicators, found everything working. He closed the main port and then looked at the clock on the instrument board.

"It's time to go into action," he said, loudly.

Every starman held his breath, at this prearranged code.

Churchill punched a button. Sixty seconds later, the Karelians keeled over. Churchill pressed another button, and air from outside swept out the gas.

It was a trick they had used to get away from the avianthropes of the planet Vixa when they had been in a similar situation.

"Do we put them in deep-freeze?" Steinborg said.

"For the time being," Churchill replied. "Later, we'll put them on the ground. If we took them to Vega II, they might murder us."

He took hold of the wheel, pulled back on a lever, and

the *Terra* rose from the ground, her antigravs lifting the fifty-thousand ton bulk easily.

"Due to atmospheric resistance," Churchill said, "it'll take us fifteen minutes to get to Aino. We'll pick up your wives there and mine—and then it's Poughkeepsie ho!"

The wives he was referring to were the Karelian women Yastzhembski and Al-Masyuni had married during their stay in Aino.

"They're not expecting this. What'll they do once we get them aboard?"

"Give them the gas and put them in deep-freeze," Churchill said. "It's a dirty trick, but we can't waste time arguing with them."

"I hate to think of what they'll say when they thaw out on Vega."

"Not much they can do about it," Churchill said. But he frowned, thinking of Robin's sharp tongue.

However, for now at least, there was no trouble. Robin and the two women came aboard, and the starship took off. The Karelians still on the ground discovered the abduction too late and hurled harmless invectives at them which they did not hear. Again, the gas was released. The women were put in the tanks.

On the way to Poughkeepsie, Churchill said to Calthorp, "According to what the spies said, Stagg was seen in a little village on the east bank of the Hudson a few days ago. That means he escaped from the Pants-Elf. Where he now is, I don't know."

"He must be trying for Caseyland," Calthorp said. "But he'll just be jumping from fire to pan. What I don't understand is how he's had will power enough to keep from going back on the Great Route. That man is possessed by something to which no man can say no."

"We'll land outside Poughkeepsie," Churchill said. "Near Vassar. There's a large clearinghouse for orphans, operated by the priestesses. The orphans are kept there until families are found who'll adopt them. We'll pick the infants up and deep-freeze them. And we'll kidnap a priestess and use a hypnotic on her to make her reveal what she knows about Stagg's whereabouts."

That night, they hovered above the clearinghouse. There was a slight wind, so the starship moved upwind a little and then released the anesthetic.

It took an hour to install sixty sleeping infants in the deep-freeze. Then they revived the head of the clearinghouse, a priestess of about fifty years of age.

They did not bother trying to get her to talk voluntarily. They injected the drug. Within a few minutes, they learned that Alba and her hunting party had left Poughkeepsie the night before on Stagg's trail.

They carried her back into the house and put her in bed.

"When morning comes," Churchill said, "we'll cruise over the vicinity where they should be. We could use black light, but our chances of finding somebody who'll be hiding under cover of trees are very remote."

The starship rose shortly after dawn from the little valley in which it had been hiding. It sped at a height of thirty meters above ground, heading due east. When it reached the Housatonic River, Churchill turned it back to the west. He calculated that Stagg could not have reached the river yet and so must be somewhere in the wasteland.

Returning, they were delayed a dozen times, because they saw people in the woods and descended to investigate. Once a man and a woman disappeared into a cave and the starmen went after them to interrogate them. They had trouble getting them out of the winding tunnels of what turned out to be an abandoned mine. By the time they had questioned them, and found out the two knew nothing of Stagg's location, they had lost several hours.

Reaching the Hudson again, the starship went due north a few miles and then began her eastward hunting.

"If Stagg sees the *Terra*, he'll come out of hiding," Calthorp said.

"We'll go up a few more meters and turn on the full power of the magnifier," Churchill said. "We have to find him!"

They were above five kilometers from the Housatonic River when they saw a number of deer riders racing pell-mell down a trail. They dropped down but, seeing a lone figure on foot leading a deer about a kilometer behind the others, they decided to interrogate the straggler.

She was Virginia, the ex-chief maiden-priestess of Washington. Heavy with child, unable to endure the hard riding any longer, she had gotten off her mount. She tried to escape into the woods, but the ship sent a cloud of gas around her, and she crumpled. Revived a short time later by an injection of antidote, she proved willing enough to talk.

"Yes, I know where the so-called Sunhero is," she said viciously. "He is lying on the path about two and a half kilometers from here. But you need be in no hurry. He'll wait for you. He is dead."

"Dead!" Churchill gasped. He thought, *So close to success. Half an hour sooner, and we could have saved him!*

"Yes, dead!" Virginia spat. "I killed him. I cut off his remaining antler, and he bled to death. And I am glad! He was not a true Sunhero. He was a traitor and a blasphemer, and he killed Alba."

She looked pleadingly at Churchill and said, "Give me a knife so I can kill myself. I was proud once, because I was to bear the child of the Horned King. But I want no brat of a false god! And I do not want the shame of bearing it."

"You mean that if we let you go, you'll kill yourself and the unborn child?"

"I swear by the sacred name of Columbia that I will!"

Churchill nodded to Calthorp, who pressed the syringe against her arm and pushed in on the button which sent a blast of anesthetic into her flesh. She slumped, and the two men carried her to the deep-freeze tank.

"We certainly can't allow her to kill Stagg's child," Calthorp said. "If he is dead, his son will live."

"I wouldn't worry about his not having descendants, if I were you," Churchill said. He did not elaborate on the statement, but he thought of Robin, frozen in the tank. In about fifty years, she would give birth to Stagg's boy.

Oh well, there was nothing he could do to change the situation, so he quit thinking about it. The immediate concern was Stagg.

He raised the ship and shot it straight east. Below, the trail was a thin brown curving line bordered by green. It went around a small mountain, a hill and then another hill; and there was the scene of the battle.

Bodies of dogs and deer and pigs. And a few human forms. Where were the many reported killed?

The ship touched ground, settling on the path and crushing many trees on either side. The men, armed with rifles, stepped out of the main port and surveyed the scene. Steinborg stayed behind in the pilot's seat.

"I think," Churchill said, "that the dead Caseys have been taken off the trail into the woods. They're probably being buried. You'll notice that all the corpses here wear Deecee clothes."

"Maybe they're burying Stagg," Calthorp said.

"I hope not," Churchill replied. He was sad because his captain, who had led him successfully through so many dangers, was gone. Yet he knew that there was a reason why he could not find it in him to mourn very much. If Stagg were alive, what complications would exist once they arrived on Vega? Stagg would not be able to help taking more than a mild interest in Robin's child. Every time Churchill loved or punished the boy, Stagg would be wanting to interfere. And he, Churchill, would be wondering if Robin still regarded Stagg as more than human.

What if she wanted to keep her religion alive?

The men separated, looking for the burial party. Presently, a whistle sounded. It could not be heard by the Caseys, because it was pitched too high. The starmen wore in one ear a device which lowered the frequency to an audible noise, yet did not block normal sound.

They came swiftly, stealthily, and assembled behind Al-Masyuni, who had blown the whistle. There, inside a ring of trees, they saw the worst: a girl and four men, smoothing out the mound of what was obviously a common grave.

Churchill stepped out from the trees and said, "Do not be alarmed. We are friends of Stagg."

The Caseys were startled, but, hearing Churchill repeat his assurance, they relaxed somewhat. However, they did keep their hands upon their weapons.

Churchill advanced a few steps, stopped and explained who he was and why he had come here.

The girl's eyes were red-rimmed and her face tear-streaked. Upon hearing Churchill ask about Stagg, she burst into weeping again.

"He is dead!" she sobbed. "If only you had come sooner!"

"How long has he been dead?"

One of the Caseys eyed the sun. "About half an hour. He bled much for a long time and did not give up without a fight."

"Okay, Steinborg," Churchill said into his walkie-talkie. "Bring the ship up and send out a couple of walking shovels. We have to dig Stagg out of this ground fast. Calthorp, do you think there's a chance?"

"That we can resurrect him? A good chance. That he'll escape brain damage? No chance at all. But we can build up the damaged tissue and then see what happens."

They did not tell the Caseys their real reason for wanting to exhume Stagg. By now they knew a little of Mary's love for him, and they did not want to rouse false hopes. They told her they wished to take the captain back to the stars, where he would have wished to be buried.

The other corpses were left in the grave; they were badly mangled and had been dead too long.

Inside the ship, Calthorp, directing the delicate robo-surgeon, cut the bony base of the antlers out of Stagg's skull and removed the top of his skull.

His chest was laid open, electrodes implanted in the heart and the brain. A blood pump was attached to his circulatory system. Then the body was lifted by the machine and placed in a lazarus tank.

The tank was filled with biogel, a thin fluid which nourished the cells swarming in it. There were two kinds of cells. One would eat away the damaged or decomposed cells of the corpse. The other was a multitude descended from cells from Stagg's own body. These would seek out and attach themselves to the mother organs and replace those which had been scourged from his body.

Stagg's heart began pumping under the electrical stimulus. His body temperature began to rise. Gradually, the grayish color of skin was replaced by a healthy pink.

Five hours passed, while the biogel did its work. Calthorp studied for the hundredth time the indications on the meters and the waves on the oscilloscopes.

Finally he said, "No use keeping him in there any more."

He twisted a dial on the instrument panel of the robo-surgeon, and Stagg was slowly lifted from the tank.

He was deposited on a table, where he was washed off, the needles withdrawn from heart and brain, his chest sewed up, a metal skull cap fitted on, the scalp rolled back over the cap and the skin sewn up.

From there the men took over. They carried Stagg to a bed and put him in it. He slept like a new-born baby.

Churchill went outside, where the Caseys waited. They had refused to enter the ship, because they were too filled with superstitious fear and awe.

The men were talking in low tones. Mary Casey sat slumped against a tree trunk, her face a Greek mask of tragedy.

Hearing Churchill approach, she raised her head and said, emotionlessly, “May we go now? I’d like to be with my people.”

“Mary,” Churchill said, “you may go wherever you wish. But first I must tell you why I asked you to wait all these hours.”

Mary listened to his plans for going to Mars, picking up or making fuel there and then going on to Vega II to settle. She lost some of her grief-stricken look at first, but after a while she seemed to fall back into her apathy.

“I am glad for you that you have something to look forward to,” she said. “Although, somehow it sounds blasphemous. However, it does not really concern me. Why are you telling me this?”

“Mary, when we left Earth in 2050 A.D., it was common practice to bring men back from the dead. It was not black magic or witchcraft, but application of knowledge that did it…”

She leaped to her feet and seized his hands.

“Do you mean that you have brought Peter back to life?”

"Yes," he said. "He is sleeping now. Only..."

"Only what?"

"When a man has been dead as long as he was, he suffers a certain inevitable amount of brain damage. Usually this can be repaired. But sometimes the man is an idiot."

She lost her smile. "Then we won't know until morning. Why didn't you wait until then to tell me?"

"Because you would have gone on home unless I told you this. There's something else. Every man aboard the *Terra* knew what might happen if he died and was resurrected. All of us, except Sarvant, agreed that if he came out of the lazarus tank an idiot, he was to be killed again. No man wants to live without his mind."

"To kill him would be a terrible sin!" she said. "It would be murder!"

"I will not waste time arguing with you," he said. "I just want you to know what might happen. However, if it's any help to you, I can tell you that when we were on the planet Vixa, Al-Masyuni was killed. A poisonous plant which shot little darts by means of air pressure got him twice. He died at once, and then the plant opened up and about twenty centipede-like insects raced out. They were enormous for insects, two feet long and armed with great pincers. They apparently intended to drag Al-Masyuni's body into the plant, where everybody—including the plant—would share in the feast.

"We stayed out of range of the darts and blasted the insects with rifle fire and the plant with grenades. Then we took Al-Masyuni's body to the ship and resurrected him, after we'd gotten rid of the alkaloid in his system. He suffered no physical or mental effects from his death at all. But Stagg's case is somewhat different."

"May I see him in the morning?" she said.

"For better or for worse."

The night went slowly. Neither the starmen nor Mary slept, though the Caseys sprawled in the woods and snored lustily. Some of the crew asked Churchill why they did not proceed with their plans while waiting for Stagg to waken. They could gas a village or two, put more babies and women in deep-freeze, and be on their way to Mars.

"Because of that girl," Churchill said. "Stagg might want to take her with us."

"Why don't we just put her in the tank, too," Yastzhembski said. "After all, it's rather delicate hairsplitting, isn't it? Being sensitive about her feelings and yet kidnaping dozens of babies and women?"

"We don't know them. And we're doing the babies, and the Pants-Elf women a favor by getting them out of this savage world. But we do know her, and we know that she and Stagg were going to get married. We'll wait and see what Stagg has to say about it."

Morning came at last. The men ate breakfast and did various chores until Calthorp summoned them.

"Time," he said. He filled a hypodermic syringe, plunged it into Stagg's huge biceps, swabbed the invisible break, and then stood back.

Churchill had gone to Mary Casey and told her that Stagg

would awaken very soon. It was a measure of her love for Stagg that she had the courage to enter the ship. She did not look around her as she was led through the corridors filled with what to her must have been weird and evil-looking devices. She looked straight ahead, at Churchill's broad back.

Then she was at Stagg's side, weeping.

Stagg mumbled something. His eyelids fluttered, became still again.

His deep breathing resumed.

Calthorp said loudly, "Wake up, Pete!"

He lightly slapped his captain's cheek.

Stagg's eyes opened. He looked around at them, at Calthorp, Churchill, Steinborg, Al-Masyuni, Lin, Yastzhembski, Chandra, and looked puzzled. When he saw Mary Casey, he was startled.

"What the hell happened?" he said, trying to roar but succeeding only in croaking. "Did I black out? Are we on Earth? We must be! Otherwise, that woman wouldn't be on board. Unless you Don Juans had her stowed away all this time."

It was Churchill who first grasped what had happened to Stagg.

"Captain," he said, "what's the last thing you remember?"

"Remember? Why, you know what I ordered just before I blacked out! Land on Earth, of course!"

Mary Casey became hysterical. Churchill and Calthorp took her out of the room and Calthorp gave her a sedative. She fell asleep in two minutes. Then Calthorp and the first mate went into the control room.

"It's too early to tell for certain," Calthorp said, "but I don't think he's suffered any loss of I.Q. He's no idiot; but that part of his brain which contained the memory of the last five and a half months was destroyed. It's been repaired, so it's as good as ever, but the memory content is gone. To him, we've just returned from Vixa, and we're preparing to descend to Earth."

"I thought so," Churchill said. "Now, what are we going to do with Mary Casey?"

"Tell her the situation and allow her to decide for herself. She may want to try to make him fall in love with her."

"We'll have to tell her about Virginia. And Robin. She may not like the idea."

"No time like the present," Calthorp said. "I'll have to give her a shot to bring her out of her sleep. Then I'll tell her. She can make up her mind now. We've no time to dillydally."

He left.

Churchill sat thinking in the pilot's seat. He wondered what the future held. Certainly events wouldn't be boring. He would have troubles enough of his own, but he would not be in Stagg's shoes for anything. To have fathered hundreds of children in the wildest and most extended orgy a man could dream of, yet be innocent of any knowledge of it! To go to Vega II and there be presented with two babies by different women, and perhaps a third if Mary Casey came along. To be told what had happened—and yet be absolutely unable to visualize it, perhaps not to believe it even when a dozen witnesses swore it was true! To have incidents of which he had no remembrance at all hurled at him during the inevitable marital quarrels.

No, thought Churchill, he would not care to be Stagg. He

was content to be Churchill, though that was going to be bad enough when Robin awakened.

He looked up. Calthorp had returned.

"What's the verdict?" Churchill said.

"I don't know whether to laugh or cry," Calthorp said. "Mary is coming with us."

POSTLUDE

Thunder, lightning, and rain.

A small tavern in a neutral area on the border of Deecee and Caseyland. Three women sitting at a table in a private room in the rear of the tavern. Their heavy hooded robes hanging from pegs on the walls. All three wearing tall black conical hats.

One, Virginia, the younger sister of the woman on the *Terra*. Now, like her older sister when Stagg came to Washington, maiden priestess of the holy city. Tall, beautiful, hair like honey, eyes so deep blue, nose curved like a delicate hawk's, lips like a wound, exposed breasts full and upthrusting.

One, the abbess of a great sisterhood of Caseyland. Thirty-five years old, graying hair, heavy-breasted, protruding stomach, and, under the robe, broken veins on the legs, tokens of childbirth, though she is sworn to chastity. In public, she prays to Columbus the Father, and the Son, and the Mother. In private, she prays to Columbia, the Goddess, the Great White Mother.

One, Alba, white-haired, toothless, withered hag, successor to the Alba slain by Stagg.

They drink from tall glasses filled with red wine. *Or is it wine?*

Virginia, the maiden, asks if they have lost. The starmen have escaped them and taken with them the Sunhero and her dear sister, heavy with his child.

The gray-haired matron replies that they never lose. Did she think that her sister would allow the thought of the Goddess to die in her child's mind? Never!

But Stagg, the maiden protests, has also taken with him a devout maiden of Caseyland, a worshiper of the Father.

Alba, the old hag, cackles and says, Even if he takes the religion of the Caseys as his, young and beautiful but ignorant girl, do you not know that the Goddess has already won in Caseyland? The people pay thin-blooded homage to the Father and the Son on their Sabbath, but it is to the Mother they pray most fervently. It is Her statues that fill the land, She who fills their thoughts. What does it matter whether the Goddess is called Columbia or some other name? If She cannot enter the front door, She enters the back.

But Stagg has escaped us, the maiden protests.

No, the matron replies, he did not escape us or the Great Route. He was born in the south and went north, and he met Alba and was killed. It does not matter that he slew a human being called Alba, since Alba lives today in this old flesh that sits with us. And he was killed, and buried, and he rose again, as it was told. And he is like a new-born baby, for I have heard that he has no memory of the life he spent on the Great Route.

Pay attention to what Alba says about the Goddess always winning even when She loses! It will not matter if he rejects Virginia and chooses Mary. He is ours. Mother Earth goes with him to the stars.

They talk of other things and make their plans. Then, though the thunder and lightning rage, and the rain falls, they leave the tavern. Now their faces are shadowed by hoods so no man will know who they are. They pause for a moment before the parting of the ways, one south, one north, one to remain halfway between them.

The maiden says, When shall we three meet again?

The matron replies, When man is born and dies and is born.

The hag replies, When the battle is lost and won.

AFTERWORD

BY DENNIS E. POWER

Flesh is an evocative title. Depending on the reader it can be either an innocuous title or a provocative one, bringing to mind images of perhaps raw meat, or of bare, naked skin. For those of a more religious bent the title may bring to mind certain biblical passages such as Mark 14:38, "The spirit is willing but the flesh is weak," or perhaps from John 1:14, "And the Word was made flesh, and dwelt among us."

While both biblical passages are certainly applicable to the novel, the latter is perhaps most apt. John refers to the incarnation, of God as taking on flesh to become his own son, Jesus Christ. By doing so God created an integral part of the Trinity, which consists of The Father, The Son and The Holy Spirit. The Trinity is of course one of the basic tenets of Christian faith.

It may seem strange to start with a religious digression, but although *Flesh* is a tale of a post-apocalyptic future, like Walter Miller's *A Canticle for Leibowitz*, it is also a religious novel. Miller's novel portrayed the Roman Catholic Church as an enduring institution that survives through post-apocalyptic barbarity to the dawn of a new nuclear age. Through civilization's fall and rise, the Catholic Church is cast as the guardian of knowledge for a human race that has yet to learn from its own stupidity.

Although *A Canticle for Leibowitz* has a religious background, it is not quite as religious as *Flesh* because there is an undercurrent of cynicism that runs through the book. The figure at the center of the novel, St. Leibowitz, was a Jewish atomic scientist who became a monk after the apocalypse in order to preserve his own life, and also to help preserve scientific knowledge from neo-Luddites determined to eradicate the learning that they believe led to the destruction of civilization. As such, the religious theme takes on a tone of pragmatism that makes it seem weaker than the religious tone in *Flesh.*

As you have seen in the novel, (that is unless you are reading the afterword first—if so, I strongly suggest you read the novel first) the reader is flung full on into the religious world of *Flesh*. Even before the main characters are introduced, we are allowed to partake, vicariously, in one of the important rites of this new world. In fact, when we are introduced to the main protagonist of the novel, he is simply portrayed as a participant in this rite, rather than as one of the novel's central characters. We quickly learn within a few paragraphs that the ceremony takes place in Washington, D.C., that the religion worships a Great White Mother, that the rituals are violent and often fatal to the participants, that the society seems to be matriarchal, and that names and figures from American history and legend are symbolic to this new religion.

In the first chapter, we have learned through inference rather than direct knowledge that the Sunhero, a man named Stagg, was part of a crew from a spaceship that landed in Deecee. The second chapter goes into more specifics about the ship and crew. The ship, *Terra*, was an interstellar exploration craft which had left the Earth eight hundred years prior to the start of the novel. The crew had been kept young through the combination of cryonics and relativistic travel. They returned to a devastated world where civilization was barely at an Iron Age level, where society was run by a matriarchy, and where the main religion was a fertility-based pantheon.

The religion was a syncretic one comprised of ancient elements combined with those borrowed from a distantly remembered American culture. Because the religious rites were so alien to what the spacemen were used to, and because the religion contained elements that seemed, to them at least, ludicrous, they had a hard time taking the religion, and its adherents, seriously.

The ancient part of the religion was based on worship of the Triple Goddess, a religion which some believe antedated patriarchal religions. In short, the supreme deity is the Earth mother, The Great White Goddess, a goddess of fertility who manifests in three physical incarnations representing her stages in life: the Nymph or Virgin, the Matron, and the Crone. They also represent the three stages of life: youth, maturity, and old age. The male aspects of these are incarnated in a singular individual, the Sunhero or Sacred King, who is both the son and husband of the Great Goddess.

The Sunhero personally undergoes within a fixed time period, which varies from culture to culture, the aspects of youth, mature man, and elder. In the case of the religion of *Flesh,* he is born at the Winter Solstice and dies at the Summer Solstice. As seen in the novel, his birth and descent into decrepitude occur as a combination of rite and medical procedure. During his rebirth he undergoes a ritual birth and has the Sunhero's antler grafted onto his skull; during his last rite he is blinded, scalped, and castrated.

Although I cannot say with absolute certainty, since Mr. Farmer is unfortunately no longer with us to confirm my argument, it seems quite likely that *Flesh*'s Triple Goddess religion was inspired by the works of Sir James George Frazer, Robert Graves, and Joseph Campbell.

Campbell's contribution to *Flesh* is evident in how Farmer framed the plotline of his main protagonist, Peter Stagg, having him literally undergo what Campbell called "the Road of Trials," in which the Hero must make a journey filled with perils in order to reap his rewards. Farmer ritualized this journey by making Deecee's Sunhero travel the Great Route from Deecee to Albany, which mythologically symbolized the journey from birth to death. Ordinarily, the Sunhero merely traveled the route and participated in the planting rites of the various towns along the way; however, since Peter Stagg was the Hero of the novel, Farmer had to insert both internal and external conflicts to plague him along the way.

Frazer's *The Golden Bough* was the work that theorized the mythic archetype of the Sacred King and discussed the importance of his role as both progenitor and regenerator. As the fleshly husband to the Sacred Goddess, he progenerated offspring and his sacrifice of blood and flesh was used to regenerate the earth; thus, he fertilized Mother Earth in death and in life.

The Golden Bough inspired Robert Graves, who was a renowned classicist as well as a poet. Graves used both of these disciplines to expand on Frazer's concepts and uncover what he perceived as the hidden truth behind myth. His research culminated in his theory about a prehistoric religion based on the Triple Goddess which permeated throughout Europe. He theorized that eventually, the kings balked at being sacrificed and began using substitutes to keep their lives and power. As the kings remained in power longer, they created dynastic reigns which led to the matriarchal religions being supplanted by patriarchal religions.

Graves dissected European mythology in his work *The White Goddess* and expounded upon his Triple Goddess theory. In *The Greek Myths*, he retold the myths of Greece in clear, accessible language. In footnotes and annotations, using an exercise we now call literary archeology, he discussed the historical and religious truths behind each myth, using his theories about the matriarchal religion as the basis for interpretation. Graves also used his theories about the Triple Goddess as the basis for his historical novel *Hercules, My Shipmate*, which retold the epic tale of the Argonauts' quest for the Golden Fleece.

Graves' *White Goddess, The Greek Myths*, and possibly *Hercules, My Shipmate* were undoubtedly influential on Farmer in his creation of the religion of Deecee, especially in terms of the Triple Goddess, the use of totemic cults, and the idea of a patriarchal society vying against a matriarchal one. One of Graves' lesser known works, *Seven Days in New Crete* (also known as *Watch the North Wind Rise*), also seems to have been quite influential.

This novel was Graves' foray into fantasy. In it a man from 1949 is transported hundreds or perhaps thousands of years into the future, to a society ruled by women and where the main religion is the worship of the Triple Goddess. *Seven Days in New Crete* is in many regards a traditional utopian novel, in that the protagonist examines the society to which he has been abruptly exposed. Despite both being matriarchies ruled by priestesses of the Triple Goddess, the societies depicted in *Flesh* and *Seven Days in New Crete* could not be more different. New Crete is far more utopian in that it has eliminated war, crime, poverty, and for the most part, disease. It also has a barter-based economy that eliminated the need for money. However, it also has a caste-based social system in which societal roles and duties are strictly defined. One of the few crimes for which someone may be executed in New Crete is to defy their caste.

Despite the differences between *Flesh* and *Seven Days in New Crete*, there are some interesting parallels between the two novels. In both novels the protagonists are men from the past suddenly thrust into a bizarre future world. Graves used the fantastical convention of a magic spell to bring Venn-Thomas into the future, whereas Farmer used the more realistic science-fiction convention of interstellar explorers returning to Earth after hundred of years due to the relativistic consequences of traveling near light speed.

Edward Venn-Thomas was intrigued, enchanted, bemused, and nearly seduced by the society of New Crete. Like the characters in *Flesh*, he was so overwhelmed by the complexities, and from his own viewpoint, the absurdities, of this society, that he failed to realize at his core, until irrefutably shown, that these people fervently believed in their theocratic society.

In both novels, the matriarchal society was formed after a devastation with oddly similar descriptions. In *Seven Days in New Crete*, the Earth was subjected to a weapon described as a bright AIRAR from Heaven. Venn-Thomas believes this was some form of artificially induced radioactive rain but that is just a supposition. A third of the Earth was devastated. In *Flesh*, the Desolation was caused by a flash of light that caused the Earth to shrivel up. Calthorp speculates that a process to broadcast power somehow ignited the ozone layer. The devastation in *Flesh* was much greater than it was in *Seven Days in New Crete*, for the New Cretans had historical accounts, if, to Venn-Thomas's amusement, erroneously jumbled accounts, whereas Deecee only had fragmented legends as their history.

As part of this jumbled history, the histories of New Crete sometimes conflated historical personages. For example, Cleopatra was considered one of the founders of New Crete who had lived at the end of the industrial age. Robin Hood was believed to have been the English Homer and most of the early ballads of the time were attributed to him. This concept may have inspired Farmer to do a similar thing in *Flesh*, wherein he made George Washington into Wazhtin, the literal Father of his Country, and made Columbia, the female personification of

America, into *Flesh*'s version of the Great Goddess.

Two other ideas that both *Seven Days in New Crete* and *Flesh* share are ritual warfare and baseball.

The society of New Crete is a very peaceful one and the New Cretans are convinced it is because of how they alleviate their violent impulses. When disagreements arose between communities, they had councils to decide whether or not to go to war. If war was declared, the war was held on Tuesday. The ritual warfare of New Crete did not involve actual battle but was more along the lines of a large game of capture the flag, with all the men of the two combating villages engaging in wrestling and quarterstaff matches as they vied to capture the other village's totem.

The world of *Flesh*, however, is as violent and deadly as our own, so the ritual warfare in this novel takes the form of the Treaty War where the various nations around Deecee signed a treaty to limit the number of incursions into one another's territories. Ostensibly this was done to limit the number of casualties, since the human race was still at a fairly low population.

In *Seven Days in New Crete*, Graves mentions that baseball had become the most popular game in New Crete, yet does not go into any detail how that came about, or even show a baseball game. However, Farmer made baseball into part of the ritual combat of the world of *Flesh* and part of the Treaty War. This makes sense because at the time Farmer wrote *Flesh*, baseball was still considered the national pastime. Baseball was considered an important component of the Treaty War because every year the Great Series was held and participants from the various nations surrounding Deecee sent a team to play for the championship.

Baseball in the era of *Flesh* was a bloody violent game using balls with metal spikes and metal shod bats. In this game, kill the umpire was taken literally.

In his depiction of baseball in *Flesh*, in the final game of the Great Series, which was between Deecee and the nearby Caseyland, and more specifically in Peter Stagg's game of One against Five against a group of Caseylanders, Farmer was able to invoke and to pay a tongue in cheek homage to Casey at the Bat, the full title of which is "Casey at the Bat: A Ballad of the Republic Sung in the Year 1888."

One of the teams that played in the Great Series was from the nation of Pants-Elf. This nation bears mentioning not only because it plays a pivotal role in Stagg's journey, but also because it demonstrates another similarity between *Seven Days in New Crete* and *Flesh*. Venn-Thomas is shocked to learn that one of the crimes for which someone can be executed in New Crete is being a homosexual. According to the beliefs of New Crete, by loving another man, the homosexual has rejected the Great Goddess.

Although it is not explicitly stated, Deecee probably had a similar policy. It seems likely that they originally may have exiled their homosexuals and in doing so they created an enemy on their borders. This may be why they instituted the death penalty instead of exile rule.

The nation of Pants-Elf, which is a corruption of Pennsylvania, appears to be an offshoot of Deecee, since it also pays homage to the Great Mother. However, the religious and social views of Pants-Elf are considered heretical by the Deecee. Despite worshiping Columbia, the Pants-Elf inhabitants thought women as inferior to men, and like some Muslim women, Pants-Elf women were veiled and covered in heavy robes. To further the Muslim analog, the Pants-Elf believed in polygamy and kept their women segregated. Men only had sex with wives for the purposes of procreation, for Pants-Elf was a society that practiced cultural homosexuality. The men were openly homosexual and the women were encouraged to become lesbians.

The modern reader might find the time that Stagg spent among the Pants-Elf a bit jarring since Farmer utilizes some stereotypical homosexual tropes to demonstrate how different Pants-Elf was from Deecee. For example, the Pants-Elf men appear to be divided into two distinct phenotypes, the short haired "butch" man and the long haired effeminate. All of the Pants-Elf men are flirty with Stagg and call each other by such terms as honey and dearie. Even the place names mentioned during this episode call out the homosexual theme. Stagg is taken to a town called High Queen and the inhabitants mention that he is to be taken to Pheelee, which Stagg points out is the city of brotherly love. Even the name of Pants-Elf could be a coy wink. Although the name is a corruption of Pennsylvania, when pronounced aloud, it is very phonetically similar to pansy. It is likely that Farmer was parodying the then-prevalent attitudes towards homosexuality, although the casual reader might believe he was pandering to them.

Another of the parallels between *Seven Days in New Crete* and *Flesh* is the sacrifice of the Sacred King. Here the similarities are not as different as might be expected. As in *Flesh*, the king is sacrificed; however, in *Seven Days in New Crete* the actual king is not sacrificed but a substitute is sacrificed in his place. It is not until near the end of *Seven Days in New Crete* that Venn-Thomas learns that the ritual sacrifice of the Sacred King is not ceremonial and that the Victim is actually killed and his flesh eaten by the Wild Women. This, more than anything, convinces him to return to his own time.

Peter Stagg, however, learns about halfway through *Flesh* that in his case there will be no substitute; when he reaches Albany he will be killed. The horns on his head have effectively shackled him to this fate since the hormones they pump into him compel him to seek out and mate with as many women as he can.

It is revealed at the end of both *Seven Days in New Crete* and in *Flesh* that the protagonists of both had been brought to their respective settings by the Goddess, or so at least the Priestesses of the Goddess believe. However, the purposes for which they were brought forth were drastically different. Venn-Thomas had been brought to New Crete so that he could be the harbinger of doom, warning the people of New Crete that their peaceful utopia was about to come to an end, for the Goddess was not always filled with love and kindness and it was time for her dark aspect to once again stride upon the earth.

Rather than foreshadowing destruction Peter Stagg's arrival was one of true regeneration. Not only did he bring some needed genetic diversity to Deecee's population in his role as the Sunhero, but by taking Virginia with him as he departed Earth, he spread the faith of the Goddess to the stars.

Graves' theory about the Triple Goddess seems to have

resonated with Farmer, for he also used it as the basis for the religion of Khokarsa. Graves' theories about the patriarchal culture replacing the matriarchal culture formed the basis of one the major plotlines in his Khokarsa trilogy, which consists of *Hadon of Ancient Opar*[1], *Flight to Opar*, and *The Song of Kwasin*.[2] Although the setting for this series is ancient Africa, one can see that Graves' *The Greek Myths* and perhaps *Hercules, My Shipmate* had some influence, since Hadon is a Jason/Theseus analog and Kwasin is an analog for Heracles.

It is perhaps appropriate that in a novel dealing with a Triple Goddess, Farmer used three plotlines to explore the religion and society of Deecee. These plotlines were based around Churchill, Nephi Sarvant, and Peter Stagg.

Once Stagg had begun his journey down the Great Route, his shipmates were released from captivity. They were told they had a month to start acclimating to Deecee society or be executed. Exile was not an option. The Asian and European members of the crew decided to try and escape to make their way to their homelands, even though they knew they were no longer remotely like the lands that they had left.

Churchill and Sarvant explored Deecee together and befriended the Whitrow family. After an evening together, the Whitrow family asked Churchill and Sarvant to be their guests. Res Whitrow was a wealthy man with powerful connections to Deecee society. His main wealth came from shipping, which greatly interested Rudyard Churchill, who immediately began

[1] Part of Titan Books' series of Philip José Farmer reissues.

[2] The latter book was written with Christopher Paul Carey; all three novels were collected by Subterranean Press in an omnibus edition entitled *Gods of Opar*.

thinking of somehow acquiring access to a ship from him. His task was made easy by Whitrow's daughter, Robin, who found Churchill intriguing. Churchill played up this interest for his own purposes but quickly discovered that he also had romantic feelings for Robin.

The Whitrow family gives a slight peek at Deecee family life. It is a very earthy society with a lack of the social graces to which Churchill and Sarvant were accustomed. At their first dinner with a Deecee family, Churchill and Sarvant were exposed to open discussions of sexuality and proof that table manners were among the knowledge lost during the Desolation. The Frats, in addition to being religious cultic societies, also functioned as lodges or other fraternal organizations did at the time that Farmer wrote *Flesh*, that is to say they were social organizations used by men and women for entertainment, charitable causes, business, and social networking. It is no coincidence that Farmer indicated that the most powerful frats were the Lions, Elks, Eagles, and Moose, since these were also among the most prominent fraternal orders at the time he wrote *Flesh*.

One of the more interesting things about the Whitrow family, and it appears in Deecee society, is the role of the father. Although the Deecee society is matriarchal and Res Whitrow had acquired his wealth and social standing through his wife Angela's family, Whitrow, like his father-in-law, was the breadwinner for the family, for he speaks of working for Angela's father, not her mother. Res Whitrow also seems to be the dominant figure in the family unit; in fact, it is noted that although Angela talked a lot, she never interrupted her husband. Her role seems to be that of a housewife. This seems typical for Deecee society, for only those women who are dedicated to religious orders work outside of the home. This is not to say, however, that women did not participate in important decision making. In conjunction with her father, Robin Whitrow planned Rudyard Churchill's career after their marriage without consulting her prospective groom.

This role is replicated in greater Deecee society as well, for although Deecee is nominally ruled by the King and Queen of Deecee, the Sunhero and the High Priestess, these appear to be largely ceremonial roles insofar as actual governance goes. The true ruler of Deecee, that is the person who actually runs things on a day-to-day basis, is the Speaker of the House. The Speaker is appointed by the High Priestess and is analogous to the Prime Minister. However, even the role of the Speaker of the House has a religious significance; the Speaker must subsume his own identity into an iconic cultic figure. There are two Speakers mentioned in *Flesh*: John Barleycorn (who died as a result of indulging too much in his namesake) and his successor Tom Tobacco. Because the Priestesses prefer a behind the scenes role the Speakers are the public face of the Deecee's government. Deecee's Speaker is the liaison between the people of Deecee and their goddess Columbia, so in a literal sense he speaks for the Goddess.

As stated earlier, Robin Whitrow had unilaterally decided her future husband's career. Instead of becoming the Captain of a sailing vessel, Churchill was to become a pig farmer. Res Whitrow explained that his sailing holdings were going to his sons, which would seem to indicate that despite Deecee being a matriarchy, inheritance could still pass down through the male lineage.

Although we only get a glimpse of the gender roles in Deecee society, they appear to be similar to the roles that were current when *Flesh* was written, that is, the man worked outside of the home and that the woman stayed at home to have children and took care of the house.

It does seem odd that in a matriarchal society gender roles remained fairly consistent with those of a male dominated society. One wonders if Farmer truly wished to make a point about Washington, D.C., by depicting Deecee society as fundamentally unchanged despite sustaining an apocalypse. Or were the gender stereotypes so firmly entrenched in American society of that era, even to a writer of his imagination, that this seemed like the only plausible depiction of women in a modern society?

If Farmer had written *Flesh* a few years later, after the women's liberation movement, would women have been depicted with more of a diverse role in Deecee society?

The plotline dealing with Nephi Sarvant demonstrates the religious traditions and structure of the theocracy as seen through its common adherents. Nephi Sarvant is a member of a sect called the Church of the Last Stand. This church seems based on a combination of fundamentalist Christianity and Mormonism. Although Farmer does not specifically state that the Last Standers were an offshoot of Mormonism, there are some pretty telling clues. Sarvant's first name of Nephi is a name strongly associated with Mormonism. The Prophet Mormon used plates written by three men named Nephi to write his book, which was later transcribed by Joseph Smith. Mormon lore also has that the Three Nephites were disciples of Jesus Christ who were granted immortality so that they could carry out missionary work until the end of the world. The Last Standers were centered in Fourth of July, Arizona. The Fourth of July oration is a famous speech in Mormon history. Also, Sarvant mentioned that he would try to get back home but Arizona, Utah, and even the Great Salt Lake seemed uninhabited. A lesser but pertinent clue is that Sarvant refers to his scripture as the Book, or the book of my faith, rather than the Good Book, so he is doubtless referring to the Book of Mormon rather than the Bible.

Farmer had a brief fascination with Mormonism, to the point of planning a novel set on a world in which the Book of Mormon was literally and historically true. Eventually, however, he abandoned the Mormon element of the novel, which evolved into *Two Hawks from Earth*. It is interesting that of all the religious beliefs that he examined in his Riverworld series, which also has a strong religious element, Mormonism was given rather scant attention. This may have been because the faith of the Ethicals seems to have been a combination of Mormonism and Scientology. One of the tenets of the Mormon Church is that in the afterlife, the faithful will become Gods of worlds of their own. In the last Riverworld novel, *Gods of Riverworld*, the protagonists reached the Dark Tower, the seat of power of the Riverworld, and had the power to repopulate the Riverworld, but spent most of the novel using the technology of the Ethicals to create mini worlds of their own.

The Whitrow family offered to guest Nephi Sarvant, but he was repulsed by their behavior. He decided that he had been placed in this time and place to bring the word of God to the benighted pagans. Since he was under a deadline to become a functioning member of Deecee society, he looked around for employment. He was told about a job as a sweeper at the Temple of Gotew. He thought that this would be a great place to observe the religion of Deecee and also where he could begin his proselytizing efforts.

En route to the Temple of Gotew, he encountered a young woman wearing a hooded robe. He discovered that she too was going to the Temple of Gotew. She was shocked that Sarvant, who was considered to be a *diradah*, that is, part of the aristocracy, because of his association with the Sunhero, would seek to take a job as janitor, but she led him to the Temple.

Upon his arrival at the Temple of Gotew Nephi Sarvant got the first knock against his preconceived notions about Deecee's pagan society. He had expected the person in charge of the temple to be a woman; however, Bishop Andi, a man, ran things. After taking the job, Sarvant was surprised to see the aristocratic woman, Arva Linkon, open her robe to a man and go with him into a curtained booth. He learned that the Goddess of Gotew was the goddess of infertile women. The afflicted women came to the temple in the hopes that some man could quicken her womb. To Sarvant's eyes this was a form of temple prostitution. His first thought was to quit, but after reflection he believed that this was a good way to start his crusade.

However, as often happens, the spirit is willing but the flesh is weak. Sarvant never really began his mission because he became infatuated and then obsessed with Arva Linkon.

His religious fervor and passion for Arva Linkon became intertwined. Her assignations with any male who could enter the Temple literally drove Sarvant insane.

One day when she was on her way home, he tried to convert her to Christianity. Sarvant was upset when she rebuked him for being a pagan and a foul blasphemer. He was even more shocked when Bishop Andi told him that if he persisted in his false beliefs, his month could be drastically shortened. Arva Linkon had told the Bishop about Sarvant's attempt to convert her because she was a truly devout woman.

When Sarvant could no longer take seeing Arva Linkon with everyone but him, he took the fertility test that would allow him to worship at the Temple of Gotew. When he took Arva Linkon to her booth, she was ecstatic because she believed that her body was the instrument that had converted the unbeliever to the true faith. When Sarvant told her that he wanted to be with her because he loved her, not because he believed in the Goddess, Arva tried to leave, calling him a pagan. Sarvant's mind snapped and he assaulted Arva. When Arva let it be known what he had done, a mob dragged him to the gallows and hanged him.

As he was being carried to the gallows, Nephi Sarvant had an epiphany that the faith of the people of Deecee was too strong for him to have overcome. They believed with an intensity that was insurmountable. He believed that had he come eight hundred years later, he might have had succeeded in getting converts when the faith had waned. Yet even in dying, Nephi Sarvant did not even consider that the reason he had failed was because their faith was stronger than his own. Or that the Deecee followed a strict moral code. Arva Linkon was a married woman forced to come to the Temple because she was barren; she did not have sex with men besides her husband simply for the sake of gratification. When Sarvant made it plain that their coupling was not to be a sacred act, she rejected him.

Sarvant's main disappointment was that he was dying a failure; he had not made one convert and he was not dying as a martyr, as he had often wished, but because he had committed rape. His last thoughts were not how he had disappointed God, but rather how he had failed himself, and so he revealed that his mission was more a measure of personal worth rather than one of absolute faith.

Peter Stagg's story in *Flesh* is as the physical incarnation of one of Deecee's religious icons, the Sunhero and Stag King, both the son and husband of the Great Mother. The Sunhero's role is to physically travel along the Great Route from Deecee to Albany, from South to North, and to impregnate as many women as he can along the way. This journey symbolically represents the sun's journey from Summer to Winter and cycle of life from birth to death.

Stagg's journey is also the road of trials that heroes must undertake. Stagg's first trial was the implantation of artificial organs that resemble transparent stag horns on his head. The horns pumped hormones and drugs into his system that increased his strength, stamina, and virility, and filled him with deep uncontrollable passions for food, violence, and sex. As he travels towards Albany, he becomes less and less able to resist their influence. His second trial was the certain knowledge that he was journeying towards his death and that there was little he could do to escape this fate. Even if he could break through his armed guards and elude them, the horns would compel him to return. His third trial was his love for Mary Casey, a captive woman who was also to be sacrificed at Albany with Stagg. Mary found Peter the man to be noble, kind, and someone she could love, but found Stagg the Sunhero to be everything she detested about the Deecee.

Fate intervened in the form of a Pants-Elf raiding party who slew Stagg's guards and took Mary and Peter captive. Peter and Mary were freed from imminent death, but had to undergo a new set of perils. This break from the Great Route effectively stopped Stagg's role as the Sunhero but set him on the path to become the novel's version of the epic hero. As the epic hero, he had to undergo another set of perils before achieving his quest.

During the course of the next few weeks, they endured a brutal captivity by the Pants-Elf until they fought free of their clutches. As they made their way to Caseyland, they encountered a bear which Stagg fought and killed, although it cost him one of his antlers. However, even with his desire cut in half, Stagg was overwhelmed by his need for Mary Casey and she hid from him. As Stagg looked for her, he encountered some Caseylanders, among them Mary's cousin, who wanted to hang him. To forgo his hanging, Stagg challenged them to a game of One against Five instead. His antler-enhanced speed, strength, and agility allowed Stagg to defeat the five Caseylanders. Mary arrived in time to save her cousin from being killed by Stagg. She warned them that she had heard the sounds of Alba's death-hogs. The Deecee had discovered Stagg's whereabouts and were determined that he perish by the hands of Alba. In the battle that followed, Stagg proved triumphant against Alba. Yet even after her followers had fled, one rider came at him. At the last moment he recognized the rider as the very pregnant Virginia.

Stagg, however, had regained enough of his humanity that he could not strike down a pregnant woman. Virginia had no such qualms and cut off his remaining antler. As a result of this injury, Stagg died, and in doing so fulfilled the Goddess' plan.

To further the mythic quality of Stagg's hero quest, shortly after his death, Stagg was resurrected and in a sense reborn.

Rudyard Churchill and several of his shipmates, in conjunction with some Karelian pirates, had overcome the soldiers guarding the armory in Deecee where Columbia had decreed that the spacemen's weapons would be stored. Armed with automatic weapons they had retaken their ship. They kidnapped several women and children, intending to leave Earth and colonize a planet. While searching for Stagg, they encountered Virginia and she told them that he was dead. Since she was carrying Stagg's child, Churchill sedated her and put her into deep freeze.

After discovering Stagg's whereabouts, they dug him up and placed him in a lazarus device, which revived him and regenerated his damaged organs. However, when Stagg regained consciousness, his entire memory of the events since landing on Earth had been lost. He was, in a sense, reborn to the man he had been before becoming the Sunhero. Prior to having become the Sunhero, Peter Stagg drank a potion that was purportedly from the River Styx. In doing so, Captain Peter Stagg of the starship *Terra* symbolically died and was reborn as Stagg the Sunhero. Having fulfilled his duty to the Goddess, she once again blessed him by letting him drink from one of her rivers, the River Lethe, which washed away all of his memory of having been Her servant.

Just as *Flesh* begins by letting us vicariously experience the Planting Rites of Deecee, it ends by taking us behind the scenes of the theocracy of the Great Goddess and lets the reader in on a rather shocking revelation. In a tavern between Casey and Deecee, three women meet. They are incarnations of the Triple Goddess in her aspects of Maiden, Mother, and Crone. The crone is the new Alba, replacing the one killed by Stagg. The Maiden is the sister of Virginia, who has taken her place as the Virgin of Deecee. Most shockingly is that the Mother is an abbess from a great sisterhood in Caseyland. She gives lip service to worshiping St. Columbus, the Son, and the Mother but really worships Columbia, the Great White Mother. She has given birth, we are told, despite having been sworn to chastity.

The three women are pleased because, despite having deviated from the Great Route, Stagg did travel from South to North, met Alba, and died. To prove that he was a worthy Sunhero, he was reborn as an innocent and he carried Mother Earth to the stars. In a sense this was literally true since the spaceship was named *Terra*. Perhaps the most telling phrase of this conversation is, "It will not matter if he rejects Virginia and chooses Mary. He is ours."

While specifically about Peter Stagg, this statement could also be taken in a broader context regarding the religion of

Deecee. The presence of the abbess from Caseyland as one of the ruling hierarchy of Deecee indicates that Deecee has made greater strides in spreading its religion through its neighboring states than we were originally led to believe. Like the early Christian Church, the Church of Columbia appears willing to incorporate the symbols of existing faiths in order to eventually convert the adherents of the other faith into the true religion. Just as Christianity had replaced the pagan religions, it appears that in the world of *Flesh*, a pagan religion is poised to replace Christianity or the remnant of it. Ultimately it does not matter whether the Columbia is known as the Virgin Virginia or the Virgin Mary, so long as people worship her.

This revelation demonstrates that Nephi Sarvant was probably wrong when he predicted that the faith in Columbia would eventually wane, since the Priestesses were slowly and carefully expanding their faith, and so their influence, over the region. It also demonstrates that unless forced, the Priestesses did not like to show their hands but rather preferred to work behind the scenes. There is a telling anomaly in *Flesh* which may indicate just how powerful and influential the Priestesses truly were.

This anomaly is in the science that the Priestesses possess. Deecee was a civilization barely above the Iron Age. The Priestesses were fundamentally anti-technology and regarded the men from the stars as both a curse and blessing. No doubt the Priestesses were interested in the genetic diversity they could bring to the relatively small population of Deecee, but also felt that their knowledge was dangerous. This is undoubtedly why they separated Stagg from his crew and then set the crew to fare for themselves, knowing it would most likely fail to become part of Deecee society in a month.

We know through the experiences of Churchill and Sarvant that the Priestesses only allow certain professions to attain any sort of literacy. By controlling literacy they also control how knowledge and information are disseminated. Also by making science heretical they restrict technology and so maintain their power.

The Priestesses, however, possess some scientific knowledge, their crowning achievement being the artificial organs shaped like horns that they implanted into Peter Stagg's head. Even if they had somehow inherited the ability to grow these organs, they still needed the ability to perform microsurgery to graft them into his tissue.

Yet this is not all that they can do. When Sarvant was cut by a knife, a Priestess covered the wound with a pseudoflesh that not only sealed the wound and would heal it, but also allowed him to use his hand as if nothing had happened. They also have the ability to tell how fertile a man is by examining his sperm; they can determine the early stages of pregnancy and also tell the sex of a child.

How are these Priestesses who exist in a culture barely above the Iron Age such wizards at biological sciences? One has to wonder how much scientific and historical knowledge was truly lost during the Desolation.

According to the Priestesses, most knowledge about the past was lost, and for most of the people this was undoubtedly true. Yet some interesting bits of Americana have been woven into the fabric of Deecee's mythology. The most obvious ones, of course, are the turning of the female personalization of America, Columbia, into the Great White Goddess, and of George Washington, into Wazhtin, the Father of his Country. I say the most obvious because there are physical representations of these two figures in the Deecee versions of the Capitol Building and the Washington Monument. In the Deecee version the Capitol has two domes which represent the bountiful breasts of Columbia and the Washington Monument has been turned into a giant phallic symbol to demonstrate that Wazhtin was literally the father of his country. The Miss America contest was used as a means of choosing the virgins who would be favored by the Sunhero. The girl chosen as Miss America became deified as Virginia, the Virgin of Columbia, the Queen of Deecee, and the chosen mate of the Sunhero. How this selection was done was never specifically stated; however, we know that Virginia was a graduate of Vassar College for Oracular Priestesses, and so had been trained for her role.

While it is possible that these were the only surviving bits of knowledge about America that survived, it also seems possible that the Priestesses tailored this knowledge to structure their religion to fit their own ends, as they seem to have done with their knowledge of biology and their transformation of the game of baseball.

It might be easy to categorize *Flesh* simply as a post-apocalyptic novel that involves a fertility cult. Although *Flesh* deals with a fertility cult, the sexual content is actually tamer than many of Philip José Farmer's other works. And as in most of his works, there is more going on than first meets the eye. As we have seen in the closing section of the book, not everything is as it appears. We leave the book with several unanswered questions, not simply about the culture and society of the world of *Flesh*, but also about some of the adventures of Stagg, Calthorp, and Churchill that were glossed over. Did Farmer simply leave these mysteries unsolved due to space considerations or did he, as I would like to think, do so deliberately, believing that in a novel about a mystery religion, there should be some mysteries left to ponder?

Dennis E. Power is a contributor to Myths for the Modern Age: Philip José Farmer's Wold Newton Universe *(MonkeyBrain Books). He also contributed several essays to* Farmerphile, *a quarterly magazine completely dedicated to works by and about Philip José Farmer. His sequel to Farmer's novel* Flesh *appeared in* The Worlds of Philip José Farmer 1: Protean Dimensions *(Meteor House, 2010). He also served as continuity editor of* The Worlds of Philip José Farmer 2: Of Dust and Soul. *His short fiction about Arnould Galopin's time traveling Doctor Omega has appeared in* Glimmerglass: The Creative Writer's Annual, Volume 1 *(2009) and in* Doctor Omega and the Shadowmen *(Black Coat Press, 2011). He was the coauthor of "Gribardsun through the Ages," which appeared in* Time's Last Gift *(Titan, 2012). His current project is a series of stories about the early life of Jules Verne's Passépartout, two of which have appeared in Black Coat Press' annual anthology* Tales of the Shadowmen. *He is the editor of the websites The El Head Homepage and The Wold Newton Universe:*

A Secret History. He holds a B.A. in History and a Ph.D. from the school of hard knocks. He lives in St. Louis, Missouri in an ancient house with an ancient guardian dog.

AFTERWORD

BY MICHAEL A. BARON

Philip José Farmer was the master of the big idea. Like all great science fiction writers, he looked at society and extrapolated. What if we went this way? What if we went that way? What if the internal combustion engine did not exist? And he did it independently of the zeitgeist or any mass societal movement. Where Isaac Asimov and John Brunner dwelt in the world of politics, Farmer dwelt at the more fundamental level of subsistence, breaking society down to its most barbarous and inserting his enlightened heroes.

He did it in his World of Tiers series, a primer on world-building, the clash between primitive and sophisticated cultures, and the inspiration for my *Nexus* saga, "The Bowl-Shaped World." He did it in the Riverworld series, perhaps his crowning achievement, reducing mankind to serfdom and letting loose some of his favorite historical characters including Sir Richard Burton and Samuel Clemens. My introduction to Burton came through the Riverworld series.

Farmer also ventured into human sexuality, daring to ask questions that other science fiction writers shunned. *The Lovers* is about a man who falls in love with a symbiotic insect that perfectly mimics a beautiful woman. He recast Tarzan and Doc Savage as sexually charged creatures in *A Feast Unknown* and several other books. As most Farmer fans know, Farmer sought to integrate the world's greatest fictional (and real life) heroes into a single tapestry known as the Wold Newton Universe, named after a meteorite that fell in Britain and may have led to genetic mutation.

Heroes of Wold Newton include Solomon Kane; Captain Blood; The Scarlet Pimpernel; Sherlock Holmes and his nemesis Professor Moriarty (aka Captain Nemo); Phileas Fogg; *The Time Traveler*; Allan Quatermain; Tarzan and his son Korak; A.J. Raffles; Professor Challenger; Richard Hannay; Bulldog Drummond; the evil Fu Manchu and his adversary, Sir Denis Nayland Smith; G-8; The Shadow; Sam Spade; Doc Savage, his cousin Pat Savage, and one of his five assistants, Monk Mayfair; The Spider; Nero Wolfe; Mr. Moto; The Avenger; Philip Marlowe; James Bond; Lew Archer; and Travis McGee. I have only claimed four influences, including Farmer and John D. MacDonald, who created Travis McGee.

Perhaps Farmer's most daring venture into human sexuality is his novel *Flesh*, about an Earth 800 years in the future. This Earth has been utterly transformed by a nuclear holocaust which destroyed civilization and gave rise to a new/old religion: worship of Gaia, the Earth Mother, elevating human reproduction to a holy imperative. Captain Peter Stagg departed with his crew from 21st-century Earth. Their faster-than-light drive meant that while the Earth aged 800 years, they barely aged a year and returned to an Earth they could barely recognize.

America has been reduced to a series of sparsely populated city-states ruled by a capital city, Deecee. The Great White Mother resides in the White House with her vestal virgins. Every year they choose a new Sun King, some unlucky stud tasked with impregnating half the available females before being put to death in a horrible manner. All ambitious youth must join a guild: The Elks, The Moose, The Elephants, The Mules, The Jackrabbits, The Trout, The Billy Goats, The Queen Bees—all known for their virility and fertility.

> "*Man, in his blindness, greed, and arrogance, has fouled the Goddess-given earth. His ant-heap cities have emptied their filth into the rivers and sea and turned them into vast sewers. He has poisoned the air with deadly fumes. These fumes, I suppose, were not only the products of industry but of radioactivity. But the Deecee, of course, know nothing of atomic bombs.*"

So says Stagg's second in command, Calthorp. Farmer's description could serve as the basis for any number of dystopian science fictions, from John Varley's *Millennium* and Frank Herbert's *Dune*, to Brunner's *The Sheep Look Up*. It's the science fiction writer's job to show the consequences of our actions. But few do it as objectively and analytically as Farmer. His brave new world is not attractive. Mankind persistently learns the wrong lessons.

Into this frothing Petri dish falls Stagg, tall and handsome, riding on a column of fire. They force him through a ritualistic rebirth and graft a pair of antlers to his forehead. When the antlers get stiff, so does Stagg. He travels from city to city amid great pomp and bloodshed, copulating with screaming virgins who fight for the honor.

> *He ran faster, now and then giving great bounds into the air and uttering strange cries. They were sheer delight, exuberance, and nameless longings and their fulfillment. They were spoken in the language of the first men on Earth, the broken chaotic feeling-toward-speech the upright apes must have formed with clumsy tongues when they were trying to name the things around them. Stagg was not trying to name things. He was trying to name feelings. And he was having as little success as his ancestors a hundred thousand years before.*

This cuts to the heart of the human experience. "Ontogeny recapitulates phylogeny"—the theory that a single organism goes through stages representing the evolution of the entire species. One of Farmer's recurring themes is man reinventing himself. A professor passes through a secret door in a closet and becomes a warrior. An astronaut returns from a long voyage and becomes a primitive tribal king. We see this again and again in Farmer's writing, and it is something he shares in common with a great many science fiction authors, from Robert Louis Stevenson (*Dr.*

Jekyll and Mr. Hyde), Mary Shelley, A.E. van Vogt, and Isaac Asimov, right up to the present day.

It is science fiction's job to examine the human experience through every lens and Farmer excels at it. He does not shy away from representations of homosexuality. A gay tribe captures Stagg and the jockeying among its members for Stagg's favors is pretty funny, until he escapes and kills about a dozen.

There are several facets of modern life that Farmer failed to envision, but no one could fault him for it, for all science fiction fans understand that life keeps getting more and more complicated. It used to be that if you got ill, you went to a doctor. Now you must appeal to a government board for treatment. In Farmer's day, there was no internet. Now it poses an addiction as serious as crack. Many modern problems are the direct result of intellectuals trying to solve problems. Farmer's worlds are the opposite—governments are stripped of their authority, and power is decentralized.

Decentralization is a recurring sub-theme in *Flesh*, as society once again grows from the ground up. But to do that, Farmer had to depopulate the world, another of his obsession perhaps best exemplified by "Seventy Years of Decpop" but also present in the World of Tiers series. Stories dealing with depopulation, such as *I Am Legend*, appeal to an atavistic impulse to withdraw. They appeal to the greatest right not enshrined in the Bill of Rights, the right to be left alone, which lies at the heart of much science fiction. Robert Heinlein comes to mind.

The sheer press of humanity, especially in cities, adds a level of stress for which the human body is not well prepared.

"Hell is other people," as Sartre observed. At the same time, Farmer correctly and sympathetically predicts the extreme effects of climate change caused by human activity. He longs for a simpler time, more specifically, the period of manifest destiny before Americans had fully tamed their new continent. It is as central to the World of Tiers series as it is to *Flesh*.

Another recurring Farmer theme is the role of religion and faith. Farmer visits this time and again, most notably in *Jesus on Mars* and *Night of Light,* and he does so here in the character of the returning astronaut Sarvant, a devout Christian determined to proselytize while fighting his inner demons. As you can imagine, things do not end well for Sarvant.

Farmer is no moralist and is not concerned with character arcs. He is a scientist and explorer mixing civilizations and ideas and observing the results. In the end, it all comes down to a savage game of baseball—in which the ball has enormous spikes, the bat is encased in iron, and it's perfectly acceptable to maim or kill your opponents within the guidelines. The heroic Stagg dies defending the woman he loves—or thinks he loves—and is buried in a mass grave.

But the remaining crew of the spaceship have had enough. Banding together they exhume Stagg's corpse and resuscitate him using the forgotten science of their day, kidnap a number of women, and decamp for sunnier climes. Earth has no hold on them.

Where does *Flesh* fall within the Farmer canon? It is one of his more serious works, rewarding the reader with insight into the human condition and Farmer's usual unsparing view of man at his best and worst. Other novels may offer more excitement, but few offer more insight and wisdom.

Mike Baron is the creator of Nexus *(with artist Steve Rude) and* Badger, *two of the longest lasting independent superhero comics.* Nexus, *about a cosmic avenger 500 years in the future, appears monthly in* Dark Horse Presents. *There are twelve hardbound volumes from Dark Horse.* Badger, *about a multiple personality, one of whom is an animal rights champion, may already be out from a resurgent First Comics by the time you read this. Baron has written for* The Punisher, Flash, Deadman *and* Star Wars *among many other titles. Baron recently published two novels,* Helmet Head, *flesh-shredding horror about Nazi biker zombies, and* Whack Job, *mind-blowing science fiction about spontaneous human combustion. Baron will publish three novels in 2013:* Biker *from Airship 27,* Banshees *from Garcia Publishing, and* Skorpio *from his own bad hands.*